MOLTEN SILVER

Delaney Silver

Nexus

This book is a work of fiction.
In real life, make sure you practise safe sex.

First published in 1997 by
Nexus
332 Ladbroke Grove
London W10 5AH

Typeset by TW Typesetting, Plymouth, Devon

Printed and bound by
BPC Paperbacks Ltd, Aylesbury, Bucks

ISBN 0 352 33137 2

All characters in this publication are fictitious and any resemblance to real persons, living or dead, is purely coincidental.

Contents

Versions of some of the following stories have appeared previously in Erotic Stories, Forum, Februs, Pleasurebound Forum, and Ludus.

This book is dedicated – with thanks – to the editors of the above mentioned magazines, to all my dear friends in the Guild of Erotic Writers, and to Cyrian Amberlake.

Party Animals

'Hi, Ellie, how are you? You're looking sensational! More beautiful than ever. Honest to God, woman, I swear you're a miracle!'

Compliments? Oh, yes, I lap them up. There's nothing that amuses me more than knowing a man desires me. I love to flirt. I love to hint. I love to promise.

And that's the great thing about parties, even routine corporate bashes like this one. Everyone is here to enjoy themselves; to eat, drink and be merry. They're here to philander, to find partners. And play games.

Ah, but I wonder what people would think of *our* party fun, my dear Rose? The games *we* like to play. Irresistibly, as ever, my eyes are drawn to you, and my flatterer follows my hungry look.

'Wow! What a body!' he murmurs, then has the grace to look contrite. 'Begging your pardon, Ellie, but that is one helluva handsome woman. Do you know her?'

Do I know you? Do I *love* you? Do I worship your abundant flesh and even now long to finger and stroke it?

'Why, yes I do, as a matter of fact. That's Rose Warren, she works for the company. She's a friend of mine.'

Friend? I'll say. An hour ago I had you naked and quivering before me, exposed and ready to . . .

'Is that so? Which division?'

'The East Coast Design Studio. She's the Executive Director.'

'Wow!'

Wow!

Oh, my sweet English Rose, you've changed a lot since we first met, but in some ways you're very much the same.

You've lost weight, of course, but you're still voluptuously lush. Breasts imposing and big-nippled, their erect state quite clear through the ruched silk of your clinging scarlet mini-dress. You're sparkling tonight, my precious, and it's no wonder. Your tawny hair shines, your creamy skin is flushed and glowing, and your mouth is constantly parted as if gasping with pleasure.

Which is probably the perfect truth.

And the men are drawn to you like flies, lured by the honey of your blatant arousal, the raw smell of sex that hovers around you despite all the Miss Dior I misted you with earlier.

I catch your eye and a fine tremor passes through your body; I see the shudder quite clearly, see the way you move your thighs uneasily, then bite down hard on your bottom lip as our secret game destroys your smooth, knowledgeable discourse on the use of comic artwork in advertising.

A man beside you asks if you're OK, and you smile brilliantly, slaying him with your fluttering eyelashes, and accept another drink. You'll regret that, my greedy little Rose. But of course, you know that, don't you?

Or perhaps not. I know you, my sweet. You like to push the envelope. Increase the risk. Make the game twice as daring. Twice as dangerous.

I begin to circulate, smiling at all, chatting to many, getting high on the secret that you and I share. Correction, the secrets. Tonight is just the latest in a long line of our pranks. I accept another drink myself, and swallow half of it down, knowing that you're watching me. In my case the increased fluid intake isn't quite as crucial. I'm not in quite the condition that you are; although I, too, have an all-too-solid reminder of our clandestine entertainment.

I fill my mind with a vision of your 'reminders' and I feel myself drip inside my undies, soiling the sheer silk of my micro-fine G-string.

Your sex must be swimming by now, my love, although you wear no panties to be spoiled. For these little outings I prefer you to be nude down below, your quim shaven and perfectly bare when I prepare you. Your nectar was already oozing, wasn't it? An hour ago, when you bent over at the waist and pulled open your own labia in readiness.

What a lovely sight. What a sublimely gross position. It's a stance you and I know so well. It was only the toss of a coin that made me the top tonight. It could have been me, now, humiliated by my own arousal, monstrously stimulated and unable to do a single thing about it in a room full of dozens of people. Although to give you some solace, my Rose, I do share a little of your torment. I deliberately brush against someone – and a movement that remains unseen makes me catch my breath.

I take another sip of my drink and wonder how the hell *you're* coping!

It's a wonder you can still stand upright – you must be coming almost continuously by now. Soon it will be time to check. And make adjustments. I catch your eye again and mime 'five minutes'. Your eyes flare bright with fear. Fear, longing, and an ungovernable, almost animal lust.

That's what I love about you, my little bitch! You're eager, game, prepared to plumb the obscenest depths in search of a thrill we can share. I catch sight of myself in the mirror behind the bar – and though my face is as pale as ever I see the same hot light in my eyes. I pat my hair, admire my make-up and my floating silk suit. I wink surreptitiously at my own image, saluting the vision that I have created.

We make a good pair you and I, Rose. Two beauties, but oh so different. Me: race-horse slim; dark, elegant and groomed to within an inch of my life. You: delectably ample; a cuddly little titian tart in your daring fire crimson frock. Oh God, if only that man who's ogling you knew what you're wearing beneath it.

Or that those beautiful breasts his nose is almost lodged between are pierced at the nipple by the finest of gold wire hoops.

Oh, how you cried the day I put those in. You whimpered so piteously, begging me not to do it. What a drama queen! You sobbed as I made you cup your own large breasts and hold them out so I could admire their new adornments. How you groaned as I made you squeeze them and drag them out further; made you part your plump, naked thighs so I could work your clitoris and make you orgasm while your nipples were in torment. Such fun! But let's be fair, I let you hurt my nipples later.

I see the guy checking out your legs now, and wonder whether he would faint if he knew what was above those lace-welted hold-up stockings you're wearing. I watch you shift your body weight cautiously – and wince – and know that you know only too well what's going on beneath that abbreviated skirt of yours. It's a miracle you can walk without groaning aloud. And why did you think I made you wear those four-inch red spike heels?

My own feet are too big for stilettos, but I still get a ghost of your sensations when I walk. It's only fair that I should wear 'something' beneath my skirt too – although my own array is far less complex than yours.

And I didn't make a sound when it went in – not a whisper did I utter as I lay over our padded leather play-bench, parted my own buttocks and ordered you to insert a thick, slightly-oiled latex dildo into my rectum, then secure it inside with thin leather straps around my body. I did purr a little, though, when you licked away the excess lubricant from my rudely stretched ring. In fact, I had an orgasm then, and you had to lick me clean from that, too!

How many orgasms have you had, my darling? There's a pretty pink flush to your throat and chest, so it could be your having one right now. It must be so difficult for you – I know how you like to scream and cry and curse when you come. How your pelvis whips to and fro, your mouth contorts, and you drool. From both ends. The tops of your stockings must be soaked with your juices by now; we'll have to slip away and clean you up or people will be able to see it trickling down your silky five-denier stockings. Yes, we'll have to mop you up, my dear, and maybe do some other things too.

I said five minutes, didn't I? Maybe I'll make you wait a bit longer than that. Suffer a bit longer. Get wetter. Get hornier. Get off again and again on the bungs inside your body.

'Oh, shit!' you cried when I had you bent over that bench – nude – and I pushed the fat black plug into your plump little bottom, working it right in so the wide part filled out your tender rectum.

'Please don't,' I said, fingering your clitoris and making your hips weave and your buttocks bob and dance.

The next step was a stopper for your vagina, another great slug of rubber with a hard little roll extruded in front – to ravage your clitoris when the dildo is lodged inside you. How sweetly you moaned when I closed your shaven sex-lips around this wicked and tantalising monster.

And you howled when I buckled up the ingenious assembly of thin steel chains and narrow white leather straps that hold the whole thing on your body.

'But, Ellie, I'll be coming all the time!' you complained.

I tightened the main strap two more notches, held you while you orgasmed, then slid you into your slip of a dress.

I had to put a gag on you in the car to stop you protesting so much – but since we arrived no one would know a thing.

Except that you're the most sexually radiant woman in the room and every single man who's here is dying to have you. I can count a dozen erections just from where I'm standing.

On a subconscious level, they will all be registering the fact you're locked into one long, almost crucifying climax; in a state of delicious precariousness from the thick prods jostling your hidden entrances – and the unforgiving chunk of latex that masturbates you with your every tiniest movement. I would like to take you somewhere where we won't be noticed and ease a little aphrodisiac cream between it and you, finger it on to your flesh until your clitoris thinks it's about to explode.

Oh, boy, am I loving this party! I could stay here all night, just getting off on our secrets, but now it's time to move on to the next stage.

I cross the room and discreetly join you. Your eyes plead for release then grow darkly desperate when I say, 'Let me buy you a drink.'

I make your choice for you, although nobody notices. A long wine spritzer. A very long one – the tall glass frosted and sparkly with ice and lemon.

'Good health, Rose! Drink up!'

It's a command rather than a toast, and I watch the tortured undulation of your milky throat as you swallow the entire drink down.

Your lower body is moving very slightly all the time now, although it's debatable whether that actually gives you any relief. You have a choice of atrocities to cope with: an acutely stimulated vulva, anus and clitoris – or a distended bladder that's being knocked and poked and constantly harassed by the solid rubber intruders inside you. I have this manic urge to reach out and prod your chubby little belly. To make you scream and wet yourself helplessly. I get as far as stretching out my long lacquer-tipped fingers towards that sweet, silk-covered curve. Your simmering eyes beg me not to, and I refrain out of respect for our secret party game.

I get you another drink, quietly suggest you drink it, then decide I'm being just a bit too mean to you. A dash of retribution is called for and I smile warmly into your eyes, indicating you should watch and see it granted.

Adjusting my skirts with as much grace as I'm able – given what's imminent – I sit down quite hard and my anal dildo bores loathsomely deep into my rectum. It's my turn to laugh gaily now, to mask my groan at the appalling blast of pleasure.

You smile back at me, still agonised in quim and bottom, yet enjoying the complicity. Knowing without having to see it that I have moistened my G-string yet again.

This party is so typical of our life together, isn't it, my love? One especially tasty scoop from our ongoing confection of sweetness. But it's time now to resolve this particular little situation, to 'tidy things up' before we return home to the slightly less deviant of our many deviant pleasures.

I nod infinitesimally towards the corridor that leads to the powder-room. A few minutes later, you join me there; sliding awkwardly into the room, eyes downcast, and locking the door behind you. Your hips are waggling slightly and your fists are clenched. You want to grab at the delicious agony in your crotch, but you daren't because you don't know if you can take it. You're balanced on the finest of edges now and you moan beneath my lips when I kiss you – desperately avoiding any pressure on your body as I plunder your mouth with my tongue.

I withdraw, take a tissue and dab away the smudges of both our lipsticks from my face. I admire my renewed state of perfection in the mirror, enjoying it all the more because you're bedaubed, smeared and sluttish. Your eyes are huge with tears and glorious with the ecstasy of submission.

'Show yourself,' I say casually, effecting one last tiny repair to my maquillage, then watching as you obey.

Slowly you skin down the stretchy top of your skimpy dress and rest your swollen breasts on the roll of red silk fabric. Without instruction you take hold of the fine gold rings and pull on them, distorting your breasts into two extenuated, conical mounds. I shudder as you jiggle them up and down, knowing how inextricably the sensations of nipple and sex are bound.

'More.' I keep my voice level, though now my own sex and anus are burning.

Weeping openly, you tug rhythmically on your fat, fruity nipples, your hips jumping in concert. I imagine the urine seeping out as you begin to lose control.

'Enough! Show me the rest.'

Up comes the hem of the red dress rolled like the bodice until all that remains is an inelegant wad at your midriff. Below it, displayed, is your enchantingly bulging stomach, resplendent in its fiendish harness of delicate chains and leather. Your quim looks pale and naked, the bare lips obscenely split by the thick black tormentor that presses so hard on your clitoris. Liquid shines on the narrow band of inner thigh between stocking and groin, and darkens the extravagant lace of your hose. I was right. You have already started peeing.

'Touch yourself.'

You need no further instruction; we have partied like this before. You turn slowly on your precarious heels and bend over from the waist, sobbing as the pressure increases, then crying out loud like a blubbering child as you reach around and caress your own anus. I ignore the noises and concentrate on the luscious sights. The thin chain caught between the fat cheeks of your bottom. The black end of the buggering dildo – so much bigger than the one I'm wearing. It holds your forbidden hole completely open. I admire your neatly manicured finger as it strokes its way around the tensioned rose-brown rim. I would like to waggle that thing inside you now, deliver the final *coup de grace* while I rub my own pulsing body to climax – but your harsh cry touches my heart.

'Please! I can't! I'm going to wet myself!'

In a frenzy of action and stolen kisses, I release you from the torturing array; your body disgorging its hideous obstructions with two heavy, audible plops. As chains, leather and rubber drop away, you glance around anxiously towards the toilet bowl.

Instead I nod towards the washbasin – and you squeak and grab your leaking crotch as I put my hands on your waist and lift you into position over it. It pays to be bigger and stronger with a luscious great girl like you, sweet Rosie.

Panting furiously, you slump against me as I take you firmly by your rounded hips and angle your pelvis carefully.

'Do it, darling,' I whisper, kissing your blushing cheek with every ounce of tenderness that is in me.

'I can't!' you wail. Fresh tears well up and I taste their salt on my tongue.

'Yes you can, my sweet. Rub yourself. It'll come.'

I hold you closer and tighter and you do it.

First it's a trickle, then a spurting flood. Jets of golden urine divide around your rubbing finger and pound against the bowl. Your legs wave wildly as you pee and pee and pee, and, weeping and babbling with pleasure, you come and come and come until your manic, jerking body can come no more.

'I love you, Ellie,' you mutter as I lift you down and pat your tired pussy dry with a soft, fresh towel. I kiss your mouth, then run water around the basin to rinse away your hot yellow flow.

'And now, my love, for you.' Your voice is suddenly strong and vibrant, and as I turn to you, I'm slain anew by your beauty. You stand before me proudly now, your full curves flaunted by the scrunched-up dress, your magnificent pierced nipples all pointed, dark and insolent.

'Over the sink!'

With a sigh, I bunch my floating silk skirts clumsily around my waist, turn, and bend to exhibit my naked buttocks for your inspection. I feel you delicately pluck the G-string cord from my crack, then ease the tiny, insubstantial garment completely clear of my body. When my genitals are bared and only my straps remain, I sense you crouching beside me, your soft breath warming my buttocks as your fingers feather an exquisite circle around the taut ring of my dildo-stuffed orifice.

You stroke me unremittingly until I'm moaning and wriggling, my bottom wagging lewdly so close to your watching eyes. My sex feels unbearably heavy, like a boiling balloon stretched almost to destruction. You reach between my legs and find me dribbling and ready.

'Turn around, Ellie,' you say softly.

And obeying you, my darling Rose, I stand up again, face you – and present my swollen cock to your ever-loving lips.

Flossie's List

Oh, dear!

Flossie Jenkins looked down at the ledger in the kitchen and blanched. Her heart beat fast in her satin-clad bosom as she studied the pencil written list. The ledger was full of misdemeanours, her misdemeanours – and any one of them was worthy of a thrashing from her mistress's fair, white hand.

It's not right! thought Flossie in anguish. She tried so hard to be a good girl, but Madam Woo was so exacting and strict. The slightest fall from grace meant a spanking. Or a strapping. Or a caning. Or the dreaded, oh so dreaded birch rod.

As she ran her finger down the roster of sins, Flossie felt her plump bottom glowing already; with a ghostly burning hotness that reminded her of her last chastisement. A slippering for 'making free' with the young ladies of the Academy, all topped off with a barehanded spanking for carelessly letting Madam Woo hear her speak the dreaded nickname.

Mrs Aurelia Woolstencraft knew full well what her staff and pupils called her, and had once – in a tender and intimate moment – told Flossie that she actually quite liked it. But even so, any mention of 'Madam Woo' in her earshot was a sovereign excuse for a punishment.

And there it was again, noted several times.

'Disrespect' – followed by that other oft-appearing crime, 'making free with the young ladies'.

'But I have to do it!' muttered Flossie, prodding at the words on the list. Most of the so-called 'young ladies' at the Woolstencraft Academy were older than Flossie herself, and were high-spirited, delinquent little chits who had been sent here for a taming before marriage. And the only way Flossie, as a housemaid, could keep them in line, and make them tidy their rooms and their clothes, was with the occasional slap or pinch. She wasn't obliged to do it in the strictly formal way that Madam always employed. That was, make them bend over the end of their beds with their posh white bottoms naked. But she certainly liked to do it that way! It was a thrill, a naughty, stolen thrill to see them bounce and cry and clasp at the redness her hand had created.

The trouble was that Madam Woo considered discipline to be her sole prerogative. When she was thinking straight, Flossie knew that Madam was the only one who could summon a bad girl to her room, instruct her to take down her bloomers, then make her bend over for a well earned smacking. Go bottom up over the ottoman, the hard chair, the edge of the chaise longue, or even, and most fearfully, over Madam's warm, strong lap. Flossie knew all that, but she still couldn't help herself.

And she had been over that lap herself, last time. She recalled the awful, breath-taking moment. She had been punished, first, over the arm of the chaise. Made to lean across it, face down, with her skirts and petticoats pushed up across her back whilst Madam made a fire on her bottom.

Oh, lor, those blows had hurt! Thick slices of stinging heat, laid on with a leather bedroom slipper, each one placed with the precision of a surgeon. Flossie had sobbed and protested, not only because it hurt so much, but because she knew how much Madam enjoyed a fuss. Her mistress's eyes flashed bright as gems when she heard a girl whimper and whine, and her pale, scholarly face would flush a most delightful rosy pink. And afterwards, in the lateness of evening, the bell would ring, summoning Flossie to Madam's private sitting room. There to perform a final and most intimate service. Oh, my! Now those moments were extremely nice, and not painful at all, but unfortunately Flossie found it difficult to think of them with the prospect of a spanking ahead. A spanking such as she had received after that session with the slipper!

'Now then, Flossie,' Madam had said, her voice soft and grave, 'let's have you across my knee.'

Oh, the shame of it! Shuffling across the room, to a fate even more painful than ever. That was something else Madam enjoyed. Her victim's ignominious progess as she crept towards her fate – hobbled by full, lacy drawers that tangled around the ankles, and clutching at skirts and frillies to keep them immodestly high. Madam required that knees be on show, and thighs, and lush glowing haunches. All that and – oh, dear! – a great deal more.

And yet there was also a certain sweet comfort in it all. Madam was exquisitely gentle when she wasn't spanking you, and her body was always warm and fragrant. Flossie gasped, remembering how it felt to be lying there, bare-bottomed and with her breasts pressed hard against Madam's firm, parted thighs.

Madam always gave you a moment to calm yourself before moving on. She let you lie across her while she stroked your hair, listened to your sobs and snivels, and tested your readiness for more. Her long, graceful fingers would slowly ride the lines on your bottom, pressing at the heat, and then sliding lightly down into the cleft. And just when you were starting to squirm for quite a different reason, she would say, 'Come come, Flossie, keep still. I'm going to spank you now. Let's not have a fuss.'

Flossie had butterflies inside her. 'I'm going to spank you,' she whispered, imagining Madam Woo's soft tones. Madam never shouted or raved, but her very quietness could chill you to the bone. Flossie could just hear her chanting all the sins on this list, her beautiful face reproachful as she slowly enunciated each one.

When she turned the page, Flossie seemed to hear the knell of doom. There at the foot of the list was Madam's bold signature and the words: *See me. The sitting room. Four o'clock.*

Like a scared rabbit, Flossie glanced toward the old grandfather clock in the corner of the kitchen. It read five minutes to four. Just enough time to run to the looking glass, straighten her cap on her untidy red curls, and smooth down the creases in her apron. Her silky black dress was a mass of crumples, too, but it was too late now to go and change it. Filled with a curious blend of fear and longing, she made her way up the stairs to the upper landing, then stood dithering, just outside the door to the sitting room. Her belly felt tight and her bosom was heaving. She wanted to run, run as far away from here as she could; yet at the same time she felt the wildest, most passionate urge to rush into the room beyond and fall down on the floor at her mistress's feet.

Torn between these two, she almost leapt in the air, when, in the distance, the old clock chimed four. It was time, and with a heart beating so loud she could almost hear it, she rapped on the dark, forbidding door.

'Enter!' answered the familiar bell-like voice, and the frightened Flossie obeyed.

'Good afternoon, Flossie,' said Madam formally as she turned away from the window, where she had obviously been admiring the garden. 'I trust you understand why you're here?'

'Yes, ma – ma'am,' stammered Flossie, as flustered by Madam Woo's beauty as she was by thought of what lay ahead.

Mrs Aurelia Woolstencraft was certainly the most handsome woman Flossie had ever seen. She was tall and slim, with a face as perfect as a Madonna. Her skin was pale and her lush, tawny hair was drawn back into a starkly-coiled knot. Her eyes were dark, and her mouth was red, and her expression was remote and thoughtful. She had a figure that managed to be both curvaceous and delicate at the same time, all clothed in a sober black dress with just the thinnest line of pure white lace at her wrists and her long, slender throat.

'Well, then, how shall we begin?' enquired Madam coolly, approaching from the window and taking hold of Flossie by the wrist.

Flossie felt pinned by that sure, intent look. Mesmerised as if by a magician or hypnotist. She was being asked to select her own punishment, decide which of many cruel implements would mark her rounded white bottom.

And there were many to choose from. The tawse. The cane. The strap. Even a whip with seven long tails. Flossie hardly dare think of them all, yet they filled her mind anyway, like an unforgettable arsenal of pain. She had been on the receiving end of all of them at one time or another, yet she knew that not one of these artificial objects could hit harder than Madam's strong hand.

'Spank me, ma'am,' begged Flossie, knowing now what she wanted most, and throwing herself ungracefully at Madam Woo's feet to plead for it.

'Get up, silly girl!' ordered Madam, looking taller and straighter and sterner than ever from where Flossie was crouched on the floor. 'Get up and show yourself to me.'

Flossie staggered to her feet, the familiar command ringing magically in her ears. She felt an unthinkable yearning in her belly. A lewd and unseemly softening. To expose herself was a thing of shame, yet she craved it, her fingers fumbling with haste as she hauled up her skirts and held them in a bundle at her waist, showing Madam her lacy white bloomers.

'All of it, please, Flossie,' her nemesis instructed in a voice as quietly calm as ever.

Struggling with the different layers of her clothing, Flossie managed to retain a hold on her skirts whilst at the same time unbuttoning her voluminous drawers. Her whole body trembled finely as she let them fall to her ankles to reveal her belly and thighs.

'Turn.'

The single word was like a blow in itself, and Flossie sobbed, just once, as she clumsily obeyed. She could feel Madam's gaze like a radiance on her bottom, like sunlight, like starlight. Her flesh seemed to shiver as if the look could burn and mark as cruelly as any spank. She felt, and heard, Madam move closer, then shook like a leaf as cool hands cupped the lobes of her buttocks and squeezed them to test their resilience.

'Do you really want to be spanked?' asked Madam, her face against the nape of Flossie's neck. 'You know I can hurt you just as much with my hand as with anything else.'

Knowing it was the utter truth, Flossie answered, her lips quaking as she spoke. 'Oh, yes, ma'am, spank me! I deserve it! Hurt me, ma'am, smack me with your hand . . . I've been so awful, and I really am sorry!'

'But we're not here to pander to your preferences, Flossie,' said Madam Woo with a faint, very silky emphasis. 'We're here to punish you for your many, many misdoings. Misdoings against me, I might add. I think I should be the one to choose the implement.' She paused then, still squeezing and mounding at the flesh contained in her fingers. 'But perhaps, afterwards, I might permit you a spanking.'

'Thank you, ma'am. I'm sorry, ma'am,' sobbed Flossie, her hips moving slowly, her bottom pressing backwards to meet Madam Woo's firm grip.

'Don't be too eager to thank me, Floss,' said Madam, softly. 'Now go to the cupboard and bring me the brown leather tawse.' With a last pinch on each cheek, she propelled Flossie forward and away from her.

Oh, no! Not the tawse! wailed Flossie inside as she edged awkwardly to the cupboard, trying hard not to trip over her bloomers. Madam Woo was a perfect mistress of the tawse, and she could make that thin band of leather do anything she wanted. Make it cover an undefended bottom with a blanket of scorching red pain. Flossie was shaking uncontrollably as she reached in and took down the implement, but even so she managed to bring it to her mistress without stumbling, falling or bursting into hot tears of terror. Eyes cast down, she held it out to Madam, then bit her lip as those pale, cruel hands took hold of it and offered it back towards her as a part of the ritual.

Still clutching her clothing, Flossie leant forward and kissed the cool, smooth leather.

'Now then, Flossie, don't prevaricate,' murmured Madam Woo as Flossie pressed her lips to the tawse and kept them there, imagining the strap all warm from her own flaming bottom. 'Let's have you over the chaise. There's a good girl.'

Feeling doomed yet exalted, Flossie draped herself carefully across the brocaded roll at the head of the French chaise longue. She felt Madam fussing lightly with her clothing, arranging the black satin and the froth of lacy white cotton beneath. She almost moaned aloud as featherlight fingers roved across the contours of her buttocks, then really did moan when the fingers withdrew. Her dark hour of retribution was almost upon her.

'Be brave now, Flossie.' The words hung in the air, and Flossie still seemed to hear them when the tawse first made contact with her bottom.

After the first second of shock, the pain was so hot

and hard and overpowering that Flossie squealed out, her voice high and clear. Her fingertips gouged deep into the cushions of the chaise, and she wiggled and shuffled to try and ease the smarting soreness.

'Keep still,' said Madam Woo, her sharp voice making Flossie even more ashamed and mortified. Why couldn't she be brave and strong for her mistress; bear her blows in stillness and quietude instead of resisting like one of the spoilt young things of the Academy who knew no better?

As she stiffened her body, another blow fell, carrying with it all the power in Madam's steely wrist. Flossie pressed her face into the upholstery, wetting it thoroughly with her tears as she struggled to contain her distress. The torment in her bottom was enormous, after just two strokes, and she didn't think she could endure much more.

'Come on, Floss,' cooed Madam Woo coaxingly, 'this isn't like you. You're usually so good for me.'

'It hurts, ma'am,' howled Flossie as two more blows fell, destroying her control altogether. She wanted to be good. Good for her darling mistress. But she seemed to have lost all her fortitude. She waggled her legs furiously as the tawse lashed down again, once, twice, three times. The pain felt like a storm of fire now, blooming in the rounds of her bottom and flowing on down through her belly and her hot, quivering privates. Sliding forward and clawing at the brocade beneath her fingers, she pressed her hungry body against the unyielding arm of the chaise. 'Wicked girl,' hissed Madam Woo, not sounding very kind at all now as the tawse began to rain down in earnest.

Flossie couldn't think straight. She could scarcely form a thought at all. She could only feel the heat and the stinging, burning pain in her bottom. Her whole world seemed grounded in those glowing lobes, and in the hand and the leather that hurt them again and again and again. She whimpered and yowled, and wriggled and rolled on the arm of the uncomforting chaise. And when, finally, Madam Woo took her shuddering and helpless across her lap, Flossie wept in both ecstasy and suffering, lifting her red bottom upwards and begging with her flesh for more smacks.

Oh, dear, thought Flossie dolefully the next day, as she stood in the kitchen with the ledger. A stroke had been put through each of her misdemeanours, a red line that ruled them out and deemed them over and dealt with. Closing her hands around her still throbbing bottom, she felt the redness of her other strokes, too – the ones that she had received from Madam Woo – and wished she could go back to the beginning. Be back in that cool, quiet sitting room, across the knee of her mistress, with her plump buttocks naked and ready.

As she dug her fingers into the soreness of her seat, she seemed to see Madam's sweet face again, her fierce eyes, and the pink-stained palm of her strong right hand as it had looked – afterwards – when she had allowed her sobbing maid to kiss it.

'Oh, Madam, how I love you!' Flossie whispered, squeezing now at the marks of her punishment. 'Even when you smack me and you spank me!'

Looking down at the crossed-out list, she made a decision, then smiled. Hobbling across to the draining board, she picked up a precious china dish, and smashed it to the floor with a flourish. Without pausing to sweep up the pieces, she returned painfully to the table and the ledger.

Kneading her sore bottom with one hand, and picking up a pencil with the other, Flossie made a start on a brand new list.

Malefico

It started with the magazine. *Decadent Life* it was called, and to say it astounded him was something of an understatement. Mark counted himself a man of the world, and more or less unshockable, but he had never seen anything quite like this before. It was pure pornography, unashamedly outrageous, and in places almost stomach-churning; a slice of delicious unadulterated perversion that made his skin get goose-bumps and his penis quiver and rise inside his underpants.

He could see it, but he couldn't believe it; he found himself touching the glossy paper as he was staring at it, trying to draw in the feeling of danger he experienced from every dark and nasty picture. He had studied the accursed rag from cover to cover a dozen times since it had first mysteriously appeared on his desk one morning; reading it clandestinely in the office because basically there was no way on earth he could take it home with him. Katie would kill him. She would call him sick. A pervert. And she would be right, he admitted. Completely right.

It was difficult, however, to read covertly in an open-plan office, especially when you were the one in charge of everyone *else*'s efficiency. The one who watched for slackers and time-wasters, and people generally not doing what they should be doing. Enthralled, and, under cover of his desk, uncomfortably erect, he turned the pages with a minimum of flick and rustle, ready at any second to slide a new sheaf of sales figures or performance indicators across them. He also felt that at any second he might disgrace himself inside his briefs because the images went way beyond what he had previously considered his 'limit'.

All eyes seemed locked on his hands and his face, watching him closely, noting his shame and excitement. How could anyone fail to see a man being changed forever as his safe, straight sex life turned to ashes?

A few days into his new obsession, Mark found a small packet lying on his desk when he arrived, heavy-eyed and exhausted, for work. He was in early because since his find he had experienced trouble sleeping – but someone else had got in even earlier than he had. When he opened the inevitable plain brown wrapper, he discovered inside it a small arrangement of black leather straps and a brief message written in purple ink on plain white paper.

You liked my magazine, it said, *now play with my toys. Wear this today. I'll be watching. I might even take notes.* It was signed 'Malefico'.

Pretentious or what? Mark thought, half of him trying to feel cool and calm and take everything in his stride, the other half panicky and wildly excited. He knew exactly what the little leather gadget was. A week ago he would have been puzzled by it, but since the advent of *Decadent Life* he had learnt quite a lot.

By the time his heart stopped racing, he could hear voices at the other end of the long, carpeted room, but fortunately the chatterers were occupied with their own far from esoteric concerns: the disaster that was the new office coffee machine, the latest petty scandals, the slender prospects for a pay rise. These topics were so all-consuming, it seemed, that no one noticed Mark sneaking away like a thief to the men's room.

When he returned to his desk the discomfort he was

experiencing was spine-tingling. Everything-tingling, in fact. He looked forward to a day of lingering and perilous stimulation which that would flex that so-called 'limit' of his, but his erection died pathetically in its bondage when he saw that the packaging and the note had disappeared from his desk.

Blushing like an outraged virgin, he looked quickly around the office, but already the coffee-drinkers and latecomers were studiously at their desks, their heads down. They were mostly women, but there were some men too; all reading reports, tapping at keyboards, jotting and frowning. Nobody was paying him any special attention at all; there was nobody who looked even remotely interested in him. As a boss, he had plenty of colleagues and underlings, but no friends, really, to speak of.

In a room full of people, he was completely alone – yet he knew that Malefico was near him. And watching.

Malefico smiled, well-satisfied with a task well begun, and wondering how poor Mark was coping with an array of leather straps around his testicles. The sorry, friendless creature appeared to be shuffling about slightly, to give himself some ease, but he was either a better actor than had been suspected, or the ball divider was not buckled tight enough. We had better see about that, thought Malefico, reaching for a sheet of white paper.

Mark's eleven o'clock meeting went surprisingly well considering his balls were swollen like two ripe tomatoes and his cock was fighting in his underpants for its freedom. The little set of straps – the divider, as he had recognised it to be – was marginally more comfortable when he sat down, and the conference table concealed his erection. The sense of being split down there was exquisite, just on the edge of being painful, but it also made him feel like a new man, at one with the dark world of his magazine. Contained by leather, he imagined himself to be a creature of the night, leading a decadent life in the bright, normal world of clean-living business and achievement. He felt almost transfigured in his strapped-up captivity – dreamy, at peace, strangely calm. That was until he returned to his desk and found another note.

Tighter, Mark. It should hurt. I want to see you squirming, with tears in your eyes.

After another trip to the men's room, Mark's eyes really were moist and his testicles were throbbing. Who was this beast who was taunting him, this Malefico who wanted him both hurt and aroused and yet who would not reveal an identity? He looked around his immediate vicinity, his supposed sphere of dominance in this clean and pleasant room. Tapping random figures into a meaningless spreadsheet, he began to weigh up the candidates.

It was a male-sounding name, but he suspected the hand of a woman. And there was Rachel, tall and sophisticated, who had a cool, hard look that fitted the profile to a T. She was cultured and smooth, clever and haughty, and with her bright hair wound back severely, as it was now, she would be the perfect, decadent mistress. He imagined her in a rubber corset like one he had seen in the magazine: her fine breasts spilling from the bra-cups, her waist compressed, her red mouth thinned and cruel. Then, just as his cock was about to betray him and spurt in her honour, he remembered that Rachel had been at the eleven o'clock meeting with him, and thus could not have left Malefico's second note. Forget Rachel – she was not a contender.

He couldn't forget the ball dividers, though. All day they plagued him, making him ache and weep thin, silky juice into his underwear. He imagined the hand of Malefico on him, tightening his torture another notch. Then another, and another. He could see a savage mouth smiling in his mind, even though it had no face to frame it. And it laughed, too – even though it had no voice – when at last he had to give in and almost run to the toilet to give himself relief.

Ah Mark, you will enjoy tomorrow, thought Malefico as Mark passed by on his way to the lift, the car park and his home. There won't as much pain this time, my boy, but something tells me you won't be in a fit state to notice the difference!

The next morning, his sense of expectation making him feel almost boyishly giddy, Mark got in even earlier than he had the day before.

And there was another brown paper parcel on his desk.

This second package was larger in area, but flatter and somewhat softer. The office was eerily deserted, although the lifts were already humming, so he took a chance, picked open the tape and unfolded the paper to expose his dubious 'gift'.

It was a pair of panties. Women's panties. Gorgeous, lace-encrusted, a work of art in rich maroon satin; and so far out of his Katie's league that they might have belonged to a different race of being altogether. This sublime erotic garment was the property of a queen, a goddess, a mistress – and to his horrified delight, Mark realised *she* had worn it!

He started to shake. His hands went clammy. For the first time since childhood, when he had once cut himself rather badly, white blotches seemed to float before his eyes in the precursor to a faint. There were one or two people trudging out of the lifts now, but even so he ran the risk and spread out the panties on his desk, his head reeling from the cocktail of odours that assailed him. A heavy perfume, something exotic and weighed down with Middle Eastern spices that he could swear he had never smelt before – and something else, another aroma, one he so rarely smelt nowadays on Katie, who was devoted to showers and to intimate deodorants.

A woman – Malefico presumably – had worn these sweet, sexy knickers for several hours at least; she had had them pressed to her perfect quim while she lusted and yearned for pleasure, her body heat baking her pheromonic signature deep into the fibres of the cloth. Mark hardly dare look at the gusset, he was too scared he would come there and then. Imprint his own pants with his essence just as Malefico had decorated hers.

The note said, *You like my smell, don't you? Now wear it. Make my knickers smell of you as well. I'll be watching*. Again, the note ended with the anonymous autograph. Malefico.

He took the brown paper with him this time, folded it and the note small, then stuffed them in his pocket. But when he returned to his workspace, his balls wrapped in satin and sex-juice, he smelt the perfume hanging in a mist above his desk: seductive, intoxicating – and so freshly sprayed that the chemical base of it almost made his eyes smart. In a funk of terror and excitement, he looked around, expecting a pair of knowing eyes to meet his.

But his diligent workers were already hard at their tasks. He watched them for a while, his glance darting from desk to desk, from industriously bent head to industriously bent head. But again there was no one watching him.

Feels good, doesn't it? observed Malefico, amused and silent, when Mark had finally given up his scrutinising sweep. The young man was settling now, that was obvious, enjoying the caress of the soft, heavy satin against his skin and the unthinkable pleasure of a woman's intimate soiling pressed close against his very male body. How long before *your* juices flow, young

Mark? Malefico pondered, waging a secret bet. An hour, but not much more than that.

No wonder women sometimes smiled so enigmatically, Mark thought, resisting a strong urge to shimmy and wriggle in his seat. It was like masturbating without even trying to, a warm-cool kiss of perfect satin-smoothness. He imagined the glorious panties encasing Malefico's bottom: embracing and stimulating her. Making her sweet fluids flow and seep, then pool in the crotch of her inanimate, pure silk lover. In seventh heaven, with his section's monthly progess sheet forgotten before him, Mark imagined the shape of the peerless bottom that had worn these pants before him. She would be pert and fruity, split like a succulent peach, her sex engorged and seeping.

He was seeping himself now, anointing the fabric that was already anointed, dampening the very square inches of cloth that had been pressed against Malefico's labia and clitoris. He imagined tasting her and licking her and felt his balls rise and tighten in her underwear. He had almost done it this morning. He had stared. He had sniffed. He had almost kissed, but had drawn back at the very last second, appalled by the deviance of the act. He had responsibilities, he was in charge of an office; he shouldn't be skulking in a toilet stall, in work time, snuffling at a strange woman's knickers.

But were they a stranger's? Malefico was close, he knew it. Not as close as her pants were to him, but nearby nevertheless, and watching. Watching and taking her own perverted pleasure in his subjugation. Wherever she was, she was creaming another pair of her knickers right now, her juices boiling and flowing, her clitoris huge, her love-lips pouting as her vagina rippled and ecstatic waves washed her sex. He imagined licking her again, mouthing her most intimate place at the moment of her crisis. Being inundated. Inundating himself.

He bit his lip, gouged his fingers along his blotter, fighting the supreme fight for impassivity as his penis discharged its pulsing load in Malefico's beautiful underwear.

As he sat in his own semen, the office junior, Penelope, brought his morning coffee. Smiling her usual unassuming smile, she was quiet and courteous. If she noticed his flushed complexion and the pungent odours around him, she gave no sign of it and her oval face remained as blank and composed as an icon.

It was her! The sly butter-wouldn't-melt little bitch! So shy and bland and mouse-like, yet a goddess of perversion within. How could he have been so blind? He almost roused again in elation, his cock a-twitch with triumph now that the tantalising conundrum was solved.

And yet, even as the idea dawned, he saw it was another blind alley. Penelope had been absent yesterday afternoon – a dentist's appointment; root canal work or something equally drawn out and painful – and she had come in late this morning, long after he had arrived himself, full of apologies for her tardiness and promises to work extra hours.

Scratch Penelope too. It had been a silly idea. The office mouse would never wear maroon silk underwear.

Soon, Mark. Quite soon now, thought Malefico, as the office manager walked by, his young face crumpled in a frown yet peculiarly alight with excitement.

Mark wasn't quite so early the next morning. He had spent too much precious time arguing with Katie. She had accused him of shiftiness, of deception and coolness, then repulsed him in outrage when he had sought ease for his inflamed libido in the silent darkness of their bed. Her vexation had begun again with the dawn, and his unsuccessful attempts to defend himself had made him late for work for the first time in years.

Unsurprisingly, Malefico had beaten him to it again.

Today's box was small and squat and square. Virtually a cube. He hardly dared to open it, and chose cravenly to read the accompanying note first.

Such fun, Mark, it said, *isn't it? But you'll soon get to the bottom of things, don't worry. Wear this today. I'll be watching*. There didn't need to be a signature any more, but there it was anyway. Malefico.

The office was already filling up, so, trying not to look surrepticious, even if he felt it, Mark took his gift to the cloakroom and opened the box behind the bolted door of a cubicle.

'No! Oh, no!' he moaned softly, painfully aware of others moving around outside.

It was another curiosity from the pages of *Decadent Life*. A fat, evil-looking, stopper-like object, a nasty blob of matte black latex, thoughtfully shaped with a useful flange at the base.

I can't, he thought, sickly fascinated as he ran his fingertips over the bulging rubber surface. It was hard, unforgiving, larger by far than the place it was intended for.

And yet he had to obey. He was drugged by Malefico and hooked on her filthy, forbidden games. He shed a real tear in the process, and stayed in the toilet for a long, long time, but eventually he unfastened the stall door, threw the box in the wastebin, and walked uncomfortably back to his desk with one particular set of muscles locked tight in a life or death spasm.

The sensations were both obscene and fabulous. He was straight as straight, he had never even touched himself there, but suddenly he started to wonder.

Was this what gay love felt like? Having something in there? Being stretched? Being filled by a man? Hating himself for loving it, he clenched his bottom around the fat black plug, then almost shouted aloud as the nerve-ends in his rectum insisted he needed the toilet. Immediately!

His bowels surged treacherously, but the message got scrambled somehow and shot to his prick like a dart of pure flame. He was stiffer than he had ever been, and he gasped under his breath, almost in orgasm as he sat down gingerly in a chair that had always been so ordinary and safe.

It took quite a while to steady his breathing; to reconcile himself with the fact that he was sitting there in his normal beehive-busy office with a slug of hideous black rubber lodged in his bottom and his cock pointing blindly at the underside of his desk. He was halfway to ecstasy – and no one around had even the faintest inkling.

He sat for a long stretch, staring at a blank white wall of sensation, poised between heaven and hell. If only Malefico would reveal herself, and touch his world with that fine, silver lining that would turn his shame and fear into freedom and joy. Malefico held the key to a whole new existence, a life of decadence and strangeness that he knew was his only rightful home.

Oh, Goddess, please come to me, he begged. See my plight, see what I suffer for you and how good it is.

But the only one who was approached was both subordinate and male.

Richard, the systems analyst and the suspect gay on this floor.

'You OK, Mark?' he enquired, his voice light and ordinary and devoid of all inflection or suggestion.

It's you, you sleazy poofter, isn't it? thought Mark, swallowing furiously and fighting for calm. He had tilted slightly in his chair and the abusive mass inside his body was pressing and jostling abominably.

Yes! Of course! The office queen was after his body – his backside, to be precise – and all these disgusting little gifts were the lure. The thing with the girl's silk knickers was a blind, Richard must have pinched them from one of the typist's sports bags to confuse the issue. It all made such elegant sense. The least obvious suspect was always the one; it was the first rule of solving a mystery.

It was also impossible, Mark realised glumly, because Richard had been on leave for two days, and only walked in a few minutes ago. This morning's package had delivered long before the man had arrived.

Mark sighed, plagued and aggravated by his own helplessness. He was a victim of the unknown. Malefico's toy. A slave to the possession of his arse and the stiff, aching bliss in his cock. He shuffled deliberately in his seat and his rectum boiled and churned. He didn't actually foul himself, but he hung right on the very edge of it, sweating and trembling, his eyes tight shut and his jaw locked with tension. In his mind, Malefico caressed him intimately, and in his briefs his tormented cock pumped and spurted. He wanted to cry with pleasure, but instead he made his face a mask and reached for a file from his 'in' tray.

Nearly there, Mark, thought Malefico fondly, studying the red-faced young man from behind a mask that was just as impenetrable.

Mark held out until four o'clock, torturing his fevered imagination with a thousand deviant visions each hour. Pictures from *Decadent Life*. Ideas of his own that were both worse and better. By four he couldn't go on any longer for fear of going mad, or messing himself, or both. He almost ran to the cloakroom and returned white and sickly with shock, the thick black intruder hidden safely in the back of his locker.

There was a note on his desk. No perverted gift this time, just a white sheet of paper, folded once.

It's time, Mark, it said. *Katie will never understand this, and she'll never make you happy. But Malefico does, and Malefico will. Remain here tonight. Remain and meet your fate.*

No signature. None necessary.

He bade goodnight with perfect normality to each of his subordinates as they left. Sounding so ordinary and wholesome, he felt filthy and aberrant. A creature of slimy darkness and forbidden, convoluted desires. But when he was finally alone, with only a small pool of light around his workstation, he felt strangely relaxed and at peace. Malefico was here. Quite close to him, he sensed. His skin seemed to prickle under a velvety presence, though he still couldn't define its gender.

'Hello, Mark,' said Rachel evenly, appearing like mist from the shadows. 'Do you have a minute?'

Mark's heart lurched, but then dropped like a stone in disappointment. She was dressed in one of her neat chic suits and carried her substantial and document-stuffed briefcase. It was work; she wasn't Malefico.

'Of course,' he said sullenly, hating all that was routine and businesslike.

'I've some projections I want to show you. Something you might like to consider for the future.' As she moved closer, her skirt swished sleekly and Mark could hear the discreet rasp of her nylons. She was a beautiful woman, but her hated her now, for not being somebody else. She snapped open her briefcase like firing off two shots from a pistol.

The manilla file she placed before him was immense and precarious. Unstable. Items slid out of it, projections for his future. Glossy magazines and brochures. Photo-sets. Catalogues. Teetering on the top was a copy of *Decadent Life* with a bound and gagged woman on its cover, but beneath were at least a dozen more similar journals. All the same; all mind-bendingly different and varied.

Intoxicated, he scrabbled through the pile, each image an electric thrill to his heart, his brain and his cock. He paused at a glossy full colour photo of a man chained in a metal frame. A man, much like himself, twisted in painful bondage, with stipes of agony on his bottom and smile of pure joy on his face.

It was only a small, evocative rustling sound that woke him from his trance of revelation.

Rachel was still standing next him, as if perusing the 'projections' over his shoulder, but her classic linen ensemble was crumpled on the floor beside her, and all that remained on her trim female form was a bodysuit of tight black rubber.

'Do you like the future, Mark?' she enquired, her voice perfectly soft and normal as she reached into the forgotten briefcase, took out a pair of long black gloves that matched her suit and began to work them on over her fingers, her hands and her arms.

Her hard face looked only strong now. Commanding, yet strangely reassuring. She quirked her well-drawn brows to repeat her question.

'Yes,' he quavered, ashamed of his weakness yet knowing it was appropriate.

'Then see more of it.' She raised her hand in a graceful gesture of summoning and two figures walked slowly out of the gloom and into the illuminated circle.

Penelope and Richard. But not as Mark had ever known them.

His mousy junior was a satin-clad cat-goddess now, her lush body gorgeous in a stylised Edwardian corset of wine-coloured silk. A corset whose matching panties were currently hidden in Mark's sock drawer at home. This deficit seemed not to bother young Penelope at all, though. Her bushy brown motte was bared to his gaze and, even as his mouth dropped open, she put her fingers between her legs and touched it.

Richard was instantly recognisable from the magazine spreads: his pale, sparsely muscled body adorned with an elaborate leather harness, his nipples pierced, and his skintight black leather shorts cut away at the front to let his long hard prick swing free. He looked completely at ease. 'Why not join us, Mark?' he murmured, his voice plummy and arch as he and his companion moved in.

'Yes, be one of us,' purred the other two in unison, also closing. 'It's a beautiful life. A decadent life. Pain and pleasure, Mark, and no limit to the quantities of either.'

Mark groaned as they engulfed him, tearing at his clothes, touching his skin, caressing and massaging him with hands and lips and sexes both female and male. He was drowning in moistures and odours, kissed by soft wet mouths. Fingered and fondled. Genitalia danced and slid across his body. He smelt rubber, leather, sweat, and strong, appetizing juices.

'But which of you is Malefico, the one who's been sending me the notes?' he asked plaintively, flat on his back as they overwhelmed him with heat and musk and delicious teasing torment.

'We *all* are,' said Penelope, her soft voice muffled by the obstruction of Mark's swollen cock.

'All of us,' whispered Richard, his slender fingertips prising open Mark's bottom and probing at the membranes within. 'And we're just three of many.'

'And you'll be a part of it, too, Mark,' murmured Rachel, popping open the crotch of her shiny form-fitting suit. 'A part of *us* –' she made a sound of husky contentment as she lowered her warm sex across his face '– when we initiate our next new member of Malefico.'

Life, the Universe and Sebastian

He was the most unusual looking man at the party. Even in a room full of Batmen, Supermen and Midnight Cowboys he stood out. His long, pale face, his peculiar golden eyes, and his slicked-back hair did remind me vaguely of a character in *Star Trek*, but he didn't seem to be in fancy dress. Unless shirt, jeans and jumper in unadorned black stood for something I wasn't aware of.

'Hello, who're you supposed to be?' I enquired, with all the boldness of two Malibus inside me as I zeroed in on him across the crowded room.

'I'm just myself, I'm afraid,' he replied, his voice amused and quite distinct in all the hubbub, 'Sebastian Sharpe. At your service.' He paused, cocked his head on one side, and gave me an appraising look. 'Pleased to meet you, Miss Peep,' he said, holding out his narrow hand towards me. 'Would you like me to help you round up your lambs?'

I felt embarrassed. Not only by my Victorian nursery rhyme costume, but because I didn't have a free hand with which to shake his. I had a glass clutched in one, and my so-called 'crook' in the other – a sort of cut-down affair made of yellowish rattan with a blue bow tied round the curly end. This had come with the costume, but looked more like a school mistress's cane to me than anything, and certainly nothing like an implement used for shepherding.

Sebastian Sharpe looked at me expectantly, then quirked one fine dark eyebrow. Shaking his head slightly, he first relieved me of the glass and put it aside, then drew the crook from between my suddenly sweating fingers.

To my surprise, he didn't abandon this straight away, as he had done the glass, but ran a forefinger assessingly along the length of it. There was an odd expression on his face as he handled the long, yellow stick; something I couldn't define, yet which definitely spooked me. The look in his eyes was far away, almost dreamy. Feeling uneasy, I held out my empty hand.

'Miranda Luxstowe. How do you do?' I said.

As if loath to tear his attention away from the crook, Sebastian offered his right hand, his left still curved around the rattan.

'I do very well, Miranda,' he said obliquely, 'and I soon hope to be doing much better.' He glanced down at the crook, balanced across his fingers, then passed it back to me with a hint of reluctance.

Sexist pig! I thought, stung by the fact he obviously realised I fancied him. And what was all that about, too? I pondered, looking down at my crook as I hung it from my sash and retrieved my drink.

'Nice party,' I murmured, resolving to invest only in a few moments' small talk, then move on to someone a tad less disturbing.

But it didn't happen that way.

In spite of our prickly beginning, I soon found myself warming to Sebastian. His manner was pleasant, he was gently and effortlessly witty, and our conversation very quickly became enthralling. We started with jobs – me, an admin clerk; him, a software development consultant – and moved on through TV, books and films, to hopes, fears and phobias, to life, the universe and everything. We both agreed that we were like fishes out of water in a frivolous, booze-sodden gathering like this, with all the raucous, seemingly atonal music and a lot of people shouting and some falling down; we both admitted we had only turned up as a favour to our hostess. I was just getting extraordinarily excited at the knowledge that Sebastian's own flat was only two floors above us, when his eyes narrowed sharply. His attention was fixed on something – or perhaps somebody – right behind me, and the look on his face was hard and dismissive, almost disdainful, as if the sight deserved his contempt.

Intrigued, I turned around.

One of our fellow guests, a girl I knew vaguely from the office, stood giggling and swaying on high heels, as she brandished what looked like a riding crop over the back of a man kneeling before her. 'Go on, Doreen, whip him!' somebody cried out, and Doreen giggled even louder and tapped her victim half-heartedly with the crop. She was wearing a short leather skirt, with fishnet tights, and a red top made of some shiny nylon stuff. Affixed to her bosom was a large, ribboned rosette bearing the crudely printed legend 'Miss Whiplash'.

I turned back towards Sebastian, wondering why he disapproved of such a pathetic, but basically harmless spectacle.

The expression in his golden eyes was more like pity now, and he was rubbing the very tips of his fingers together as if testing the texture of his skin. Questions surged to the tip of my tongue, but before I could ask them he said, 'I've had enough of this. Come on, let's leave.'

'What's wrong?' I enquired in the lift, fiddling with my crook, whilst Sebastian seemed pre-occupied.

'I –' He paused, watching me fidget. 'Some people . . . They get ideas . . .' He paused again, and smiled wryly, almost helplessly.

'What ideas?'

'You wouldn't understand.'

'I might!'

He looked at me very steadily, very intently, his large

golden eyes bright and fiery. I sensed him thinking very carefully about something, weighing possibilities, assessing me all over again. 'You might at that,' he conceded at length. 'Yes, perhaps I ought to give you a chance.'

In spite of my protestations, I hadn't a clue what he was talking about. I understood nothing, but I had a feeling I might be learning pretty soon.

Sebastian's flat was just the opposite of the chaos we had just left; it was elegant, spare, and silently and beautifully tranquil. There was a leather-upholstered settee, a desk and several book cases; the air seemed to hum with knowledge, and with a quiet, civilised peace. As I crept around, awestruck, examining prints and the spines of his books, Sebastian fixed drinks and put on some music; a light, but very stately piece by Mozart.

I didn't drink neat whisky as a rule, but after a moment, I found myself enjoying it. Needing it. Sebastian had picked up my crook from where I had left it on his desk, and was twirling it slowly in his fingers.

It gave me a very queer feeling in my stomach to see him handling the thing so. His hands were very white, yet looked strong. Capable. The weirdest thoughts began to pass through my mind, and when he swished the crook through the air, then smacked it against his palm, the hairs on the nape of my neck seemed to stand up one after another.

Blushing furiously, I looked away, then sat down on the settee and picked up a book from his coffee table. I flipped a few pages, to try and cover my nervousness, then realised I had made a huge mistake.

Sebastian's beautiful coffee table volume was full of pictures of people being beaten. Women being beaten, their bare white bottoms lifted up and offered to a variety of punishments. As I stared down at a woman being thrashed across a table with a cane, a huge lightbulb came on in the space behind my eyes – and I understood about life, the universe and Sebastian.

'Those people, downstairs at the party . . . You realise how little they know, don't you?' he said, a heartbeat later, as if my revelation had been flashed up on a screen.

'I – I think so . . . I'm not sure.' I looked down at the caned woman in the picture, then across at my crook, its length revolving slowly between Sebastian's pale fingers, its true nature not at all hidden by that absurd blue ribbon.

Horror and fear must have shown in my face, because Sebastian laughed. Very quietly and very kindly.

'Oh no, not with this,' he said, taking a step towards me, still twizzling the cane. 'I would never start a girl off with a cane. And this –' he paused, that look of distaste resurfacing on his elegant, rather aristocratic features, '– this "thing", is quite unsuitable anyway.' With a swift, ruthless gesture, he snapped my *faux* crook in two pieces, then dropped it into the waste-bin beside his desk.

'A girl's education should always begin with the hand,' he observed, steepling both of his before him at waist level. 'The hand is very intimate. The contact is skin to skin. There's no better way to gauge the effect of a smack, and thus modify the force of the next one.' He looked at me very steadily, his gilded eyes unblinking, then nodded infinitesimally. Like an android, I rose to my feet.

Mozart played on softly, but all of a sudden I was in a new and surreal dimension. Sebastian Sharpe could control me with the very slighest gesture, and as he walked smoothly towards the settee, then sat down just a couple of feet away from me, I turned to face him, my head meekly bowed. He was lower than me, seated whilst I was standing, but in all things he had the upper hand.

'So, Miranda Luxstowe, do you want to understand what those others are so woefully ignorant of?' He reached out, took hold of both my hands, then held them in one of his. He let his free hand slide lightly down my thigh, tracing its shape imperfectly through my petticoats. Sensing that he required it, I looked up and met his eyes, realising he was far older, and far wiser, than I had thought. I nodded, knowing instinctively what I had let myself in for, and feeling both fearful and curious in equal parts.

'Good,' he said, smiling thoughtfully, then let his hand slip beneath my full skirt and its petticoats. 'Are you wearing anything beneath these?' He plucked at the long, lace-trimmed Victorian pantaloons that peeked out from beneath my hem, then flattened his hand, slipped it upwards, and cupped the rounded cheek of my bottom.

'N – no,' I quavered as he squeezed. I had expected to get the costume grubby at the party, and as I would be laundering the whole thing anyway, I had decided to be naughty and go without extra knickers.

'Excellent!' His eyes gleamed. 'Now lift all these skirts up for me. There's a good girl.' He released my hands and nodded to my Bo Peep dress and all the frippery beneath it.

'But . . .'

Sebastian didn't speak, but his old-fashioned look spoke volumes. Trembling, I reached for my hem, then hauled up my skirts and held the whole lot in a frothy bundle at my waist.

'Back *and* front,' he specified. I obeyed with a graceless scrabble, then closed my eyes as he gripped my pantaloons, whipping them down to my knees with one smooth, efficient jerk.

'Lovely,' he said softly. I could feel the heat of his gaze on the curly triangle of my sex, like a therapy that made my hidden folds tingle. 'Now turn around for me.'

Shuffling, I presented my bottom, keenly aware of its plump, curvaceous shape.

'Perfect,' he whispered, and I heard the leather upholstery creak as he shifted position. I was quite disappointed that he didn't try to touch me.

'Turn again.'

I complied.

'Open your eyes.'

Again, I did as I was told, aware that my whole face was scarlet.

Sebastian was sitting comfortably on the sofa, his posture strong-looking, his knees spread a little apart. 'Do you know what to do?' he asked, regarding me steadily.

I bit my lip. I knew, but I couldn't say it.

'Come on. It's easy. Come across my knee. I won't bite you.'

I wasn't worried about him biting.

Slowly, cautiously, I laid myself across his lap, letting his hands guide me into exactly the right position. My balance seemed precarious, and I felt vulnerable and dizzy, my head down and my bottom rudely up. I couldn't imagine how I had let myself get into this pickle. What the devil had I been thinking of? One minute I'd been flirting, non-commitally, with a moderately attractive man; and the next I was face down across his knee, about to let him spank my bare buttocks. How could I have been so reckless, so foolish?

I moaned when Sebastian started touching me.

'You have a remarkably nice bottom, Miranda,' he commented, conversationally, like a connoisseur appraising an *objet d'art*. His fingers palpated the muscle of each of my bottom cheeks in turn, pressing them firmly as if testing their resilience. 'Firm flesh. Soft, pale skin. You'll mark very well, I imagine . . .' His fingers slid dangerously downwards, between my legs, then retreated and settled delicately on the very crown of my left buttock. 'Oh, yes, my dear, I'm going to make you pink.'

I yelped noisily when the first spank fell. I was expecting just a tap, and the full power of his hand was astounding. I could almost feel the shape of it – four fingers and the palm – scorched furiously into my right cheek where it had landed. My lungs filled, and I opened my mouth ready to protest and stop things going further, but then he spanked again, and my brain couldn't function. The second smack singed my left cheek, making it a match for the other one, and already my eyes were filled with tears. Half-blinded, I reached around to protect my flesh.

'No,' said Sebastian, soft and low, and the single word froze me to immobility. My bottom was tingling, glowing, itching, yet I dare not move a muscle to try and soothe it. Sobbing, I felt my two hands once more gathered in one of Sebastian's, then pinned gently, but with no nonsense, behind my back. I couldn't believe I had only taken two strokes, but very soon the first two became a memory, submerged in the growing pain that seared my buttocks.

The spanks landed briskly, methodically and without mercy. I could feel Sebastian's meticulous attention to detail; the way he was working his way around in a pattern, covering the entire surface of my bottom, making every bit of me hurt and turn red. While he belaboured me, he talked to me constantly, his soft voice unruffled and hypnotic.

As his palm and his fingers turned my skin and flesh to flame, he described the regime he would impose on me in future.

Spank! I would be taken across his knee regularly, for treatment like this, but somewhat more stern.

Spank! I would be beaten with implements when I was a little more experienced; when my bottom and my temperament were better seasoned.

Spank! I would taste the strap, the hairbrush, the ruler. And I would cry.

Spank! I would be stripped naked, gagged and bound, and take the cane.

Spank! Spank! I would suffer, at great length, and endure.

By the time Sebastian's hand fell still, I was weeping freely, my mind a mass of wonders.

My bottom was a swollen, throbbing war zone. I couldn't believe that anybody would seek this condition more than once. It seemed ludicrous. Yet the thought of *not* following the strange path that Sebastian had laid before me was upsetting, too. I felt confused, out on a limb, bereft of purpose. The idea of losing him, or displeasing him, was frightful.

I whined pitifully when he turned me over on his lap, and his black jeans chafed the soreness in my bottom.

'There, that's better, isn't it?' he said, wiping away my tears, and stroking my jawline and my brow.

Better than what? I wanted to ask, but then immediately realised that I *did* feel better than I had before. Despite all the torment in my hind parts, I felt relaxed and peculiarly at peace.

Back at the party, I had been edgy, worried about meeting someone, and nervous about how I looked and what I said. I had felt competitive, combative, forced to assert myself and be part of a scene I wasn't sure I really liked. Now I felt calm, serene, and quite detached from all my former fears. From this day forward, the only thing that mattered was doing well, here in this room, for Sebastian. Life was simple. My world was straightforward. All I had to do was to receive as much punishment as he could give, and he would be pleased. I wanted to kiss him to show I understood.

But I didn't need to. As I looked up, his great golden eyes shone down like stars. Just as before he had read my feelings effortlessly from my face.

'You've done well, Miranda,' he whispered. 'I'm very pleased with you. But I think you already know that.'

With a low laugh, he shifted me on his knees and adjusted our positions, kissing my swift groan of anguish off my lips.

'And now, my darling, it's time you had a reward for being brave,' he said as he lifted his face again.

Then he smiled, and I smiled; we both knew I hadn't been brave at all. Even so, he placed his hand between my legs and began to reward me.

The Gamesters of Harquin Hall

'Oh, boy,' murmured Marisa, as she slid into the room and let the door swing shut behind her.

'What the devil's been going on here?' She hesitated, grinned, then detangled a single, stunning item from the strange mass of clutter on the bed.

Marisa had never much cared for underwear, even now she had given up her wild child ways, and come home to Harquin Hall to settle down. She preferred her handsome shape untrammelled: no bras, no pants, no itchy tights.

But could *this* be classed as underwear? she asked herself, staring down at the garment in her hands and wondering what a friend of her father's could be doing with it.

Nathaniel Caufield, their latest house-guest, was obviously into fetish games, and was trying to make his girlfriend like them too, it seemed.

Marisa held the white leather basque against herself, intrigued by its smoothly-grained texture and the way the hide seemed to cling to her fingers. Turning it this way and that, she examined its fastenings: at the back, a lacing of criss-crossed silk cords, and at the front a line of tiny hooks and eyes.

It was short, too; very short. She guessed it would probably only reach down to her belly button, while at the top, the bra cups were just shelves. Narrow, silk-lined crescents that would support the wearer's breasts to perfection, yet hide nothing from the beholder's hungry eyes.

A cheap version of the same basque would have been unutterably sleazy, but this 'real thing' was both beautiful and elegant. The stitching and construction were neat and meticulous, and each seam was trimmed with a narrow lace piping that had the unmistakable sheen of pure silk.

The woman who wore such a garment would be worshipped. Her scantily clad body would be adored, lusted after, yearned for. Marisa giggled. A woman wearing this would inspire a thousand aching wrists, too; there was not a single shred of doubt about that!

Then again, she reflected, picking up several other items – a number of small, buckled leather straps – the basqued one could also be a victim. A vulnerable, tightly-trussed delicacy to satisfy some man's warped desires.

'Oh, God,' she whispered, as the second image stirred her profoundly. She suddenly saw herself in the severe white corset; her body bound and helpless, her mouth stopped with a bridle-like gag. There was a flesh coloured vibrator on the bed, too – a vulgar thing, and impossibly large – and she imagined it pushed rudely inside her while unseen hands increased its buzzing speed.

Next to the dildo were several sets of tiny metal clamps. Now where might they go? she mused, picking up one and testing its grip. Ears? Nipples? Somewhere else? Unable to help herself, she scissored her thighs and shuddered, then dropped the little toothed clamp back on the bed.

Dear me, he's really into this, isn't he? she thought, examining more and ever stranger paraphernalia. Legstretchers, handcuffs, a bulbous rounded object that made her bottom clench and quiver as she handled it.

I wonder if this was what did it? Marisa reflected as she fingered the horrid little plug. Caufield's girlfriend had driven off in a taxi just an hour ago, with an expression of furious anger on her face.

Silly bitch! thought Marisa, then retrieved the basque for a second appraisal. Looking at her body, behind the corset in the mirror, she considered things she had done in the past. You're playing *my* game, Mr Caufield, she thought smugly. I bet I could teach *you* a thing or two.

Dropping the basque on a chair, she started to unbutton her dress, fumbling and impatient in her haste.

The smooth white leather seemed just made for the honey of her skin. The laces would take just a second or two, although all those hooks and eyes were infinitely more tricky.

But you're all sweaty, Marisa, she told herself, hesitating. You've been in the garden in the sun all day, and less than half an hour ago – well, you were 'at it', weren't you? She touched the pristine satin lining of the basque, then imagined her sticky body against it.

But I could always wash, she thought with a smirk.

'Nice one, Marisa,' she murmured as, naked, she rubbed Nathaniel Caufield's monogrammed face flannel against the silky flesh she had stimulated earlier. Life had been dull since she had abandoned the good life, and she had had little or no sex ever since – except what she had provided for herself.

Swaying dreamily against her fingers and the facecloth, Marisa let her mind float free.

Had Caufield noticed her? she pondered. She had certainly gone out of her way to make him, even with his wimpy girlfriend at his side.

As Marisa considered the possiblilites, a noise in the bedroom made her jump and drop the facecloth. She *wanted* to be caught – how else could the game begin? – but now the moment was here, her heart pounded.

Holding herself perfectly motionless, she listened for

a voice, or voices, but heard none. There were only the very faint sounds of movement, and the clink of a bottle against a glass.

Come on, you bastard! she called out silently, but her answer was the clinking glass again. Drunken sot! she thought witheringly, willing him not to drink too much. Moving silently, she inched towards the door to the bedroom – and reached it the very instant it opened.

Caufield's face was a picture. Clearly the last thing he had expected was a naked nymphette in his bathroom, but judging from the strained look about his eyes, and the whisky-filled tumbler in his hand, he was sorely in need of female comfort.

Her father's houseguest was an engaging looking man, even if at present he appeared a bit raddled. As Marisa eyed him warily – framing meaningless excuses – he pushed a hand through his thick, greying hair and regarded her in total amazement. Neither of them spoke, but as Marisa took another step forward, Caufield took a long pull of his drink.

'I . . .' Marisa began, then faltered when he drained his glass, reached for a towel, and casually held it towards her. She was just about to take it, when suddenly he seemed to change his mind, and instead of just passing her the bathsheet, he moved to one side, unfolded it with a single, loud flick, and draped it around her bare shoulders.

'This is an unexpected pleasure, Lady Marisa,' he said smoothly, his voice a little blurred but still suave, 'but I can't quite see what I've done to deserve it.'

'Neither can I,' answered Marisa pertly.

'Well, Milady, does your father know you wander around his guests' bedrooms stark naked?' He looked quizzically at his empty glass as if debating a refill.

'I live here,' answered Marisa, proud of her cool as she adjusted the towel to show her breasts to advantage. 'I can go where I want!'

'Is that a fact?' Caufield enquired, his eyes – which were a deep smoky grey – clearing as he seemed to shake off the effects of the whisky. 'And does that also mean you can pry into people's private things?'

Marisa felt the pit of her stomach go as soft as melted syrup. She had always had a thing about confident, well preserved older men who took excellent care of their bodies, and Nathaniel Caufield was bang in that category. She estimated him to be in his early fifties, but he was still fit and slim in his sexy blue jeans. His yellow cotton shirt was unbuttoned at the neck, and the throat it exposed looked both strong and, somehow, strangely vulnerable. There was an appealing, outdoors-man ruggedness to him, and a touch of devilment around his mouth and his eyes. He had a sense of adventure, Marisa decided. Not a bit like her father's usual, stuffy-minded friends.

She decided to be honest. 'It's a little hobby of mine, Mr Caufield. I like to know what makes people tick, so I snoop around. Find out about their quirks from their stuff –' she looked up at him from under her lashes, then glanced towards the doorway, and the bed '– and stuff like yours? Well . . . Clearly you've got more quirks than most!'

'You think so?' murmured Caufield, insinuating himself behind Marisa and, with the lightest of touches to her towel-clad back, guiding her firmly through into the bedroom.

'I've got quirks, have I?' He shot her a glance when they reached the disarrayed bed. 'And what do you usually do when you've found out people's secrets?'

'Not a lot,' lied Marisa, then eyed the objects still spread out on the counterpane. 'What is your secret? Do you wear corsets and stick things up your bum?'

Caufield's eyes cooled. 'You're an arrogant little slut, aren't you? Young lady of the Manor . . . Daddy's golden girl with a mind like a sewer.' Too right, thought Marisa, as she watched her opponent's mouth narrow.

'It seems to me you need taking down a peg or two, young lady. You need a lesson in minding your own business.'

'Maybe I do,' said Marisa softly, evading Caufield's hand, and swinging her hips as she walked around the bed. 'This is amazing!' She picked up the basque and, as she did so, let her towel drop away. Turning, she held the white leather against her, and watched Caufield's eyes blaze with sudden lust.

'It's glorious,' she continued, twisting this way and that as if posing in front of a mirror. 'I could wear something like this.'

'Then why don't you?'

'What do you mean?' she countered. 'Would you like me to put it on now? I'd need some help.' She ran her fingers down the intricate lacing.

'I'll help you,' he growled, and in a flash he had her clumsily in his arms, with basque squashed flat between their bodies. Looking down into her eyes, he pushed his hardened crotch against her belly. 'I could teach you that lesson, you know. And you don't want your father to know about your nasty little snooping habits, do you?'

It wasn't really blackmail, thought Marisa as his mouth bruised hers. He wouldn't say anything – because he was the one with most to hide – but these things fared better with a structure. A reason, however flimsy, to play the game.

The basque stuck to her breasts as they kissed, its boning digging into her midriff while Caufield foraged in her mouth with his tongue. Marisa could feel her vulva opening up like a flower, and her entire body growing heavy with desire. It would be quite something to confine all this in a corset, she realised, and be constricted instead of loose and free. Greedy to move forward, she wriggled herself out of Caufield's arms, then held out the basque towards him.

Her father's friend smiled, a slow, almost voluptuous, smile as if anticipating the depravity ahead. With a adroitness that suggested this wasn't the first time – by far! – that he had handled such garments, he slackened off the lacings, then lifted the basque above her head and indicated she streamline herself into it.

Marisa felt a tingle just from having the thing slide down her body. The sleek silk lining seemed to coast along her skin, and she got more little shocks of stimulation when Caufield's fingers repeatedly touched her. With a discriminating accuracy, he settled the corset loosely around her waist, then lifted her hands so she could hold it in place.

As she had suspected, the basque left her belly, her quim and her bottom quite bare, and though the cups would have covered a fraction of her breasts, Caufield arranged her so she was completely on show. His touch on her now-aching globes was rough and seigniorial, as if he enjoyed manhandling her, and as he propped each rounded breast on its platform, he squeezed her nipples and pinched them almost cruelly.

It was a treatment that drove Marisa frantic. The small pains made her swollen sex ripple, and her hips waggle wildly to and fro.

'You're a horny little madam, aren't you?' he hissed in her ear, still squeezing with one hand while with the other he let down her blonde curls.

Marisa's own fingers felt itchy. They seemed filled with a peculiar electricity, a mad urge to stroke her own body. She wanted quite desperately to masturbate, but she knew she needed Caufield's 'permission'. It was his game – or so he thought – and he had wrapped her up like his leather-clad love doll, a slavish bimbo who was his to command.

'Turn round,' he said suddenly. 'Lean forward, spread your legs, and brace yourself against the bed. I'm going to lace you.'

Just the words made Marisa sweat and burn, and as she obeyed she felt a tiny plume of pleasure. Intensely aware of exactly what she was showing, she almost came from the indignity of her stance, and her defencelessness. She was bent at the waist, with her stiff arms holding her up from the bed and her curvy rear thrust backwards towards Caufield. Without a word, and as if taking something that was rightfully his, he squeezed and crudely handled her bottom cheeks in the same way he had played with her breasts. Taking a lobe in each hand, he moved it around strongly and demeaningly, then let her smooth flesh bounce and shake as he released it.

'Lovely,' he murmured after about a minute, then turned his attention to the tightening of the laces. Adjusting the tension from the small of her back to the middle of her ribcage, he took hold of them and started to pull.

The effect began almost immediately. Marisa felt her internal organs being compressed forcibly downwards and pushing against her sex from within. Her vulva seemed to pout like an over-ripe fruit, and her juices trickled slowly down her legs.

Or is it juice? she thought wildly, suddenly wishing she had taken the chance to use the toilet. There was a deep, delicious aching in the region of her bladder, a discomfort so acute it was exquisite.

When Marisa was sure that the corset was as tight as it could possibly be, Caufield began another round of pulling. She felt her breath start to shorten, and her belly harden like the surface of a drum. Her sex was so full and wet it felt ready to explode, and she was convinced that any second she would pee.

When Caufield was finally satisfied with the lacing, he pushed her forward on to the bed and instructed her to kneel up like a dog.

'Gorgeous,' he whispered, running his hands over her

leather-bound body. Marisa gasped as his fingertips traversed her fevered skin; every inch of her seemed doubly – no, trebly – sensitised, and even the areas that were covered felt his touch.

He was examining her, she realised, testing the textures and responses of her body. Seeing how warm she was; how wet; how sweaty and how slick with her nectar. His hands moved indiscriminately over both sexual zones and others; one moment digging carelessly in her furrow, and the next, shaping reverently around her foot.

'Move about a bit,' he instructed in a low, gruff voice. 'Waggle your hips, that's it . . . Spread your legs and exhibit yourself.'

Exhibit herself? Even the words made her giddy. Going forward on her elbows, Marisa gyrated her hips in a circle and imagined what Caufield would be seeing. Her round, well-shaped bottom, framed by the corset and its edging of lace, and the centre, her dark, fruity quim. The idea of it made Marisa tremble crazily, and when two fingers went inside her, she squealed.

'Be quiet, you minx,' he whispered, leaning over her, his breath lightly scented with whisky. 'You know you want it; you're wet through. You're one of these women that's always on heat, aren't you? Always looking out for it. Always dripping and randy.'

Marisa smiled at how so right he was. Flexing her spine, she pushed herself back on to his hand and gripped his fingers with the muscles of her sex.

'She-cat . . . Horny little whore,' he murmured, rubbing his face in her soft, tousled hair and nibbling at her earlobe as he pumped her.

Groaning, Marisa fell forward against the bedspread and felt an orgasm rampage between her legs. It was quick, hard and shocking, and as her inner flesh worked on Caufield's fingers, she bit hard into the fluffy chenille spread.

'So easy,' hissed Caufield, jiggling his fingers insultingly inside her and making her chew at the cloth between her teeth.

But just as she was soaring on their motion, the long, pleasuring fingers were withdrawn. 'That's enough for now,' said Caufield, his voice mock-severe, 'You've been caught doing something you shouldn't. You're not here to enjoy yourself, young lady.'

Try and stop me, thought Marisa, her sex still fluttering as Caufield rolled her over. As she lay inert on her back, he arranged her body: pushing apart her thighs, pointing her toes, and laying her arms stretched out above her head. Her vulva was open and unguarded, and her breasts were lifted up, her nipples pointing. She was spread like a star before her captor, every part of her accessible and exposed.

Marisa's whole body screamed silently for attention, yet, almost callously, Caufield ignored her. Turning away, he prepared himself another drink, picked up and studied various items from the bed and, after a moment, disappeared into the bathroom, to blatantly answer nature's call.

Listening to the long, heavy gush of his urine, Marisa squirmed her hips and bit down on her lip. The demands of her own bladder were extreme now, but perversely the sensations were exciting. The swelling in her belly seemed to chafe a thousand nerve-ends, and each one was connected to her clitoris. She imagined wetting herself, here on the bed, and masturbating furiously while she peed. The orgasm would be as messy as it was massive, and perfect to incur Caufield's wrath.

Or his pleasure, she thought slyly, not knowing which of two outcomes she wanted most: to be punished by Caufield, or to have him play with her clitoris until she came. In lieu of either, she cupped her hand around her pubis, and rocked it against the fluid massed within.

'Wicked girl,' said Caufield sternly from the door. 'No pleasure for you until I say so.'

'But I need to pee,' Marisa pleaded, injecting a little girlish whine into her voice.

Caufield's eyes brightened.

'You'll have to hold it in, my dear,' he said, moving across so he could stand right next to her. Reaching downwards, he pressed the heel of his hand lightly into her belly, and rolled it to and fro against the fullness.

'No . . . Oh, no . . .' moaned Marisa, kicking her legs at the luscious, bursting jolt.

Caufield pressed again, and she felt a few tiny drops seep out, but no diminishment in the pressure on her sex.

'We need to work on this, don't we?' he murmured, his expression unwavering and absorbed. Looking up, Marisa could see a strange near-rapture on his face, a focusedness that was inward and profound. This game – having a woman at his mercy with her bladder full – wasn't just a turn-on, but a dark, obsessive rite.

As Caufield moved around the room, making his preparations, Marisa let her mind drift back towards the past. She thought of her wild days in the city, and Jake, a rich, spoilt, and rather lunatic youth who had been both beautiful and sexually precocious. They had tried everything, he and she, and then some, but always come back to games like these.

She remembered a day when he had tied her to the seat of his sports car, and driven several hundred miles in one haul. For his own comfort he had stopped now and again, and pissed boldly at the side of the road, but he had not allowed Marisa the same privilege. To make matters worse, at each halt he had made her drink large amounts of weak beer, wine spritzer, or just water; holding the container against her lips and tilting it, because her hands were pinioned tightly at her sides.

After hours and hours, when Marisa had been almost beside herself, he had pulled the car off the road and driven along a track to a small secluded clearing. Marisa had groaned, and almost fainted, when he had helped her get out of the low, bucket seat, and set her down with a jerk on the turf. The thump of her landing had made her yelp, and she had felt urine trickle betrayingly down her thigh. As he had led her across the clearing, she could only waddle awkwardly, clenching every muscle in an effort not to wet herself.

When they had reached a young, narrow-trunked tree, he had untied her arms and ordered her to strip naked, then bound her to the tree with leather belts: her bare back and bottom jammed tight against the bark, and her thighs spread and flexed around the trunk.

Then he had made her drink again, ignoring her groaning and her crying as her body had seemed to swell out before her. When there was nothing more to drink, and Marisa was writhing like a mad thing and almost wrenching her every joint in her struggles, he had begun fondling and feeling her all over. Caressing her everywhere but her sex, his fingertips had been as light as airy thistledown. He had kissed her breasts, her arms, and her neck, and all the while he had stroked her bulging belly.

And when – finally – he had touched her clitoris, she had screamed, climaxed savagely, and her piss had been a torrent down her legs. She had still been a throbbing, dribbling maniac when he had entered her and called her his 'beloved'.

Marisa whimpered as she emerged from her memories, as exalted now as she been with Jake. Her bladder was a distended ball inside her – pressing hard against the nerve-knot of her clitoris, inducing pleasure and distress in equal parts.

Caufield's last refinements were almost unnecessary, but Marisa grunted as he turned the final screws. Placing towels – and a cushion – underneath her, he smeared her sex lips and her cleft with dabs of gel.

'No! Oh no!' she protested when he picked up the big

dildo and placed it at her entrance. 'Oh, please, no!' she keened when he started pushing it remorselessly inside her, and made space where there was little to be had.

When her quim was a filled as it could be, he let her catch her breath, and as she lay there, panting, he seemed to be considering his next move.

Yes, goddamnit, what next? she cried inside, almost delirious at the thought of anything more.

Yet there was more. Sobbing and biting her lips, she felt Caufield tilt her body upwards and begin slathering her bottom with the gel.

Then, with a barely audible exclamation of triumph, he was pushing something else inside her – and she recognised the stubby, rounded plug. Clawing at the bedspread, she felt the loathsome object slide into her anus, and when it lodged, she lost a tiny jet of piss.

'Naughty girl,' whispered Caufield almost kindly, his finger dancing lightly on the bung.

Helpless, Marisa peed again, and as it happened Caufield craned his body over her, to kiss her lips while he fumbled for her breasts. With his mouth moving skilfully on hers, and her hips waving uncontrollably, she felt him fit the metal clips on to her nipples.

After that, she couldn't really have said whether she was conscious – or drifting in some bizarre, hyper-stimulated limbo where Caufield seemed to mutate, for moments at a time, into Jake, then change back again to simply being himself. With every tender part of her assaulted, Marisa's senses seemed to focus in her clitoris. It ached, it pulsed, it glowed, it almost sang a song – and if he touched her there, she knew she couldn't bear it.

In the end she had no choice. Virtually in a trance, she felt Caufield lift her from the bed, and carry her, already peeing, to the bathroom. Wailing with relief, she squatted in the shower stall while he fingered her, and drenched his hand with her streaming golden flow.

And when at last the pandemonium was over, she stumbled from the stall and lay down upon the bathmat, breathing deeply. As her composure gradually returned to her, she sensed Caufield moving around – somewhere close beside her – then heard a rustling as he quickly shed his clothes.

So, what next? she thought, smiling smugly and coming up on all fours. Arching her back, and jiggling her glistening, still-stuffed rump, she presented her corsetted body to her lover. Caufield was on the mat now, too, snuffling at her haunches, and Marisa laughed when she felt him kiss her bottom.

You're mine now, all mine! she thought triumphantly, as she both offered and demanded everything.

In this game, there was no way she could lose.

Darling Nikki

Roger Nelson could hardly believe his eyes. He took another look, but he had been right the first time. The woman across from him was masturbating. Tossing herself off in broad daylight; unashamedly making love to herself in the foyer of the po-faced St. Vincent Hotel.

He had had been sitting in this secluded corner for quite a while now, sorting out his briefcase and feeling pretty full of himself about the nifty deal he he had just clinched. Success had always made him horny, but when he saw what the foxy little piece opposite was doing, his libido went clean through the ceiling. Why he hadn't noticed her when he had first arrived he simply couldn't imagine. But he had noticed her now, with a vengeance. She was gorgeous!

Gorgeous, and teetering on the brink of an orgasm, he guessed. The magazine draped across her lap was dancing, her painted eyes were closed, and tiny panting gasps were coming from a mouth that was as perfect as it was Gothic red.

Roger had never got hard so fast in his life; and when her long legs stiffened, her booted heels gouged the carpet, and her hidden hips rose high into the air, he nearly shot off himself in sympathy!

After several hard-grinding seconds, the girl seemed satisfied; subsiding into her chair with a creamy sigh and casually withdrawing her hand from the shield of her open magazine. Roger's cock was at full stand already, but when she looked him in the eye, smiled, and slid her finger between her brightly painted lips, it jumped in his pants for joy.

'Hi! I'm Nikki. Come and sit with me.' Her voice bore no trace of embarrassment – and Roger did as he was told. He had no real idea why he had obeyed her, or what he might to say to her, but for the moment it seemed OK just to sit there.

The mysterious Nikki was a medium-sized woman, but apart from that there was nothing medium, moderate or average about her. Her hair was a mad mop of dark red Rocky Horror curls, and her skin was as white as skimmed milk. The eyes she ran him through with were narrow, tilted up at the corners, and either black or a very dark blue.

Her clothes were twice as outré as her face and even more of a reason to notice her. Everything seemed to be vinyl. A chunky, stud-spangled bomber jacket swamped her narrow shoulders and the dress beneath it was an absolute sweetheart; plunging low, nipping in, then flaring out in an abbreviated excuse for a skirt that floated on a fat black froth of paper-nylon petticoats. Her dainty ankle boots had heels like needles, and her only entirely non-plastic items were a pair of black lace fingerless mittens and her smoky fishnet hose. Stockings, thought Roger ecstatically. How else could she get to her sex?

'Yes, they are,' said Nikki, suavely knocking him for six. With no qualm at all she hauled up her dinky skirt and revealed broad, black clingy lace welts and ice-white thighs beyond them. 'And to your second question . . . No, I never wear them.'

How in heaven's name had she known he was thinking about her panties? Or the lack of them?

'What do you want?' he croaked at last, his body on fire and his mind full of pervy, unthinkable thoughts.

He had first seen this woman a minute ago, but now he wanted to fall at her feet and worship her. The idea of kissing her shiny little bootlets seemed like kissing the Holy Grail. He wanted to lick them, even; smooth them with his tongue until his mouth ran dry of saliva. Even worse, he wanted to tear off his clothes and show her his body. Exhibit his sex and his arse. Then shudder when she deemed him pathetic.

'To have some fun,' she answered evenly. 'Come along, stranger, I've an afternoon to kill. We'll go to my room.' The convenient magazine fell away as she rose and Roger bent down to retrieve it.

What the hell am I doing? he asked himself numbly as he climbed the stairs behind her, dividing his attention between the possibility of seeing her pussy and the contents of her truly astounding magazine. He stared down at its pages as she fished in her pocket for a key. The pictures were like nothing he had ever seen before. Men in chains and straps. Men trussed up in elaborate, torturous bindings. Men being smacked. Men being beaten and demeaned and hurt.

'Give me that!' she said sharply, snatching back her property and pushing him into the room. Roger felt an insane urge to cringe and wondered why on earth he wasn't already at his next crucial meeting.

'Welcome to my castle!' Nikki said gaily, flinging off her jacket, then closing the thick velvet curtains. For a moment the room was totally lightless; but then, with a eerie lack of collisions, she seemed to glide through the darkness and switch on a couple of small lamps.

As Roger's eyes adjusted to the gloom, his sense of unreality grew. He was glad he couldn't see too clearly, because the bed, the chairs and the table were strewn with the same litter of obscene sexual gadgetry that he had seen in the weird magazine; every kinky, pervy or nasty device that hard-earned money could buy.

He was staring transfixed at a contraption of buckled

rubber and chains when Nikki tapped his shoulder. She was holding out a heavy black ledger and a quill pen.

'Sign your name on the dotted line, Roger. You want to be listed among the brave and the bold, don't you?'

It wasn't until she had flung the book on the settee that he wondered how she knew his name.

What now? his befuddled mind demanded. And who was she? A prostitute? A nymphomaniac? A sex fiend from an alien galaxy?

'You don't know what you want, do you?'

Nikki was standing in front of him now, her small feet planted squarely, her gloved hands fisted on her slender hips. Without her jacket he could see she had a pair of truly beautiful breasts: all high and firm and fruity. They were spilling right out of her bodice, and without thinking he reached out towards them.

'Oh no you don't, buster! That's not what you're here for . . . Even if you *think* it is!' Confounding him, she cupped her own breasts in her hands, massaging them vigorously and with evident pleasure. 'Take your clothes off, Roger. Come on, look alive! Jump to it!'

With more of that incomprehensible obedience, he started to strip, feeling clumsy and foolish as he tripped over his trousers and struggled with his vest and his socks. The sight of her sexual fondling made his movements more awkward than ever; and when his underpants came off, and his cock lurched up like a spring-mounted flag-pole, he had never blushed so hard in his life.

'Put these on.' A bundle of tangled black leather came zipping across the room towards him; hitting him hard in the chest and making his cock bounce foolishly as they fell to the floor at his feet. 'And then we'll take a look at you.'

Roger bent and picked up what she had thrown to him: a thin, unadorned black collar, wrist cuffs the same but wider, and a kidney-shaped eyemask with holes cut out for its wearer to see through.

'I'd prefer it if you hurry.'

Her voice was light and silky, but her moody-blue eyes made him shake. He had never felt like this before in his life and he could not understand how his fear and confusion was having such an effect on his penis. It reared out from his groin like a stiff, jutting rod and his balls felt like twin spheres of lead.

What am I doing? What am I doing?

The internal questioning was constant now. Why he was standing stark bollock naked in a strange hotel room before a bossy, vinyl-covered woman he had never even met before? Why, for the love of Mike, was he struggling to buckle on the offensive accoutrements of her dominance? And why, if she asked him to dress and leave right now, did he think he might break down and cry?

After much fumbling, the straps were on and he stood before her, as straight as he could, the cloak of submission as real to him now as the leather at his throat, wrists and eyes.

Nikki prowled around, surveying every inch of his body, her blue-black gaze probing like a laser, searching the chinks and folds of his anatomy and panning like an arc-light to the rampant length of his prick. He could feel her stare there like a weight – feel it cruising the veins and grooves, and assessing the taut, bulging head.

'I had hoped for more,' she murmured dismissively.

Roger felt both crushed and elated in one glorious fusion. Weird urges grabbed him and shook him. Humility. Exhibitionism. The desire to display himself grossly, jiggle his cock and make it bigger in order to please her. He had already achieved his hugest erection ever.

'Not yet,' she said, making him giddy with her ability to read him. The idea that she might allow him to masturbate was intoxicating, but he fought to stay still and dead calm. He had to stay presentable and strictly at attention – to make sure he pleased his mistress.

'Turn around, Roger. Show me your arse.'

Taking small steps, keeping his hands at his sides, he turned.

'Not like that! I said show me your arse!'

The horror – when he realised what she meant – was so luscious he almost erupted. Unsteadily, he spread out his legs and bent over.

'More.' An immaculately shiny toe nudged first one ankle then the other.

Balancing carefully, Roger widened his stance – fighting an urge to tense up his buttocks. His balls felt enormous now, hanging between his thighs like two furry, conspicuous fruits. He wanted her to touch them, enclose them, roll them slowly in her half-gloved fingers – but he knew in his heart she would not do it. Why should she, darling Nikki, his sudden goddess, soil her hands on a poor worm like *him*?

Again his thoughts amazed him. He had been searching for this all his life, he realised dimly, yearning for this odd, inversed delight in being exposed, exhibited and humiliated. And the thought of more of it – and worse – was like a drug that went straight to his brain.

'I want to see everything. Do you understand?'

He did, and he sobbed aloud with the knowledge.

'Very quiet now,' she said, and Roger thought he heard a hint of kindness. Of caring. That idea seemed most unlikely but it gave him a fresh burst of strength.

Bracing his thighs, he reached around and parted his cheeks. Cool air wafted over his crack, and the hole within pouted and winked.

'Such a naughty little thing,' Nikki murmured, 'So sweet and tight ... I think we should investigate this, don't you?'

Roger didn't know what to think – because he couldn't think. He was just an orifice now, a channel to be examined for her bizarre amusement. His whole consciousness seemed to settle in the groove between his buttocks, and when he heard several thin, sharp snaps, he couldn't for the life of him identify them.

'Relax now, Roger. Don't fight me. Hold still . . .'

As a statue, darling Nikki! he told her soundlessly, alarmed and eraptured by her easy perception of his thoughts.

Hypnotised, and with his every nerve-end screaming, he stared through his own spread legs at the more delicate and slender ones beyond. With the acuteness of extreme panic, he saw the flawless finesse of her skin beneath the coarse dark net of her stockings.

He gasped when her hand settled softly on his back, fingers splayed and enclosed in what he guessed was an ultra-sheer surgeon's glove. His cock leapt in exquisite repulsion. Any second now, he would be plunged into the deepest of all pits.

'Open, my angel.' Her husky coo was tender, almost loving – but when it entered him the finger was cruel. Consummately so. But not in the sense of force or roughness. It was its slow, sly, abominable wiggliness that sent out such unthinkable messages.

'Open, my sweetheart. Bear down.'

He did weep then. He really cried. Teardrops oozed out from beneath his mask and on to the carpet below; pattering like rain as her rubber-sheathed digit went deep into his shrieking passage. Through a watery blur, he watched the progress of his other seepage. A silvery cord of juice was suspended from the tip of his prick, its fat head kissing the floor just as Nikki found the core of his bowel.

'Don't be such a baby,' she said briskly, massaging the small of his back as if he were indeed her infant, 'it's only one tiny little finger. If you don't stop making such a fuss, I'll put something much bigger inside you. And when it's in there it might have to stay there!'

Sniffing furiously, he fought to endure the sensations. To accept both the unprecedented pleasure and the nightmarish urges to shit. His guts were in ferment and his thighs were twitching in waves. His cock felt twice its normal size. Huge and bursting, it hung between his legs like a monstrous newly grown limb. The longing to touch it made his arms ache and his fingers tingle – but instinct said he needed permission. With a stifled gasp, he pushed himself backward and bore down as his mistress had commanded.

At the very moment he expected to scream, shit, come, or do all three things at once, the demonic finger receded – and, unbelievably, he found himself mourning its loss.

'Stand up and turn around.'

He heard the snapping of the gloves again, and by the time he had stood up and faced her, she was tossing them coolly away, revealing the lace mitts beneath.

His cock hadn't really doubled in size, but it was definitely bigger. Enflamed and empurpled, it stood out at a high, sharp angle, and was pointing directly at Nikki.

'That's much better, isn't it?' she purred, striding from one side to the other and viewing her prize from all angles. 'Now we'll really have some fun!' Her fingertips hovered within inches of his fat reddened prod.

Desperate for comfort, Roger jerked his hips towards her.

'Oh no no no, wicked boy!' Her laugh was light, but deliciously menacing. '*I'm* not going to touch it. You're going to do that yourself. I want to see you bump those sexy hips, Roger. Pump that big stiff prick. You're going to grind, little man. Take a handful of that beautiful tool and grind and grind and grind until you come on my shiny black skirt.' Whirling away from him, she did a sudden, elegant spin – and for one breathtaking hundredth of a second showed the pretty red curls of her snatch.

'You'll have to lick it off yourself, of course.'

Reaching out, she touched a finger to his quivering mouth. 'And if you do that properly, Roger, I might even let you watch *me* grind again!'

It was twelve hours later when Roger woke up, and he was alone. There wasn't even a trace of Nikki. No leather, no ledger, no magazines, no nothing. No reminder at all except the ache in his cock when he moved.

'You're going to grind,' she had said – and he had ground. He had wrenched at his most sensitive organ like a madman. Pounded and pummelled and pumped it, then disgorged its white product – as ordered – on the slippery black surface of her skirt.

And when he had licked his own seed from her vinyl garment, his goddess had put on *her* performance. He had watched, agog, while she had fingered her body and teased it; he had wept again as she had coaxed her splendid, satin flesh into climax after climax, her thighs wide open to show him her inner spasms. Not once in the whole exhibition had she allowed him to touch her – but watching her, *being* hers, had done far more to Roger than the mundane simplicity of contact.

Had he imagined her? He couldn't tell. His senses told him she had entered his body, stolen his soul, and left him possessed and broken. He could still hear her harsh, feline cries when he trudged down the poorly-lit stairs; still see her pale, fantastic beauty, her dripping pink slit, and the working blur of her juice-covered, masturbating fingers.

In his trancelike state he nearly didn't see his own salvation. A tiny scrap of paper on the very last step.

Thanks, it was funky, it read. *Call me – 0171 999 666 and we'll grind again.*

He heard a faint, swishy sound as he paused, the rustle of plastic on plastic; but all there was before him was a lighted phonebooth in the darkness of the long hotel foyer.

He should have tried his answerphone – to see if he still had a job! – but a devil within took his fingers and his sore cock rose up and throbbed.

He dialled, waited, died and lived again . . .

'Hello? Is that you? Oh, God, my Nikki . . . my darling, darling Nikki!'

Belle and the Candyman

'To the prettiest pussy in the world!'

Arabella Destry raised her glass of champagne and knocked it back without even tasting it.

You've done it again, Belle, she told herself smugly. Blown their minds, and earned a whole heap of money by doing it. Most celebrities produced a book eventually, and now it was her turn. But there had never been a book like this before.

Sweeping her lustrous black hair out of her eyes, she poured out more champagne, then sank tipsily to her knees to study her latest project.

Portfolio was not so much a book as a succession of sublimely horny images. In the simplest of terms it was high-toned, beautifully photographed pornography. Pictures of her fair self, of course: posed with models and props in explicit tableaux of bondage, sadomasochism, lesbianism and sometimes just plain sex. Each and every photograph pushed the envelope and hinted at much, much more.

The launch had been tonight at an exclusive London gallery. She had had the most outrageous photographs blown up to life size and exhibited on stark white walls, then graced the event for ten minutes to be surrounded by her fans and the image of her own sensational body.

But now, much later, she had banished her adoring public and was alone in her flat for a Garbo-esque one-woman gloat: just Belle, soft lights, a magnum of champagne and a single copy of *Portfolio*.

It lay on the coffee table now, open at a shot of herself in chains, having her naked pussy petted by two oiled and musclebound skinheads. Both men had a hand between her legs. The atmosphere in the studio had been clinical and detached but, seeing the shot now, Belle forgot all that. Her sex simmered as if those brawny tattooed fingers had genuinely brought her off, and her clitoris twitched in the perfumed darkness beneath her long spangled gown. She had gone pantie-less to the launch tonight – as she often did – and her juices were oozing like treacle in her slit and overflowing down her immaculate silky-smooth thighs. In *Portfolio* they had used a glycerine gel for effect, but this was the real thing and Belle moaned out aloud at the delicious sensation.

'Yo, bitch, right on!' Drunk on champagne and her own imagination, she lifted her shimmering skirt and popped a finger straight into her pussy. Rubbing delicately, working her hips, she gazed at the monochrome images before her.

In one, a knife was being held to her full white breast and she was being 'forced' to suck the fingers of a latex-clad dominatrix. The crotch had been ripped from her white lace teddy, and protruding from her exposed pussy was a thick black dildo. It was fiction but, even so, seeing that menacing object lodged in her perfect body made Belle's vagina ache to be filled. Her breasts tingled in the elaborate wired bra that shaped her beneath her dress, and without thinking she dropped her glass, took a nipple between her fingers and worked it in the same furious rhythm she was using on her clitoris.

'Bitch! Horny bitch!' she groaned, staggering as her hips pumped and her quim pulsed in the soft, wet heat of an orgasm.

'That's true!'

With her sex still throbbing, Belle froze and looked

wildly around the room. The apartment was fitted with the most sophisticated security system currently available, and was supposed to be impregnable; an intruder was an impossibility.

Yet, just when she had started to breathe again, the supposedly impossible became actual. A shadow unfurled itself from a chair in the corner and rose slowly and elegantly to its feet.

'Who's there?'

Terror made her voice a scared Olive Oyl squeak. The world was full of nuts out to get famous people, and sometimes the nuttiest were so clever they actually made it. Something like this had only been a matter of time.

The standing shadow shifted, became a figure, then moved forward as a slight, thin-faced young man wearing a shabby pin-striped suit and an expression of pure, unholy glee.

No!

Bile rose in Belle's throat. The bastard must have been sitting there in the gloom all the time, watching her jerk off over her own stupid book!

'Who the hell are you?' she shouted, a rush of anger tamping down her fear.

'Names don't matter, Belle. But if you like you can call me the Candyman.' The voice was flat, almost metallic, but as he spoke the stranger smiled a small, odd smile.

'What the f –'

'Please yourself.' The thin grin widened. 'It's something you're obviously good at!' Belle's heart lurched and her body went weak in a traitorous surge of lust.

But when the Candyman's hand slid into the folds of his jacket and brought out a long-nosed automatic pistol, her eyes widened in terror. His dark coat gaped in the wake of the draw, and she caught the brown gleam of leather. Her guts seemed to drop in her belly and she felt a sudden sharp urge to pee. The bastard was a professional. He was toting a holster!

'Wha – what do you want?' She crouched by the long, smoked-glass coffee table, her arty fuck-book forgotten.

'I've come to test a theory, Belle.' He gestured towards *Portfolio* with a languid sweep of gun and hand. 'You might say I've come to call your bluff.'

Belle glanced towards the phone, but he tracked her with a reptilian speed and his eyes narrowed warningly.

'Unwise.' Tilting the gun towards his own face, he tapped it against his lips as if it were a stick of rock, not a sullen, fat-barrelled killing machine. Hypnotised, Belle saw that quaint little smile again, saw him first sniff the gun, then flick out his tongue as if he were going to suck the damned thing!

'Don't mess with me, Belle . . . All I want is the truth.'

'What do you mean "the truth"?'

Belle was a tough woman and normally scared of no one – but now she was terrified. The Candyman was obviously a nutcase, hell-bent on some kinky mission of his own devising. And yet there was a silvery sparkle in his eyes that was strangely alluring. The crazy shit was unbelievably sexy! There was a hard, dark cuteness to his sharp, foxy face, and even his fondness for his mean, black firearm was a turn-on. Belle felt her sticky body flutter. The Candyman might shoot her any second, but she couldn't help wanting him to touch her.

'This is so pretty . . .' He dropped to a cat-like crouch beside the coffee table and its open book. His head tilted as he studied the picture, and Belle saw the glint of gel on his tangled dark-red hair. It was a nondescript shade, but the way he had scraped it into a ponytail reminded her of the models she had used in the book. Come to think of it, he had much the same 'look' that they had. Lean and ambiguous. A pretty boy with gangster pretentions.

But the boys in the book really were only boys. Faced with the Candyman here, they would probably run screaming home to their mothers!

With his gun-free hand he reached out and pressed a finger to the image of her violated quim. 'Pretty pictures, Belle . . .' He looked up, thinning his eyes and swivelling his finger suggestively. 'But what about reality?'

Belle's cheeks warmed and moisture welled in the fold between her legs. This was so weird! She had never done any of the scenes in *Portfolio* for real – but right now she actively wanted to!

With him.

It would be a true danger and a truer sex than she had ever had in her life. Tied up by the Candyman, she would be just an open female orifice: quivering and available to intrusions both luscious and foul.

And she would love it, love it, love it!

'Well?'

He lifted the gun infinitesimally.

'But I have!' She pointed to her spreadeagled image.

'Pictures, Belle. Just pictures.' His grin was boyish as he holstered the automatic with an accomplished twirl. 'Would you *really* like it? Imagine it, Belle . . . Being bound, then touched? Being utterly helpless while a total stranger fingers you to orgasm.' Empty-handed, he seemed more frightening than when he was armed. 'Think about it, Belle. Being rubbed and rubbed until you come over and over again . . . Until you've come so much you can't bear it any more?'

Belle moaned. It *was* what she wanted. To be tied up, then fondled by those slender assasin's fingers. Her body ached. Her sex-lips bulged. Her juices dripped. She heard her idiot mouth say, 'Oh yes!' and the Candyman smiled.

'Then let's begin!'

It was unthinkable but it was happening. He was a criminal in her home and she was letting him play games with her. She remained meek as he swept her precious book off the coffee table, then rose to his feet and smiled down approvingly at the toughened glass sheet and its chunky stainless steel legs.

'Perfect,' he murmured, shimmying off his jacket and flinging it away. Underneath, he wore a dark, form-fitting polo-necked sweater. The garment was thin and silky, and over it the gleaming holster hugged his wiry shoulders like a glove. The gun sat neatly beneath his left armpit; just ready to be drawn and fired in the space of half a heartbeat.

At the Candyman's slight nod, Belle rose and moved towards the table.

'Good girl!' he praised, taking her arm and making her lie on the narrow glass panel. It was the first time he had actually touched her, and Belle was surprised by the coolness of his skin. There was a strange, quiet pleasure in the smoothness and gentleness of his fingers.

Feeling doll-like, she let him place her – and rip four long strips from the hem of her two thousand dollar dress to bind her. He tied her hands loosely together beneath the table, then fastened her legs widely apart, bending her knees and securing her ankles to the table's metal supports. The flexion in her body made her loins rear up invitingly – and the Candyman took a fat satin cushion from the couch and tucked it beneath the small of her back. He wedged another behind her head; then leant over, placing a hand on either side of her face, and kissed her squarely on the mouth.

It was a peculiarly tender kiss, although his tongue pushed immediately between her lips. He possessed her mouth in the way she suspected he would possess her sex in a simple fuck. The kiss seemed to invade her face and melt her flesh against his. She felt its effects between her stretched out thighs, too; her quim swimming with liquid just as her mouth swam with their blended saliva.

And as his tongue fought hers, so her head seemed to fill with a familiar but unexpected perfume.

The guy really does smell of candy! she thought in

wonder, sucking on his flexible tongue as if it were a lollipop. The Candyman both smelt and tasted of a hundred different sweetnesses. Parma violets, peppermint, honey; but over and above all there was a pervasive tang of aniseed, not unlike one of those obscure Parisian liqueurs or the smell of an old-fashioned liquorice stick.

'Candyman ...' she whispered dreamily when he released her lips.

'That's me, pretty lady.' He stood up lithely then shucked off his holster and its deadly cargo. Belle trembled like a reed as he crouched beside her again and whipped up her glittering skirt, bunching it deftly before easing it from beneath her buttocks and out of the way. Apart from her spike-heeled sandals, she was left completely nude from the waist down.

'No panties ...' He twisted a tiny coil of her pubic hair around his middle finger. 'That's nice, Belle, really nice.' He nodded in the direction of the discarded book. 'Maybe it is all true, then?'

Blood roiled in her chest, throat and face. In *Portfolio* she was bared for all the world – but having her sex exposed by the Candyman was like being stripped a thousand times over. Her quim would be visibly sopping by now, she realised; free-flowing juices would be glinting on the soft black floss of her pubes. The Candyman compounded her shame by sliding a finger daintily into her slit and paddling it around in her goo. He stirred slowly at the slick bath of lubrication but hardly touched the flesh itself.

'Please,' she groaned as his forefinger settled momentarily to her clitoris, then withdrew.

'Patience, my sweet!' His thin white smile twinkled like a knife-blade. 'We mustn't forget your pretty boobies, must we?'

With one hard yank, he wrenched open the top of her dress and sent sequins skittering in all directions as he tucked the whole bodice crudely beneath her heaving breasts. Her lacy bra got the same ruthless treatment, and in seconds the Candyman was folding aside its underwired cups to expose the swollen slopes and puckered nipples of her truly world-famous bosom.

'Ah yes,' he purred, taking the tip of each breast between a finger and thumb and dragging remorselessly upwards to make two long, exaggerated cones. The pain was intense and the arousal unbelievable. And as he pulled on her aching teats, he seemed, also, to be jerking on a pair of fine, tensioned wires that stretched inward from her nipples and were wound a hundred taunting times around her naked, throbbing clitoris. Each measured tug set it jumping madly, and her hips waggled in a helpless syncopated rhythm.

'Please, baby! Stroke my clit!' she begged. The ghost of a climax seemed to haunt her quim, screaming in silence for the pressure of the Candyman's fingers.

'I'm not your baby!' He grinned, then made the words a lie by swooping down, taking one tortured nipple in his mouth and sucking on it like a starving infant. The sweetshop odour rose in waves from his hair and Belle felt first faint, then mindlessly excited as orgasm flared simultaneously in her breasts, her vulva and her brain.

'Oh, God, oh, God, oh, God,' she whimpered, her body still spasming as he spat out her nipple, then rose in one swift graceful movement and glanced searchingly around the room.

'We need a toy,' she heard him mutter; and when she managed to focus, he was studying *Portfolio* and the image of her stuffed by the fat black dildo. 'I've the perfect thing.' Almost absently, he reached for his fallen holster and its fearsome payload.

'No! Please, no!'

'Hush,' said the Candyman silkily, kneeling beside her again and cradling the automatic in his dangerously relaxed fingers. Belle sobbed as he laid it on her belly, her flesh goose-pimpling its smooth, faintly greasy texture.

'There's nothing to fear.' His light voice almost sparkled and his unusual eyes were lit with a steely demonic light.

'Don't! Please!' The urge to urinate rushed back and soared to a hard, spiky pain as the Candyman slid the barrel of his gun into his mouth and sucked it in a horrid parody of a blowjob.

'There's nothing to fear,' he repeated, looming over her now and edging the pistol between her labia.

Belle couldn't speak. She could barely even think. She just stared at his lips so close to her face; lips that were ringed with a black line of gun oil and puffing her with his sweet, faintly aromatic breath.

'Nothing to fear . . .' Going lower, his lips moved on her belly as the gun barrel pushed deeply and obscenely into her.

'Nothing to fear . . .' He rose again to a kneel, and, to Belle's horror, reached his free hand between her legs and took her clit in a tight, pinching grip. Working it up and down, he matched the precise, measured frigging to his slow, sticky shoves with the gun.

Belle mewled and drooled, jerking in her bonds and hating herself for the pleasure that boiled in her crotch. She hated her body as it bucked on the designer table, grotesquely aroused by the lethal weapon rocking steadily and remorseless in her vagina.

But most of all she hated the Candyman! Hated him like acid as he jiggled her defenseless clitoris and seemed to know how exquisite it felt to her. She hated him utterly and absolutely as she came like a train, her vagina grabbing at the black cylinder inside her while her bladder let go and hot urine poured out between her legs. Locked in an intense, unstoppable orgasm, she wailed like a banshee and waited to die as she felt his finger flex then depress the fatal trigger.

There was a dull, mocking 'click' – but nothing else.

Belle whimpered, her body a wreck of fear and loathsome bubbling pleasure as the Candyman withdrew the gun from her vagina and held it in front of her eyes. She couldn't look away, no matter how much she wanted and needed to. Mesmerised, she watched him do something that was as unexpected as it was curious. Taking the pistol in both hands, he exerted a swift twisting pressure and snapped it cleanly into two separate pieces. The grip, the trigger guard and trigger and its mounting he discarded, while the thick, menacing barrel, still smudged with her various fluids, he wiped slowly and carefully on her gown – leaving glaring black smudges on the pale, sequinned fabric.

'I told you there was nothing to fear,' he said, and proceeded to break off a thin sliver of something from the gross black object in his hand.

Then, before Belle could protest, or even understand what he was doing, he had coaxed open her mouth and popped in the mysterious fragment.

Sweetness exploded on her tongue: thick, runny and loaded with spices and aniseed.

Jesus Christ, it's made of candy! Belle laughed in wonder as reassuring childhood flavours filled her mouth. As relief and hysteria bloomed, she felt the Candyman push the rest of his bizarre sweetie back into her oozing vagina; then saw him rise to his feet, retrieve his belongings, and retreat like a faerie into the shadows from whence he had come, waggling his fingers at her as he went in a cheeky, childlike farewell.

'Bastard!' she hissed; then smiled, gloating over tomorrow's headlines. *Portfolio* was outrageous, but wait until she was found trussed up like *this*! The publicity would be priceless beyond measure!

There was one question that still nagged at her, though.

'Hey, come back, you little shit!' she shouted into the

darkness, squirming her bottom as something thick and sugary dripped out on to the already disgusting table. 'Come back, Mister Candyman!' she called out imperiously. 'I want to see if your prick's made of sugar-candy, too!'

Malefico: The Queen's Gambit

They hadn't played this game for a little while, and it came as both a shock, and a relief, to see the familiar single chess-piece on his desk.

It was the Black Queen, and Mark smiled because he knew what that meant. He was being 'moved' – commanded to action by his sovereign – and it thrilled him. His heart began to pound as he opened the crisply folded square of white paper on which the chess-man had lain, and trepidation trickled through his belly.

Beneath the ornate, curlicued 'M' that stood for Malefico there was the notation *Kn-QR4*, in purple ink. Mark shivered, half entranced and half horrified – by both the logo and the instruction. This actual combination had never come up before, but he had always been expecting it. Knight to Queen's Rook Four meant an engagement between himself and Richard, and it would be the first time they had ever played alone. The code also indicated Knight 'to' Rook, not Knight 'take' Rook, and he shuddered again. The implications of that particular transaction made his innards churn and flutter, and his cock stiffen instantly in his pants.

Richard Kendall was the office nance, a tall blond aesthete who was effortlessly and beautifully camp. He had the narrowest, limpest wrists imaginable; but even so, Mark knew full well that the man was also as strong as a lion, and had a prodigious sexual appetite. The two of them had been close and naked together during earlier Malefico diversions – but always in the company of the others. They had often taken an equal share in the pleasuring of one of the women, and thus touched each other's bodies in the process; but they had never ever been alone and one on one. Just two men. Doing the things that two men always do.

As part of Malefico, the fact that Mark actively wanted this to happen was something that shouldn't have troubled him; but somehow it still did. There was still a small corner of his psyche that lingered in the old world of boring, everyday life and meaningless, humdrum relationships – even though it was several months now since he had joined the mysterious union of eroticism that was signified by the Gothic letter 'M'.

Mark looked at his watch and wondered when the chess-piece had arrived. There were no real time limits in their Malefico entertainments, but soon, very soon, he would have to present himself to Richard, and accept what the blond man had in store for him. With a dry mouth and a hardening cock, he tentatively took a black knight from his pencil caddy.

You know what's going to happen, don't you? he told himself as he made his way into the computer suite – where Richard worked – with a randomly chosen pocket file tucked beneath his arm. In their most recent frolics, the man had made increasingly more flagrant overtures towards him. Stroking his thighs and bottom while he was making love to one of the women. Kissing him fulsomely in greeting whenever Malefico convened. Ogling him hungrily if they happened to meet in the real world.

As he opened the door to the suite, and met a bank of softly humming technology, Mark saw Richard immediately. The blond was sitting before his terminal, loafing languidly in his chair as if the data on the screen was meaningless. He looked as if he was waiting for something, and Mark felt a small plume of anger that – as usual – he was the last to find out about a game. He knew he was still a novice by the standards of this particular chapter of Malefico, but nevertheless he wished they wouldn't always treat him as such. Even Penelope, the office junior – and in this context, the pawn – was always in the know before he was.

At Richard's desk, he burbled something meaningless about figures and projections, then handed the blond the file. Richard flipped it open with one long, pale finger, then fished out the chess-piece and the note. It took him barely a second to assimilate the message, then he stood up, stretching his lean frame eloquently, and nodded the slightest of nods to his left. Mark looked across, and saw the door to the paper store, then nodded in return. His head felt light, but his belly and his bowels lurched dangerously.

'Chess', and other similar diversions, were always played discreetly, so he didn't go straight to the paper store. Instead, he returned to his own office area, composed himself for a second, then spent some time in the washroom preparing himself. He splashed cold water on his face, and used the toilet, scrupulously. There was sweat flowing freely beneath his arms, he realised, despite his expensive deodorant; but there was nothing more he could do about that now.

In the paper store, Richard was already waiting, a suave, cat-like smile on his beautiful, fine-featured face. He was a favourite of the Queen, Mark knew, mainly because his primarily homosexual proclivities did not prevent him from also pleasuring her when the situation demanded it. And in Malefico such situations were frequent.

As Mark closed the door, he felt overwhelmed. Losing his will entirely, he let Richard take hold of him. He quivered as the blond man kissed him violently on the lips, then felt the touch of those graceful, roving hands.

Mark moaned around the tongue in his mouth, and wriggled beneath the fingers that probed his hips, his crotch and his bottom. Was this what the women felt when *he* caressed *them*? he wondered, shimmying beneath Richard's uninhibited fondlings. It certainly felt no less delicious having a man hold his prick through his trousers than it did a woman: a man play slow, teasing fingers down his bottom crease; a man cup his balls and jiggle them. He felt the same urge to be nude for Richard that he did for the Queen herself. He wanted to show himself to this man, exhibit his flesh and his erection, tantalise his own body for the delight and arousal of another. He moaned happily as Richard found his belt and his zip, unbuckling one, and whizzing down the other. He felt tears spring to his eyes, tears of joy and submission as his trousers and briefs went down to his ankles, and his bottom and crotch were laid bare. Meekly, he took the flaps of shirt in his hands, lifted them up, then cried out loudly as his ravisher took hold of his penis.

'Beautiful,' whispered Richard, the first word he had spoken since Mark had given him the chess-piece. Mark whimpered and shimmied as the other man slicked at the length of him, coaxing out the fluid from his love-eye and coating him to halfway down his shaft. 'Beautiful,' murmured Richard again, his voice effeminate and sultry. 'I do love a nice, sticky man.'

For a moment, Mark thought his expectations had been wrong, and that Richard might suck him, or yield up his own slim bottom; but in the next instant he realised that was not the case. He began to shake like a leaf as the blond man handled him with surprising strength, gripping him by the hips and turning him bodily around.

There was a pile of boxed paper just in front of him, and Mark bit his lips, holding in a sob as he was urged face down over it, his nude rump up and presented. His stiff cock was pressed hard against the carton just beneath him, and as his terror excited him even further, he rubbed his glans against the cool, rough-textured board.

'Yes, little slut,' said Richard archly from behind him. The blond laughed softly, and Mark heard the rustle of clothing, then the familiar small tearing noise of a condom being freed from its packet.

'You want it, don't you?' the other man went on as Mark imagined the picture of wafer-thin latex being rolled on to a strong, reddened shaft. There was another noise then, an uncouth spitting sound, and after a second he felt moisture being applied to his crease – Richard's saliva as a makeshift lubricant.

'Oh, please,' Mark heard himself whisper, even though he wasn't sure whether he was pleading for a reprieve or for sodomy itself. All he did know was that there was suddenly an intense, unrelenting pressure against his anus; a cruel, graceless push from a mass that felt slick and enormous. He cried out frantically, then shrieked as the huge thing entered him, forging up his passage like a knot of white fire that burned and seemed swell in his bowel.

The sensation was terrifying. Appalling. Yet still the greatest pleasure he had ever experienced. He wanted Richard to plumb him ever deeper; yet, at the same time, he wanted to turn around and kiss the man passionately on the lips. He wanted to embrace Richard, howl out his affection and gratitude, praise the man's name and adore him, and beg him for more, more, more.

It was over with an inevitable quickness. As Richard pumped smoothly in the newly opened channel, Mark howled and mewled in ecstasy. Within seconds, he felt his loins melt and his trapped prick leap against the cardboard. He was coming, ejaculating, spurting – and he was perfectly and wonderfully happy. He felt his heart close to bursting with elation when the man in his arse cried out, too; jerking and plunging repeatedly, then collapsing in a heap across his back.

They lay together gasping and trembling for what seemed like hours, but could only have been two or three minutes. Surprising himself, Mark was the first to recover. He was able to stand when Richard slid off him; and he was fastening his trousers, smoothing out the crumples in his shirt, and running a grooming hand lightly across his hair, while his friend – and now lover – was still slumped, breathless, on the floor. Tidy again, Mark stepped across and smoothed his partner's tousled golden locks.

'Your move, I think,' he whispered, as Richard smiled sleepily up at him. 'We mustn't keep the good Queen waiting.'

Richard studied the chess-men that lay in his desk tidy and considered what the next move should be.

There were no rigid conventions in this game of theirs, but they were playing the Queen's gambit today, and her wishes were always pre-eminent. It had been her desire that Mark's experience be broadened, but who knew what other whims and whimsies were on her mind. Richard had seen her earlier, and she had shown not the slightest sign that she even knew a match was in progress, much less that it was her own match. Her face had been cool and expressionless, and perfectly made-up. Her sharp, pin-striped suit had been as immaculate and creaseless as ever, and her bright hair sleek and gleaming. No sign had there been whatsoever of the screaming, sweating love-goddess who so loved to climax against his mouth.

That image gave him his idea, but he decided to add a twist, and involve the fourth of their number. Eyeing his rook, he resolved that their Malefico Queen certainly would have a mouth to honour her. But not his. The pleasure would be given by proxy – so, with a calculating smile, he took up his pen, reached for his noteblock and wrote briefly on the top sheet. Picking up the small square of paper and the rook, he rose and, whistling as he walked, made his way to the large general office. In search of their willing black pawn.

Penelope looked up from a mountainous pile of filing, and felt infinitely relieved to see Richard. Especially Richard with such a promising look on his face. That sexy, sleazy expression which told her Malefico was loose, and that she was no longer simply the underpaid undervalued office junior in this company, but a fully fledged, libertine participant in a life-enhancing game of the senses.

'Good morning, Mr Kendall,' she said pleasantly, then listened with little attention to his spiel about computer anomalies and problems with the network server. She had ears only for the sensuous inflection of his smooth, slightly girlish voice, and eyes for nothing but the neatly carved ebon-black chess-piece that he had innocuously dropped in her 'in' tray, along with a familiarly cryptic note. When he walked away, she watched his bottom for a few seconds, then returned her attention to the chess-man, picking it up and twirling it in her fingers, then stroking it slowly and thoughtfully as if it were quite another object entirely.

Where would Richard be waiting? she wondered, then rose with a surprising self-confidence from her small and not very prestigious desk. She walked quickly towards the door that led to the landing but, once outside, she lost her momentum. Where could he be? There was no sign, no indication. All it had said on the note was *RxP*. Rook takes Pawn.

Just then, the door to the ladies' room opened, and out walked Rachel, her immediate boss. Penelope blushed, every nerve in her body firing crazily. She wanted to faint, sigh, touch herself. Throw herself to the carpeted floor and gaze upwards at the beautiful woman before her. She wanted to worship that gracious, cultured face, those fiercely red lips, that vivid, glossy hair coiled tightly in the most chic of styles. Rachel was regal and confident, worthy of the deepest, deepest respect, and Penelope wanted to sing as her mentor nodded slightly towards the toilet.

There seemed to be not a soul inside. The tiles shone as usual, and one tap was dripping, but the mirrors reflected only Penelope herself. She frowned and patted her hair, wishing it was as brilliantly titian as Rachel's, then looked down at the chess-piece and the scrap of paper that she still had clutched in her hand. Was there really a game on? Sometimes Richard played pranks of his own, childish but harmless little japes that were entirely unconnected with Malefico.

As she debated, the door of the furthest toilet cubicle swung slightly open. There was still no sound, no indication that she had company, but even so Penelope strode forward, dropping the rook and the note on the floor.

Richard was sitting on the flipped-down lid of the toilet, his handsome face split by a wide, white grin.

'Hello again, Penny. Ready to play?'

Feeling weak-kneed already, she sank to the linoleum floor and crouched between his splayed-out legs. Her mouth, and her other, more tender parts were already watering, as she remembered the rich, gamey taste of him. Richard's sexual preferences were confusing to say the least, and she knew he often went with men. Despite that, he didn't seem to mind which gender sucked his prick. Only last week, he had begged her again and again to use her mouth on him, employing all his many charms to win her over. Unable to resist, she had indulged him: kissing and sucking and nibbling and swallowing until her jaws had ached with the effort.

Afterwards, he had used a vibrator on her until her poor little clitoris was raw, and she couldn't hold a thought in her head for longer than fifteen seconds. It had been another two days before she could stand to have an orgasm; and two further days before she had even needed one.

As she reached for his fly, he brushed away her hand, and slid his own down around her curvy body. With the strength that always made her tremble, he lifted her up and placed her on his lap, squeezing her breasts and her thighs as he arranged her.

'I've had mine,' he murmured, pushing at her skirt. 'I'm satisfied. I want to give you something.' He paused, stroking the skin at the top of her thighs, in the gap between her stockings and her panties. 'But only if you'll play the next move as I tell you.'

'Oh, yes . . . Yes!' she replied, her voice cracking and faltering as his fingers moved inexorably higher. 'Anything!' she wheezed as he pressed her pants into the niche of her sex, rubbing at her core through the thin layer of cotton-lined nylon.

'Promise?' he whispered, kissing her throat as he adjusted her weight. She felt his free hand curve neatly round her ribcage and its palm touch her breast. For a man who claimed to like men best, he certainly knew how to handle a woman.

'Promise,' she said faintly, wriggling on his lap as, inevitably, he tugged at her panties, then skinned them down her thighs to her knees.

'Good. Now look into my eyes while I diddle you.'

Richard had blue eyes, a blue as strong and bright and unwavering as the screen of her brand new word processor. When she looked up, they seemed to burn into her soul. Hold her. Restrain her. Keep her controlled and immobile as his fingertips dived through her bush and sought out the soft place within. She cried out hoarsely as he found her clitoris, but she stayed still. She groaned, then grunted uninhibitedly as he delicately pincered the tiny tag of flesh and worked it to and fro and up and down. She gurgled, tears filling her eyes and trickling down her face, when he gripped her breast in time to his tugging. She screamed out – uncaring that someone might come into the ladies' room at any moment – as her tormented quim pulsed and seemed to liquefy, brought to climax by her strange, foppish lover. Her bottom squirmed of its own accord – even though she tried with all her might to stop it – and as her whole sex fluttered, she could feel the dew oozing freely from her body. Richard's pale designer trousers would be soiled, but Penelope didn't give a damn. All part of the game, she thought, feeling giddy; then she stopped trying to think altogether as another wave crested and claimed her.

'So, what is it you want me to do?' she enquired shakily, some time later. She was still lying stretched across Richard's linen-clad lap, but by now she had gained a hold on her senses. It amused her mightily that, despite his claims of satisfaction, she had just felt Richard's cock leap and spurt beneath her bottom. More mess for those posh fawn trousers.

'Tsk tsk,' he murmured almost drowsily, his voice soft and peachy in her ear. 'Don't be impatient, little pawn . . . I still haven't finished *this* move yet.'

She moaned as two fingers slid inside her.

When the knock came, it sent tingles right down Rachel's spine. She had been wondering how long this particular strategy would take to develop, but as usual Malefico had surprised her.

So much, so soon, she thought, grinning. Her players must all be grand masters!

Penelope's face was pink and flushed when she walked in with one of those ubiquitous manilla folders that were so useful for things other than memos. Rachel kept her features impassive as she opened it, and even retained her cool when the tiny black pawn tumbled out. The folded, accompanying note read *P-Q1*, Pawn to Queen One, and she hoped Penny would interpret the play well.

'Will that be all, Miss Elliot?' enquired Penelope, her soft voice unusually formal as she stepped around the desk and stood beside Rachel.

Rachel spun in her red executive chair, and faced her subordinate, well pleased. 'There is something, actually...' She reached down and took the hem of her pencil-slim skirt. 'It won't take a minute ...' That was true, because she was already dripping with excitement, the product of her pleasure in the game. 'If you'd be so kind ...' Sliding up the crisp grey fabric on its silky lining, she lifted her bottom from her seat, then bunched her smart skirt around her waist, showing a dreamy-eyed, open-mouthed Penelope that beneath it her Queen wore only a pair of super-fine black crotchless tights.

Throughout the end-game, Rachel kept her eyes closed, picturing other manoeuvres, other ploys and even stranger and more complicated contests. Her Pawn's tongue was nimble, moist and clever, and as it finished her, she screamed and clawed her desk, scrabbling blindly amongst her papers and her pens.

But of course, the thing she sought was now elsewhere; which was the single, glaring flaw in Malefico 'chess', and in this, her own gambit, in particular. By sending her black queen to someone else, she had conceded her dominion and her power, and lost control of far more than her body.

I had better start a different game next time, she thought wildly, as her beleaguered flesh leapt, then leapt and leapt again.

We'll play 'dominoes' – I always win at that!

Wilhemina's Correction

A pastiche for Cyrian Amberlake

Life is just a series of bearable compromises, at best.

Now where the dickens did I read that? Wilhemina wondered, reflecting on its truth in her case. Living in someone else's house, because her boyfriend had oh so tactfully but comprehensively rejected her, was most definitely one of life's bitterest compromises, but it was also, she now admitted, quite bearable. All thanks to a certain special someone.

When she had seen the card in the newsagent's window, she hadn't really held out too much hope. Still nervous from her rejection, and out of funds from living in a hotel, she had rung the telephone number hopefully, but also been prepared for disappointment. A free room in an academic's house, in exchange for light domestic duties, sounded far too good to be true.

And yet luck had been with her. A cultured voice had answered, said the room was still available, and would she care to come around and inspect it? Wilhemina had almost stuttered with excitement, and answered that she would *love* to see the room!

The house in Lavender Road was beautiful, and Wilhemina knew, the instant she saw it, that things were looking up in her life. Even the tuneful doorbell seemed to cheer her, as she rang it and waited for an answer. The soft grey stone looked strong and peaceful, and the polished black door reassuring. The whole place had an air of quiet order, a steady calm that her frazzled nerves needed.

And the cultured voice – from the phone call – was matched by an equally cultured face. When the front door swung open, she found herself confronted by a tallish man with a long, studious face and a pale complexion – a man who looked youthful, and peculiarly mischievous, despite, or perhaps even because of the white streak in his thick chestnut hair.

'Hello, my dear,' he said, holding out his hand. 'I'm Darius Brent, and you must be Wilhemina?'

Already quite awe-struck, Wilhemina took the proffered hand, and allowed hers to be shaken very firmly. She was most surprised by the strength in his grip. For a rather fine-boned man, Doctor Brent seemed decidedly powerful.

'Y – yes,' she stammered, holding on to his fingers, 'I'm Wilhemina Woodforde. I've come about the room and board.'

'I know that, my dear,' replied Doctor Brent, his eyes twinkling as he reclaimed his own hand. 'Please come in, and we'll discuss the details over a nice cup of tea.'

Blushing at her own gaucherie, and looking around her in excitement and wonder, Wilhemina followed the academic inside, then allowed herself to be led into what she presumed must be his study – a cosy room, richly appointed but welcoming, which was filled with antique furniture and what seemed like a million books.

'Do sit down, my dear,' said Doctor Brent, gesturing to an elegant Victorian nursing chair, set by the fire, and across from what she sensed was 'his' chair – a more imposing, high-backed, broad-armed affair, 'I'll get our tea . . . I'll only be a jiffy.' Then with a smile, and slight, courteous nod, he was gone, and Wilhemina was all alone.

It was difficult to know what to think about; the good Doctor or his beautiful house. Wilhemina was equally affected by both of them. The room she was sitting in was both august and beguiling, and the same might be said for Doctor Brent. He wasn't the sort of chap she would have called her 'type,' but she realised her type had now changed. She had only seen the man for a moment or two, but she was melting. Almost moonstruck. Going dreamy over a man who was lanky, seemed a little effete and was clearly almost twice her age ... Doctor Brent wasn't a 'big' man in physical terms, but he had an aura that was immense and imposing, and there had been a grace and presence to his movements that even his loosely-cut suit couldn't hide. It was strange, and he made her feel quite scared somehow, but in a way that made fear seem quite pleasant. To distract herself, she gazed around the room.

There was a fire burning in the hearth, even though the day was not exactly cold, and a grandfather clock that ticked comfortingly in the corner. Between their two chairs was a low hexagonal table; across the room was a huge master's desk. Books and journals were crammed into the heavy oaken bookshelves that lined the room, and others were scattered over the desk and on the floor. Wilhemina noticed a number of sepia prints on the portions of wall that weren't taken up with bookshelves, but from where she sat, she couldn't make out their subject. What she could make out, however, as she looked more closely at the wall-space nearest to her, were some objects that rather alarmed her, all arranged in an artistic, almost heraldic composition. Feeling strangely guilty, she got up to take a look.

Lying horizontally, on a set of rests of some kind, was a long, thin, yellow rattan cane. Beneath it were what looked like two slender, leather-bound whips, their shanks crossed to make a shallow, flattened X; and under these, hanging downwards and suspended from a pin in what appeared to be its handle was a thick strap of polished brown hide, with its tail split into two equal tongues.

The fearsome arrangement made Wilhemina quiver. All these objects were quite clearly instruments of discipline, but whatever were they doing here? Doctor Brent was a scholar, he held a seat in the Classics – or was it philosophy, or perhaps literature? He wasn't the headmaster of a strict school for boys. Or even girls, she appended, aware that her shaking had increased.

'Beautiful, aren't they?' said a soft voice behind her, and with a squeak of fright, Wilhemina swung round.

Doctor Brent was standing just a few feet behind her, but she had never even heard him come in. He must move like a cat, she thought, noticing that he had set a tea tray on the small table by the fire. Now how on earth had he managed to do that without her hearing him?

'They're very interesting,' burbled Wilhemina, looking nervously from Doctor Brent, to the cane and the whips, and back again. The academic's eyes were glittering intensely, their unusual bright gold colour just as cutting as the whips must surely be.

'So, you find implements of correction interesting?' he said thoughtfully, almost to himself, then reached out to guide Wilhemina towards the tea. The pressure he exerted was ineffably light, but she got the impression it could have been far greater. Doctor Brent might not be a very athletic-looking man, but within him she sensed a steely strength. An implacableness. A single-mindedness. She realised she would not like to cross him.

'Er – yes . . . I suppose so. It's the first time I've ever seen any,' she said, sitting down, and trying in the process to look elegant. As elegant as Doctor Brent himself.

'Hmmm . . .' he said contemplatively, taking his own seat, his eyes on her face as he sat. 'That's good . . .' He steepled his long fingers in front of him. 'Perhaps you would care to pour the tea? That is going to be one of your duties; preparing my morning tea just how I like it. Pure Assam. Quite strong. A dash of milk. No sugar.'

Wilhemina's hands shook as she filled his cup, and a little tea sploshed out into the saucer. Immediately, she looked up shamefacedly, knowing, even before she met his gaze, that Doctor Brent was regarding her intently.

'Don't worry . . . You'll learn,' he said very softly. 'In this house you'll learn very quickly. There will be plenty of incentive to improve . . .' He held his hand out towards her to take his tea.

Wilhemina passed the cup, her arm almost aching from the tension of controlling it.

'Now then, Wilhemina Woodforde, I think I know you, don't I? I've seen you at work in the library.' The implication was, somehow, that 'seen' meant 'watched', and it became even harder to control the teapot. Wilhemina poured in too much tea and left room for only the smallest drop of milk. To make it more palatable, she reached for the sugar tongs, then snatched back her hand as if burned. Doctor Brent's faint, barely perceptible frown told her exactly what he thought of young women who had a sweet tooth.

'Er . . . Yes,' said Wilhemina nervously, 'I have a part time job there . . . I – um – I like it, but it doesn't pay all that well.'

'Does money matter a great deal to you?' murmured Doctor Brent over the china rim of his cup. 'I wasn't planning to pay much in the way of a salary; just a little pocket money, really, in addition to board all found –' he paused, his eyelashes flicking down and up like fans, '– and maybe a clothing allowance . . .'

'Clothing?'

'Yes. Clothing, Wilhemina,' said Doctor Brent gently, as if he were explaining a very simple fact to an even simpler child. 'I often receive visits from colleagues . . . Old-fashioned colleagues who appreciate the niceties of convention and form. They prefer the door to be answered, and the tea to be served, by a maid in a traditional domestic uniform.'

'U – uniform?' stammered Wilhemina, wishing desperately that she could answer the distinguished doctor in something other than her current moronic fashion. She simply wasn't being too impressive.

'If you don't care for the idea, you don't have to accept the position, you know,' he replied somewhat airily. 'I do have other young women to interview.'

Wilhemina's disappointment must have shown on her face, because Doctor Brent smiled and looked at her more kindly. 'Although it would be a shame if I had to send for one of them . . . I rather think you'll do very nicely.'

'I'd love the position, Doctor Brent,' she replied earnestly, sipping quickly at her tea and barely noticing it was still quite hot. 'And I'd be happy to wear a maid's uniform. I'll wear it all the time, if you like.'

'Now that would indeed be splendid,' said the doctor, favouring Wilhemina with a truly devastating smile. 'Yes, quite perfect. I knew you were just the right girl.' He held out his cup, and Wilhemina stared at it numbly for a few seconds, before realising he was requesting more tea.

Still shaking, but happily not too hard, Wilhemina negotiated the teapot again, and managed to serve them both without the tiniest spill. Doctor Brent smiled benignly as he took his, and Wilhemina smiled back – quite sure now that the future would be rosy – as they discussed the details of her brand new position.

The uniform was another of life's compromises, but after a day or so Wilhemina managed to accept it. The plain black dress had a certain sober charm, she supposed, but she was constantly in fear of dirtying her pristine white apron and cap, and thus incurring the displeasure of Doctor Brent.

And it was certainly worth a little compromising for the pleasure of living in such a house. Every room was a haven of old-fashioned comfort and understated luxury, even Wilhemina's own bedroom. It was furnished like a frilly Victorian boudoir, and more suited to a favoured niece, or a pampered mistress, than someone who was simply hired help. All she was here to do was a bit of dusting and tidying – a 'woman who did' took care of the rest – and the occasional serving of tea.

Not that very much of that had been done, except to Doctor Brent himself, whose attitude was friendly but spine-tinglingly watchful. There had been no 'colleagues' as such to be waited on as yet. In fact, the only visitors had been a succession of rather nervous-looking young women, who were all ushered immediately into Doctor Brent's study, to stay about an hour, and who were not offered any refreshment at all.

Wilhemina wondered about these female guests. Wondered quite a lot, if truth be told. They were all in their early twenties, all quite pretty, and none of them carried the books or files that would have marked them out as Doctor Brent's students. This lack of the usual accoutrements of study was especially odd, in view of the fact that whenever one of these fresh-faced young visitors arrived, the good doctor would don his rusty black academic gown, as if his intentions at least were instructional.

His students mostly looked extremely fearful when they arrived, and some of them looked quite teary when they left, and all walked down the drive very slowly and with the appearance of considerable discomfort. Some of them, however, though walking with the same careful, almost ginger, gait, had a quite different expression on their faces. A look that was quite beatific, quite exalted. As if *they* were just as much in love with Doctor Brent as Wilhemina already was, and he had done something that had made them love him more.

None of this accounted for the noises, though, and one day while she was dusting, Wilhemina was shocked – and intrigued – to hear a sequence of rhythmical swishing sounds, and shortly after a soft female cry. At first she thought she was imagining things, but after surreptitiously finding it necessary to re-polish the decorative brasses that hung on the wall just next to the door to Doctor Brent's study, she heard the strange noises repeated. Again and again and again. A whistling swish. A chillingly solid thud. And a high-pitched, very feminine yelp.

What on earth could they be doing in there? thought Wilhemina, then, suddenly, she remembered the frightful armoury that hung on the wall, and her heart clamoured as the penny finally dropped. 'Oh, dear Lord, he's spanking them,' she whispered to herself, and then, as if to confirm her suspicions, the study door opened, and the latest victim – miscreant? – came scuttling out, her hands clasped to her flannel-covered buttocks. The young woman's face was tear-stained, yet somehow also radiant, and Wilhemina heard her thank Doctor Brent – who was standing just behind her – in a voice that was both timid and adoring.

Wilhemina was so amazed by what was happening, and so unnerved, that as the chastised young woman walked awkwardly past her, she stepped rather clumsily out of the way and her elbow caught a vase she had dusted earlier – the one which stood on the Jacobean sideboard in the passage – and sent it hurtling to the floor with a crash.

Squatting down, and scrabbling around for what seemed like a thousand pieces, Wilhemina braced herself for the Doctor's shout of anger. Like everything in the house, the vase was exquisite, and clearly very valuable. What was more, the good doctor seemed to cherish his every possession most highly.

He'll dismiss me, she thought dolefully, gathering the

shards in her apron, and quaking as his soft step drew near.

But there was no angry reproof. No harsh word. Just a light touch on her shoulder when he reached her. Blushing, Wilhemina looked up from her ungainly crouched position on the floor.

'Oh, dear,' said Doctor Brent gently. 'What have you done, Wilhemina? That vase came from China and was centuries old.'

Transfixed, and feeling like a rabbit in the headlights of a car, Wilhemina looked up in amazement. There was no fury in Doctor Brent's handsome face, not even a trace of irritation. He looked calm, as composed as a saint. In fact, she could almost have believed that he was pleased that she had destroyed his costly vase.

'I'll pay for it, Doctor Brent,' she muttered wanly. 'I'll go without my allowance. I'll manage somehow . . . I don't need much.'

'I doubt if your allowance would cover the required amount in a lifetime, Wilhemina,' said Doctor Brent serenely, as he reached down and helped her to rise. The touch of his long, strangely warm hand seemed to burn her right through her dress, and in her confusion, Wilhemina lost her grip on her apron. The pieces of vase cascaded to the floor again, and as they did so the doctor laughed softly and released her.

'You had better pick those up – again – Wilhemina,' he said, his voice sounding almost excited. 'And when you've disposed of them, perhaps you could return to my study, and we'll discuss a more appropriate restitution.'

Although her heart knew what was going to happen to her – and what 'restitution' meant – Wilhemina's conscious mind refused to accept it. She had accepted Doctor Brent's enormously sweet smile, then hunkered down again to get on with her task, hearing the study door snick shut as she had reached beneath the sideboard for the very last piece. She had ignored all thoughts of her fate while she had disposed of the ruined vase, then made her way to her room to prepare herself. She had kept her mind blank as she had used the lavatory, washed her face and hands, and combed her hair; and thought of nothing as she had replaced her grubby apron with a new one, and used hairgrips to secure a fresh white cap.

But now, outside the study door, poised to knock, her heart and her mind came together.

Doctor Brent was going to spank her for smashing his vase. She knew it, and she suspected that Doctor Brent knew she knew it. Her pulse thudded as she tapped for entrance.

'Come in, Wilhemina.' To Wilhemina's ears, that pleasant voice sounded just like the tolling of a bell. The dreaded knell that announced anguish ahead. She entered the room, closing the door behind her, but kept her eyes down, unable to look at him. Unable to face the brilliant eyes of her accuser.

'No need to be afraid,' said Doctor Brent encouragingly. 'We both know why you're here, don't we? And I think we both know it's really for the best . . .' He paused, and Wilhemina heard the tiny sounds of him sliding his arms into his voluminous black gown – which she had noticed lying ominously across the table. 'Now then, Wilhemina,' he continued, moving past her to sit down in the nursing chair she had occupied at her interview, 'look up. Show me your pretty face.' She obeyed, feeling as dazzled as she had that first time. 'That's better.' His eyes were almost kind now. 'Now come here – and come across my knee.'

So this was it. What she had been hearing. What she had been imagining. Corporal punishment for her grievous misdoings. The flat of Doctor Brent's pale, graceful hand across her bottom. It would hurt – the young women's cries attested to that – and his hand might be only the beginning. Nervously, she glanced towards the wall, where hung the cane, the whip and the strap – each one of them the very devil of an implement.

'It's the only way to learn, Wilhemina,' he murmured, his voice husky and suddenly quite seductive. 'After a spanking, you'll be more mindful, more careful . . . You'll remember to look after my things properly. To be a better and more thorough maid, and not to hang about eavesdropping in corridors, when other, equally undisciplined young women come to visit me and receive their lessons.'

With that he set his strong legs slightly apart, and reached out and took hold of her hand. Then, pulling gently, and controlling her effortlessly, he brought her face down across his lap, settling her neatly and making her lift up her bottom.

'Oh, please, don't!' she whimpered, as with a flick of his wrist, he had her skirt and her fluffy, lacy petticoats in a thick folded bunch around her waist. And then remained only the inevitable, final shame of it – and she struggled in vain as he pulled down her white panties.

'I'm afraid I must,' said Doctor Brent, one hand moving lightly across her bottom cheeks, as the other rested in the small of her back. 'It's the only sure, effective way. Charming as they are, your panties would blunt the blows . . . Steal their fire. And a bare bottom also adds shame to the equation. Don't you think so?' he enquired as he palpated her flesh.

Wilhemina nodded woefully, already sobbing before the first smack had fallen.

But when it did fall, she yelped like a baby!

It hurt! It hurt so much! She couldn't believe how a man's hand could sting her. The heat was enormous, the pain a pure shock, and as soon as she was recovering from one smack, she was getting the next, and the next, and the next.

Doctor Brent was as methodical and fastidious in his

spanking as he was in the whole of his life. Through the tingling red fires in her belaboured bottom, Wilhemina sensed a consummate perfectionist at work. He spread the smacks with all the finesse of an artist, balancing the hot flaring crimson exactly. No part of her formerly white backside was left unattended, and after a few minutes, she perceived the soreness as uniform.

'Well, now we've raised a lovely glow,' he observed, running his fingertips across her to prove it. Every place he touched seemed to smart with equal fervour, and every touch made her desperate to wriggle. There was no way she wouldn't be careful now. 'But I think it's time that we really went to work.'

Wilhemina gasped, and began to squirm in panic as Doctor Brent tipped her further across his knee. She felt herself sliding, slipping, falling, but a strong hand on her back kept her steady. 'Hush, hush, my dear,' he whispered, his voice a benediction, 'you're safe here with me . . . We'll soon get you seen to. Don't worry.'

At the sound of this soothing pronouncement, Wilhemina let her stinging flesh relax. She *did* feel safe. She *did* feel cared for. And she trusted Doctor Brent completely. To set her life to rights with the stiff palm of his hand.

The smacks began to fall again, and this time they were far harder and far more effective. Striking her just on the peachy underhang of her bottom, their impact was particularly intense, stirring flames of pain in the already tender flesh. Each spank was exquisitely aimed, and perfectly delivered. Each spank made Wilhemina see stars. She yowled at each stroke, and she sobbed like a baby, but lifted her bottom to improve the doctor's aim. Because one sweet thing made the agony all worthwhile.

Every time his hand fell hard on her bottom, Doctor Brent spoke a little word of praise. He called her 'a good girl', 'a brave girl' and 'a clever girl who learnt her lessons well'. Wilhemina couldn't restrain her anguished tears, but even as she shed them, and she snuffled and groaned uncontrollably, she knew the fuss had not one cause but two. Doctor Brent's words were just as moving as his hand.

'Do you think you've had enough?' he asked at last, as his fingertips traced her fire-filled cheeks. 'Do you think you'll remember to take care with my possessions from now on, and to refrain from snooping and spying on me?'

'Y – yes, Doctor Brent,' Wilhemina stammered, her self-control shattered by his touch.

'Are you sure?' he persisted, the pads of his fingers pressing at her soreness. 'Really sure?'

'I think so . . .' Wilhemina felt doubt now, and sensed that he wanted a different answer.

'Wouldn't you like to know for certain? I can think of a way to convince you . . .' He was squeezing her now, squeezing firmly.

'Yes – Yes, Doctor Brent. I'd like that,' she answered cautiously, but knew that 'like' wasn't quite what she meant. How could one like the idea of being chastised?

'You'll have to be brave, Wilhemina,' he said, as he urged her off his knee, then held her secure as she stumbled. The pain in her bottom was atrocious now, but to her chagrin, she knew it was nothing. She winced like fury as he arranged her to his liking: her face buried in her folded arms, against the seat of the chair, while her bare buttocks were offered up as his target.

'And the only way for us to be really sure that you're trying,' he continued conversationally, as he adjusted her legs, and parted her thighs, 'is for me to spank this –' he touched her simmering left cheek, and made her gasp, then gnaw her lower lip and slowly sway '– every, single day. And sometimes . . .' He paused, and Wilhemina imagined him looking thoughtfully towards the wall. 'As perhaps now, I fear. I may also have to employ one of my implements ... Do you think you can bear that, Wilhemina?'

I'm going to have a flaming red bum for the rest of my life, thought Wilhemina dreamily as she quivered. I might never be able to sit down comfortably ever again. I'll have to sleep every night on my face.

In a life filled with hard-to-bear compromises, this was the biggest and hardest she could imagine, but she realised that she would simply *have* to bear it. And be brave enough to earn this man's respect.

'Yes, Doctor Brent, I'm sure I can,' she answered fervently, and surrendered her bottom to her beloved for all time.

Ice

Miranda Litherland stared intently at the document, and especially at the single word 'no'.

The deal had been bungled, all her efforts wasted, and goodness knew how many thousands had been lost.

Yes, all *my* efforts, she thought. All those phone calls. All those carefully worded reports. All that research. If it had been down to me, we would have clinched it, I know.

The loss of the contract was partially her fault, though, she supposed, weighing the situation with her usual rational calm. She should have watched Jonathan more closely, made sure he was pushing and dealing, but instead she had taken his efforts all on trust.

Unwise, Miranda, she thought, as her mind began to run on retribution. On revenge and punishment. And how someone must suffer for this lapse.

The idea of a salutary lesson made Miranda's heart beat a little faster. The very words had a certain grave charm. Yes, she decided, touching her tongue-tip to her glossy red lips, if Jonathan Harcourt had been a little sharper, a little cooler, this situation would never have arisen and the firm would have been a good deal better off.

Steepling her long, polish-tipped fingers, Miranda reviewed her strategies. Her fantasies. A course of action in view of this setback. And as she did so her thoughts were clear as glass.

As the plan and the fantasies came together, Miranda realised something that almost unnerved her. Almost subconsciously, she had begun massaging her crotch against the desk. Gasping with irritation, she stepped away smartly and smoothed down her skirt. This was no time for casual self-pleasuring – she must contain herself for the challenge yet to come.

Checking her immaculate appearance in the office mirror, Miranda smoothed a stray blonde wisp into her chignon. She was well aware of her nickname – the Ice Maiden – but what the others didn't realise was she liked it. It pleased her to be sternly untouchable – with an inferno of white heat deep inside.

Some time later, at home, after a long, hot shower and change of clothing, Miranda poured herself a large gin and tonic.

Jonathan would be home now too. How convenient. It was time his shortcomings were discussed.

Standing before her long antique mirror, Miranda sipped her drink and studied her reflection. She had let down her thick, straight, almost white-blonde hair so it hung in smooth sheaves to her shoulders. She had re-applied her make-up, made it fierce and stylised, then slid into clothing more appropriate to her mood – a black nylon fitted shirt worn without a bra, and a pair of leather jeans-cut trousers that clung ferociously to the contours of her thighs. Beneath these she wore a G-string, a tiny scraplet of flimsy black lace that, she realised ruefully, was already well soaked.

'Not so icy now,' she observed to herself, slipping her feet into her favourite short boots. Having placed one or two choice items in her attaché case, she shrugged on her black leather trenchcoat, then rang for a taxi to take her to Jonathan's.

There was no need to ring or knock when she got there, for the key was already in her pocket. She simply ran lightly up the stairs, abandoned her coat on the landing, then strode with cool confidence into the bedroom. Lying on his bed in just shirt and suit trousers, Jonathan was waiting for her, an icy drink on the chest of drawers beside him and a magazine open across his lap.

'I thought you might be ready?' Her voice was silky, and her face neutral, but she might as well have screamed out profanities. Jonathan leapt from his bed like a startled rabbit, his sandy hair flapping as he did so, and his magazine cascading off the bed. He was handsome in a bland sort of way, Miranda reflected detachedly, but as he stood beside his bed, visibly trembling, his face was a mask of fearful lust. He cringed, too, his stance pathetic – but his erection was bulging unmistakeably, quite inappropriate for a man who had done wrong. Miranda felt like taking a stick and beating his penis until he howled, but it was a little early for the direst of severity.

As she watched him evenly, Jonathan struggled with the buttons of his shirt. His blue eyes were enormous with fear and excitement, and he bit his lip as he fumbled and got entangled with his sleeves.

'And those?' said Miranda when the shirt was off, nodding faintly towards Jonathan's lower body.

She never shouted during encounters such as these. Controlled tones were far more effective. She felt violence – it was like an elixir inside her – but she never let anyone see it. Or detect her wild, seething state of arousal. As she prowled slowly around the room, placing her slim black case ominously on the bed, she felt joy in her own cool control. Her nipples were like stones, and her vulva was dripping, but she behaved as if her body meant nothing. The only need she acknowledged was for a drink.

Still tasting the gin she had drunk earlier, Miranda poured herself a measure from Jonathan's decanter. There was something about the silvery resinous spirit that seemed to suit these sessions to perfection. Its flavour was steely and unyielding, and its power flowed like mercury through her veins. She imagined dipping her finger in the glass, then touching the clear fluid to her clitoris. It would bite. It would sting. And she would hiss through her teeth as she climaxed. Turning away from Jonathan, she smiled slyly. It wouldn't do for him to see evidence of her thoughts.

'Still dressed?' she enquired, swinging around.

Jonathan was only just unzipping his trousers, clearly embarrassed to reveal his stiffened penis. Miranda could imagine how he felt right now. He had a nature that craved humiliation, and a puny pride that always resisted it. His own urges fought and jostled inside him, leaving him directionless and so easy to control.

As his grey designer trousers slid down to his ankles, Miranda gave a soft, contained laugh. Instead of his own boxer shorts Jonathan was wearing a pair of *her* French knickers. Pink and frilly, they would have looked silly enough under normal circumstances, but now they were pushed outwards at the front. The loose legs gaped under the pressure of his erection, and his pubic hair, and his balls, were on show.

'Hmmm, not bad, I suppose,' murmured Miranda disparagingly.

Wearing only the revealing pink panties, Jonathan hung his head and stood before her, waiting. There was a spreading damp patch on the fine, silky lace and Miranda relished the evidence of his wetness. His cock was weeping now, where it butted against the fabric, but before long there would be other, sweeter tears.

Slowly, at her leisure, she strolled forward, placed her drink beside his, then took hold of the waistband of the knickers. For a moment, she simply stretched the elastic slightly, looking directly into Jonathan's liquid eyes, then, with a measured, almost infinitesimal unhurriedness, she began easing the flimsy silk downwards.

It wasn't usual for a mistress to perform such tasks, or to half-kneel before her awe-striken victim, but Miranda loved these little variations. They increased the tension, and kept Jonathan off-balance. He sobbed like a baby as she licked his red shaft, but when he pushed forward, she leapt up and danced away, leaving her lingerie at half mast around his knees.

'Are you proud of that?' she enquired, reaching for her drink and taking a small sip. For a moment, she considered holding the gin in her mouth while she sucked Jonathan's penis. The blend of flavours and resulting loud screech would be diverting; but he would also probably come far too soon.

'Well?' she persisted.

'I – I don't know,' he stammered, looking down.

Jonathan's erection was so extreme now that it pointed straight upwards towards her, the flesh itself as solid as old oak.

I could hang something on that, she reflected whimsically, then considered a few likely items. The knickers, perhaps? She could make him step out of them, then drape them on his shaft himself.

What about her G-string? A good idea, but she didn't want to be naked just yet. That, too, would make him come prematurely. He would spurt for sure if her fragrance touched his tip.

Not that it wasn't dripping already. A line of clear fluid was stringing out from the end, and crawling down towards the carpet like a silky resin exhuded from a branch. Miranda knew she should have expressed disgust at this juncture – her rôle demanded it – but as ever her feelings were maverick. She would have liked to catch that glistening thread on her fingertip, then conveyed it to her mouth and her tongue. She imagined the flavour exploding on her taste-buds, and the texture gelatinous on her lips.

Instead, however, she merely said, 'Deal with it.'

Jonathan looked vaguely sickened but, again, he

knew what to do. Reaching down he caught his own sticky product and lifted it quickly to his mouth.

How silly you look, thought Miranda, feeling her blood warm and her mettle start to rise. She remembered how Jonathan had been when she had very first met him: his carefully nurtured self-importance; his petty ego-tripping; his preening and his puerile body language. He had been so easy that she had snared him in seconds.

'Enough. Mustn't be greedy,' she reproved gently as he made to repeat the action. 'Make it dance for me instead; I'm getting bored.'

Wearing an expression of acute unhappiness, Jonathan bent his knees and rotated his hips, making his stiff flesh bounce cheerfully in front of him. Miranda could well imagine the effect this rhythm would have in him: the humiliation, and the slow, caressing drag.

'More,' she urged, then turned away, moistening her suddenly dry lips. Jonathan might be an ineffectual, incompetent idiot, but his penis was nothing to be ashamed of. Miranda could feel her vagina fluttering; soft, slippery fluid welled up in her furrow and flowed out across her labia and clitoris. The lace of her G-string was soaked through already just from watching Jonathan's absurdly lewd contortions.

The temptation to rub herself was exquisite, but resisting it aroused her even more. The pit of her belly was like a ball under pressure; tight, out-swelling, and alive with an unstoppable craving.

'It's not very impressive, is it?' she observed, dismissing the very flesh she longed to envelop. 'It looks rather bare . . .' She cocked her head on one side, eyeing him, and noted a minute increase in hardness. 'Should we dress it up a little, perhaps?'

'Oh, no!' he whimpered, 'Please, no!'

'Oh, yes,' murmured Miranda, the tension in her own loins increasing.

The next part of the game was something Jonathan didn't like. But as Miranda herself enjoyed it mightily, it was an element they always included.

Snapping open her attaché case, she drew out a small contraption made of thin leather straps and tiny, cruel looking buckles. Without a word, she handed the device to Jonathan, then nodded imperiously at his cock.

His fingers shook as he took the harness, and he dropped it. Miranda gave him a steady, old-fashioned look, and, crouching, he bent to retrieve it.

'Continue,' she bade him, reaching for her drink and draining it.

Clumsily, haltingly, Jonathan strapped the leather around his genitals. As he fastened the last buckle, he looked beseechingly towards her, but she nodded, indicating he tighten the strap another notch. He sobbed softly, but still he obeyed. Then obeyed again and again and again as she repeated her implacable instruction.

As a female, Miranda had no way of knowing what a cinctured penis felt like, but she believed she could imagine the sensations. Jonathan's flesh must be a bar of fire by now, aching for release just as her vulva ached for its orgasm. He certainly looked profoundly uncomfortable; his shaft was trembling, and coloured up to a violent, veined crimson. It jutted upwards and towards her at a sharp, unlikely angle, and his testicles were swollen like two plums.

'Very good, Jonathan,' she said almost cajolingly, then paused to pour herself more gin. 'And you may step out of my underwear, too.'

As she mixed her new drink, Miranda silently commended her victim for having a large supply of ice. She was burning up in every way now, and the coolness of the gin was sublime. Flicking an ice cube with her tongue, she imagined what it would feel like to push the melting chunk right into her sex. Or rub it back and forth across her clitoris. It would be excruciating, but still she was tempted.

With a small sip of gin came a large rush of wickedness, and Miranda looked back towards Jonathan. Her thoughts were too rude, too fanciful, she knew that, but she wasn't called the 'Ice Maiden' for nothing, was she? Swirling her glass and watching the ice cubes twinkle, she considered their irregular dimensions.

Refining her plan, Miranda smiled and took another sip of gin, then signalled the quaking Jonathan towards her. From her case, she took out a pair of perfectly standard office bulldog clips, then held them up before his fear-widened eyes.

Jonathan shook his head, but Miranda nodded hers. She could see sweat in the hair along his brow-line, and drops of it gathering on his lip. His relationship with the clips was like his relationship with her; he was half in love with them, but hated them, too.

'Dear God!' he cried as she applied them, closing their grips on his nipples one after the other.

'There . . . Isn't that pretty?' she asked as tears trickled down his sweating face. His penis seemed to jerk, as if to reach her, but neatly she stepped back a single pace.

Standing with legs parted and her hands resting lightly on her hips, she felt the devil stir inside her. This stupid, grovelling creature had almost certainly lost them good business, and suddenly she longed to see him suffer.

'Kneel on the bed,' she ordered coolly. 'Facing away from me, please,' she added, knowing that her politeness only frightened him all the more.

When he was in position, head bowed, she took a long silk scarf from her case and tightly bound his hands behind his back. Eyeing a second scarf, she debated gagging him. The scarf would be an insult in his mouth, a subtle torment, but she so loved the sound of Jonathan's moans. With a shrug, she left the second scarf alone.

'Forward now,' she said, pushing firmly on the nape of his neck. 'Press your forehead against the cover, but don't let your penis touch the bed.' She let her hand drop delicately on to his bottom. 'Or I'll thrash you to within an inch of your life.'

Jonathan's arse was really his best feature, thought Miranda dispassionately, admiring the hard muscle, and the narrow, shaded groove. When she stroked him, his anus seemed to pout at her, and she took that as a subconscious invitation.

I wouldn't encourage me, if I were you, she told him silently, her free hand swirling blindly in the ice bucket, as she fished out more cubes for her drink.

'Relax,' she whispered, taking a taste of her watery gin and sucking a small chunk of ice into her mouth. Slithering it around, she softened its edges then slipped it out into the palm of her hand. 'Relax,' she whispered again, then before Jonathan could protest, or even flinch, she pushed the chilly morsel deep inside his rectum.

'Oh, no! Oh, no!' he keened, and it was clear he understood the awful truth.

Oh, yes! thought Miranda exultantly, entranced by the waggling flesh beneath her. 'Stay still!' she ordered, pushing in another cube, then another and another, whilst still stroking him gently with her fingers.

After a minute or two he was a gasping, panting wreck, his chest heaving and his bottom cheeks taut. Each time he seemed about to lose control, Miranda stopped packing him and concentrated on fondling, touching his balls or his pulsing anal ring.

'Please . . . Oh God,' he pleaded as she inserted yet another cube, but Miranda couldn't tell whether that meant 'stop' or 'more'. As he jerked and jiggled, she decided on the latter.

When she gauged that his poor, chilled innards couldn't take any more, she ignored the ice cubes and turned solely to caressing. Slowly and tauntingly, she slid her fingertips all over his hind parts, rubbing his bottom, his perineum and his balls.

Jonathan was sobbing uninhibitedly now, and pushing his face into the tear-sodden counterpane. His thighs were rigid with effort, his belly distended, and his cock diamond-hard and drooling freely. Almost mesmerised by such a vision of blissful misery, Miranda had never felt so aroused in all her life. She shifted her position, to reach around beneath him, but as she did so, her jeans' seam grazed her clitoris and she orgasmed immediately, with a silent, stifled scream. Without a sound, and with her free fist jammed tightly against her lips, she climaxed magnificently without revealing the fact to Jonathan.

The spasms took some time to subside, and to calm herself she watched the slow twitch of his bottom. The strain must be killing him, she thought, feeling mellow. She had once had an enema at a health farm, and vividly remembered the delicious sense of terror. She hadn't been able to keep still for a second as the slowly gathering fluid had swelled inside her, but despite her fears she had experienced the deepest pleasure.

Jonathan's buttocks were tensing, then relaxing, tensing, then relaxing, in a regular, almost hypnotising rhythm, and his penis was a red, unbending rod. From its tip there hung a silver stream of juice.

Orgasm had purged Miranda of her anger, and in its place left magnanimous indulgence. Let the little worm have *his* fun now, she told herself, feeling loose and voluptuously genial.

'Right, that's it, my sweet, you can go and do what you have to,' she said, then touched him cautiously on his agitated flank before making short work of his narrow silky bonds, 'But be quick. I'll want you back here in a minute.'

While she waited, Miranda saw visions. Jonathan, scuttling like a crab across the room and clutching himself, his anguish an exquisite turn-on; herself, in a stiffly boned corset, selecting a whip with a smile on her face. Jonathan, bound naked to a rack, his mouth gagged and his eyes covered with a mask; herself again, encased in something made of rubber, while an unknown man pushed ice into her.

The creak of the bathroom door put a stop to her provocative fantasies. Miranda took her hand from her crotch – where it had naturally settled – and looked up towards the source of the interruption.

Jonathan was a sorrier sight than ever. His hair was wet, his body blanched and shaky, and his penis was a tiny, shrunken stub. He had achieved his climax, but in shame and sickly, trembling weakness. It was the only way he liked it, Miranda observed wearily, her earlier fond feelings a little dissipated. Jonathan sadly was a wimp and a coward. In the same situation she herself would have had far more resilience.

But even so, he still had his uses.

'Come here,' said Miranda resignedly. Spreading her legs, she hutched her bottom forward to the edge of the bed and set her booted feet flat on the carpet. 'You know what to do.'

Jonathan slunk forward, then hovered a few inches from her knees. Closing her eyes, she let herself go limp and tried to ignore who it was who first fumbled with her boots, and then with her skin-tight trousers. As her mind flew high and free, other, more mysterious, hands seemed to work on her tiny, sopping G-string.

'Get on with it,' she said when she was uncovered, her hunger made spiky by her dreams, 'Make yourself useful.'

A tongue settled clumsily on her clitoris, but it didn't matter any more whose it was, because reality had slid away into the void. A digit bored rudely into her bottom, and another smoothly entered her quim. Hard teeth nipped cleverly at her clitoris; then, more softly, a pair of playful lips worried it, and rolled it to and fro and back and forth.

Rolling and thrashing and kicking him, Miranda saw rainbow colours behind her eyelids and heard distorted sounds pounding in her head. Orgasm grabbed her loins like a hard, squeezing fist, and one noise rose to the surface of the others.

The familiar, ragged tones of her voice.

'Yes! Yes! Yes!' she screamed as her whole sex clenched, and her belly seemed to dance with leaping fire.

A flame that melted the very last scraps of ice.

The next morning she was at her desk early, but Jonathan didn't arrive until gone eleven. She saw him regard her without reaction as he passed through the office, but his indifference didn't ruffle her in the slightest. There was nothing now to agitate her composure.

A short while later, the intercom buzzed, and when she pressed the receive stud, his familiar voice floated out.

'I'll have my tea now, Miss Litherland,' he said briskly, although Miranda detected a quiver in her name.

'Will that be *iced* tea, Mr Harcourt?' she asked – the cool, perfect secretary – then laughed as she distinctly heard him groan.

In the Air Tonight

It was my first formal party in the village, and I was going to have a wild time or expire in the effort.

'I can help if you like, Flora,' Morwenna had said with an evil twinkle in her eye. 'I'll mix you a special perfume. A real love-brew. The men won't be able to keep their hands off you.' She had given me that look then, that special sideways leer of hers that always made me melt and want to kiss her. 'And for that matter, neither will the women.'

I had believed her then, but now, here at Rawnsley Hall for the Midsummer Night's festivities, I wasn't so sure about Morwenna's herbal magic.

My clever friend had never let me down before with her concoctions. Her pot-pourris were delectable, her remedies and recipes always worked to perfection, and even her organic compost made my vegetables come up jumbo-sized and choice.

This aromatherapy perfume she had mixed for me, however, wasn't nearly as sweet-smelling as I had expected. It wasn't gruesome, but it wasn't exactly Chanel. There was a bitter, woody sort of tang to it, an edge of smoke and an undernote of earth. I had scrunched up my nose as I had sniffed it, then applied it, but even so I had decided – as ever – to trust her. I was still suffering from the tail end of a nasty summer cold – which another of Morwenna's remedies had helped to soothe

– and my sense of smell probably wasn't working as it should do.

But even with my misgivings, I was glad to be at the party. Rawnsley Hall looked wonderful in the twilight. The air was warm, the light was golden, and, unsurprisingly, almost the entire population of Marwick Magna was either in the house, or strolling in the gardens. There were drinks in abundance, and there was food around somewhere, and classical music was playing from a PA system. There was only one thing to spoil the rural idyll – and that was the defiant and irritating presence of droves of midges. Even this early, the village was already plagued with them. I could see them dancing in the air as I looked towards the garden, and every now and again, someone would slap at one impatiently when it landed.

Any minute now, I thought resignedly, looking down at my bare shoulders in my strappy, bra-topped ball gown. I was just a walking landing ground for the hungry little blighters; an open buffet for their tiny jaws to munch on.

'Hello, sweetheart, I've been wondering when you'd get here,' said a purring voice behind me, and I instantly forgot the airborne insects. I turned around to find a handsome, smiling face and proffered glass of wine.

'Hello, Marshall, how are you?'

Marshall Fox was Marwick Magna's premier man of letters, a best-selling novelist who wrote carefully-researched, critic-pleasing thrillers as well as deliciously filthy pornography on the side.

'Great. Wonderful. And all the better for seeing you.' He paused, eyed me up and down. 'Flora, darling, you look gorgeous tonight, quite edible. In fact, I'd like to eat you right this minute.'

I blushed furiously, caught unawares by his heavy double-entendre. Lean-bodied, dark-eyed Marshall was pretty gorgeous himself, it had to be said, and I had engaged in certain 'dealings' with him earlier in the year. His brilliant imagination served him well as both a writer and a lover; and his hands, his cock and his long, eager tongue were all equally as mighty as his pen.

He stared at me for a moment, as I drank my wine too fast, then he shuddered and seemed to come to a decision. Taking my glass from my hand, he placed it on the parapet with his, then slid a proprietorial arm around my satin-clad waist. 'Jesus, Flora, I've been wanting us to get together again,' he muttered, almost panting as he hustled me along the terrace in the direction of the rose garden, 'but I didn't realise quite how much until just now.'

Being swept off my feet was quite thrilling, and as my body stirred I silently thanked Morwenna. Her aromatic compound might smell peculiar to my nose, but it seemed be working wonders for Marshall. Beneath a tree and out of sight behind a high rose hedge, he began kissing me and struggling frantically with my clothes.

'You're so beautiful tonight, Flora,' he gasped, his mouth against my neck and his hands dragging up my long full skirt. 'There's something about you . . . You make me feel like an animal. I'll go mad if you don't let me touch you!'

Far be it from me to drive a man crazy, so I hauled helpfully at another flounce of skirt. Within seconds, he was tugging at the elastic of my panties, and a moment later they were down around my knees.

'Oh, Flora, Flora,' he chanted, rummaging through my fleece, then pushing his strong fingers deep into my wetness. Without hesitation, I eased apart my thighs.

That first sweet touch was quite magical. So longed-for it was uplifting and sublime. There was something in the air for me tonight, too, it seemed, because I was slippery and as mad for sex as Marshall. I moaned as he rubbed my vulva roughly, my voice uncouth and my actions even more so. Working my sex on his hand as if

I were possessed by a demon, I chanted obscene words as I bumped and jerked and swayed. I could hear him gasping, my dress rustling, and the distinct, liquid slicking of my juices. And when I climaxed, I shouted, 'Oh, dear God!' and bit his ear.

Fortunately it was only a nip, though, and when I could think straight, I murmured, 'Sorry,' and kissed it better.

'Not there,' said Marshall huskily, placing his hands on my shoulders and pushing downwards.

It seemed only fair to undo his zip and kiss his cock.

A few minutes later, I left Marshall dozing like a zombie on a bench in the rose garden, while I ventured towards the house to find a drink. My mouth felt thick and sticky with a familiar salt-ammonia taste, and though I liked it, I found it made me very thirsty.

Despite the unrelenting army of midges, not many party-goers had retreated inside. I nodded to one or two as I passed through the open entrance hall, but I didn't stop because I didn't want to talk. I needed some space now, a refuge and time to think. Grabbing a glass of wine, I made my way towards the library.

Morwenna's mixture was working, without question. Marshall had always been a gentle and enthusiastic lover, if a little on the kinky side, but never before had he seemed so manic, so driven. The bitter herbal perfume must have played havoc with his senses, just as surely as it was doing the same to mine.

The library was quiet and cool and tranquil, with not a midge or voracious lover in sight. I considered lighting one of the candles that stood waiting in their candelabra, but changed my mind and sat down gratefully in the darkness.

Now it was my turn to drowse, my mind swirling dreamily with sensual memories and expectations. Marshall had been the perfect taster, an erotic *hors d'oeuvre* for the banquet that lay ahead. My body was still warm where his fingers had touched and stirred me, my soft folds moist and already swollen with fresh desire. Pressing my hand against my crotch, I began to drift into fantasy.

'Miss Swain? Flora? Are you all right?'

Confused, realising I had almost fallen asleep, I opened my eyes – and before me stood a vision of sleek, blonde hair, smooth, immaculate make-up, and an elegant patrician body draped in a black crepe Jean Muir. It was my hostess, Amelia, Lady Rawnsley, someone with whom I had also had 'dealings'.

'Good evening, Flora, my dear,' said a second voice, close by. 'Such bad manners to fall asleep at one's party, eh?'

I swung around, swivelling on the leather sofa, and found Lord Rawnsley himself just behind me, his cool blue eyes glittering and intense. In his exquisitely cut dinner suit he looked every inch an earl, and his prematurely silver hair only added to his air of distinction. I had learned quite a lot from His Lordship since my migration to the country; and as he and his wife sat down – one on either side of me – it looked suspiciously like I was going to learn some more.

'I'm sorry, M'Lord,' I said, unable to resist a defiant little grin. 'Work hard, play hard. You know how it is.'

'Indeed I do,' replied Crispin, his voice silky, and his hand on my thigh. 'And what, pray, have you being playing so hard at, my dear?' He squeezed my leg, his fingers almost cruel through my skirt and my petticoats, and as he did so, I felt Amelia pressing closer.

The Rawnsleys, like many aristocrats, were as decadent as they were anciently blue-blooded. The notorious 'English Vice' was their favoured peccadillo, and Crispin in particular loved young ladies for their round and tempting bottoms.

'Have you been doing something naughty that I

should punish you for?' He was sliding my skirt up now, like Marshall before him, and as before, I wasn't making any protests.

'I – I don't know . . .' I stammered as my clothing reached my waist. I could hear my petticoats crackling as he folded them and bunched them, then a soft gasp from Amelia at my side.

'Well, perhaps we should humble you anyway,' he suggested, plucking delicately at my pants.

Suddenly, I heard voices. We all heard them. There were people in the corridor, outside the library door, people who might come in at any second and find Milord and Lady *en flagrante* with a guest.

I tried to push my skirt down, and Amelia tried to help me, but Crispin carried on exploring my nether regions.

'Crispin, please!' Amelia muttered urgently. 'Someone may come in!' She batted at her husband's hands, 'Someone who – who doesn't understand.' She seemed scared, but excited, in just the way that I was, her picture-portrait features brought to life with naked hunger.

'Don't fuss, Amelia,' said Crispin, his voice determined but uncharacteristically ragged. By this time, my panties were at my ankles. 'I'm not going to let this luscious young woman escape us now. She's a treat. A torment. A feast. I've got to get my hands on her or I'll simply just expire!'

A part of me was still listening for those voices in the corridor, but the rest of me was thrilled by Crispin's outcry. He had never been this passionate before, this desperate. His seductions were usually civilised and laconic in the early stages, then a little cruel when he really got the flavour. Morwenna's love oil had altered things completely.

'Let me touch you,' he purred in my ear, 'Let me look at that glorious, peachy arse of yours . . .' His hand slid beneath me, gripping rudely and squeezing, then he shoved lightly upwards to lift me to my feet.

'Crispin,' hissed Amelia, protesting but no longer really meaning it. She wanted to share me, and my body, with her husband; her bright eyes and her pink cheeks betrayed her.

The voices faded, and with them went all our inhibitions. The two Rawnsleys slid apart on the leather couch again, making room for me to crouch, lengthways, between them. Amelia's lips settled on mine as her hands caressed my shoulders, while her husband slid my dress up and bared my rump.

'Beautiful, beautiful, beautiful,' he whispered, running his face across my cheeks as if he were nuzzling a beloved cat. He nosed my bottom-cleft, my anus and the insides of my upper thighs, then kissed the underhang, where a veil of sweat was forming. The night was warm, and the mood, now, even hotter. I whimpered as his teeth closed lightly, nipping my left buttock while his fingertips probed my rosebud.

'Yes, oh, Flora, yes,' he whispered against the crown of my bottom, pushing, pushing, pushing, with one finger only now, to enter that dark, forbidden portal.

'Please don't,' I gasped, meaning 'please do' as I pushed backwards and relaxed.

'You're such a little slut, my dear,' he said in my ear, leaning over me to kiss Amelia. My head went down, and I arched my back in pleasure, knowing that above me their mouths were fused and ravenous. I could feel Amelia fumbling around blindly as she kissed, struggling with the top of my dress so she could release my aching breasts.

My zip whizzed down, the thin straps slithered off my shoulders, then the boned front of my ball gown fell away. My breasts swung free, the nipples hard and pointed, and Amelia reached beneath me to cup them in her hands.

The Rawnsleys broke apart then, and both eased a

little way from me without releasing their respective holds on my body.

'Isn't she perfect, Ammie, my love?' said Crispin archly, twisting his finger very slowly in my rectum. His intrusion into my bottom was dangerous, insidiously arousing. I could feel deep spasms beginning to pulse through my vitals. 'So wanton . . . So willing . . . It was a good day for everyone when she came to us. She's such a trollop, she's been with everyone already . . .' He paused, then pushed deeper, making me grunt. 'And done everything and more with them, no doubt.'

Being spoken of as if I were just a object made me shudder. This was one of Crispin's better games, this induction into the sly pleasures of being shamed. He enjoyed acquainting young women with their baser, cruder natures, and it was down to him that I had discovered my darkest side.

'You like this, don't you?' he questioned silkily, pumping hard now.

I bit my lip, played stubborn, and tried to fight back the thick waves of pleasure. I felt Amelia hurting my breasts now – palpating and pinching – and I made a low, vulgar noise as I climaxed.

They spanked me then; Crispin taking me across his knee and trouncing me, while Amelia held my hands to calm my struggles. My pretty ball gown lay discarded on the Persian rug beside us, and I was punished wearing just my lacy hold-ups. My panties were still tangled round one ankle.

It hurt, because Crispin was superlatively good at everything he did, and as I finally struggled back into my dress and my petticoats, I winced and clutched my buttocks from time to time. On previous occasions, either Milord or his Lady had always helped me to get dressed again, usually stealing a few kisses and gropes along the way, but tonight – as had happened earlier – things were different.

It seemed as if what they had done to me, or perhaps even just my presence, had aroused Crispin and Amelia to distraction. The minute they were finished with me, they fell on each other like a brace of starving dogs, and as I left they were already entwined, half-naked on the rug. The last thing I saw was Crispin's bottom beginning to clench.

The next hour was one long haze of licentiousness. I made love with Declan, my next door neighbour, on a bench behind the shrubbery, then felt up Simon, the Rawnsley's butler, in the pantry. When I found myself being eyed up by Lucy, the village librarian, and then wondering what it would be like to kiss her vulva while her beau of the night fucked me, I decided it was time to get away again. The only things at the party that didn't seem to want me were the dancing, flitting midges, so – hot and shaky – I headed for the asylum of the conservatory.

And found Morwenna – at last! – inspecting the vast array of exotic house plants.

'Where have you been? I've been looking everywhere for you?' I half-lied, thinking how lovely she looked in her earth-green chiffon dress, with her black hair a shining fall across her shoulders.

'Oh, it was Robert, as usual, just when I wanted to get here early and catch you,' she murmured, shrugging and smiling a small mysterious smile. 'He'd lost his cufflinks again . . . Are you all right? You look a little flushed.'

I *felt* a little flushed. Morwenna's dress was both abbreviated and thin, and I could see every bit of her lush shape through its sheerness. Her breasts were round and firm, and her waist and hips were slender, and even after everything, I couldn't help but want her.

'It's this perfume of yours – this aphrodisiac potion. It really works! You won't believe what a time I've had already.'

Morwenna laughed. Not a giggle, or a titter, but a full-throated, body-shaking belly laugh. Her fabulous bosom quivered and her unbound hair rippled, and she dabbed her face to wipe away her tears of mirth.

'Oh, Flora,' she said, still laughing as she stepped close, and slid her arms around me. 'That's why I wanted to find you. To talk to you. You picked up the wrong mixture from the counter.'

'But it works,' I protested again as she pushed her hips against mine, and massaged my belly with her thinly-clad pubis. 'It works. The only things that can't resist me are the midges.'

'Yes, it does work,' whispered Morwenna, pressing my breasts with hers as she kissed me. 'But not in the way you think it does.' Her words were puzzling, but her actions were unambiguous. She was stroking my bottom where Crispin had made me tingle, and nibbling lightly on my ear as I pondered.

'What do you mean?' I asked breathlessly, wanting to know, but also longing for the pair of us to be naked.

'Flora, the bottle you took was full of insect-repellent,' she murmured, sliding down my zip and flipping my straps off my shoulders, just as Amelia Rawnsley had done an hour earlier. 'The only ingredient that's driving people crazy here is Flora Swain!'

I didn't argue – because she was kissing my breasts now and running her tongue across the hard crests of my nipples – but I wanted to.

Surely there must be something else in the air tonight but me!

A Day and a Night

On the morning of the first day, at precisely eight o'clock, the penitent began her momentous journey. She was dressed exactly as her Master had previously specified: a black velvet bustier, lace-top stockings, spindle heels. To maintain her modesty, she wore her trench coat over these, but following orders she didn't fasten the buttons, merely crossing it over her and belting it loosely at the waist.

As she ascended on to the train, she felt her vulva tense then quiver, her fear arousing her as she thought of what was coming.

Settling into her seat, she filled her mind with her Master, thinking of his low voice, his handsome face, his strong, strong arm. He hadn't struck her yet – that was the thing that lay ahead of her – but he had described it and she had believed every word he had said. It had been a little more than a fortnight since he had first entered her shop and bought something, but it seemed as if she had belonged to him forever.

The Gothic *prie dieu* had been the beginning. His courtship of her had been perfectly normal, until then, and perfectly rational. But then he had whispered in her ear, and said he would like to see her bound across that dark wooden prayer stool, her buttocks raised and naked, while he whipped her with a lash of twisted leather. The idea had astounded her, but it had made her vulva ache – and when he had touched her panties they had been sodden with hot juice. Then he had laughed at her and proposed this trip today.

While she was musing and watching the swiftly passing countryside, a young man came and sat beside her. Glancing at him from under her eyelashes, she saw a beauty that reminded her of her Master. She imagined herself leaning over, her face pressed against the grubby moquette seat, whilst this young angel pressed his fingers into her orifices. Her Master had told her she was nothing – just a plaything, a slave – and that she should allow any male she met to enjoy her favours. For which she would be punished, of course, as sure as night followed day. Taking a tiny pad and pencil from her handbag, she wrote a note and passed it to the pretty boy.

Waiting for him in the lavatory, she began to stroke herself, her head filled with images of abasement. Perhaps she should lean over the sink and offer him her bottom? Her fingers slick and sticky, she slipped off her coat.

When he squeezed sideways into the lavatory, his eyes popped. She was teetering, balanced on one leg, whilst the other she had lifted and had draped across the filthy sink. She was holding her shaven snatch open with her fingers, and without a word, the young man unzipped and put his cock inside her heat.

'Oh, Master, Master, Master,' she chanted as he fucked her, her excitement so immense she climaxed quickly.

When they returned to the carriage she allowed him to put his hand beneath her coat and masturbate her, and by the time she reached her destination, she had come six times. Her thighs were wet and slippery with both their juices.

The station was cold, very crowded, yet unfriendly. She felt vulnerable with a naked bottom beneath her coat. At any moment, a tricky breeze might come tearing through the mall from across the tracks. Her coat would billow up and a hundred strangers would see her sex. A pussy that had been shaved on her Master's orders; a pussy that was dripping with the seed of an unknown youth.

Feeling a sense of panic, she began to have strange fancies. She imagined her Master's voice, over the Tannoy, ordering her to lift her clothing and display herself to all. 'Caress yourself, whore,' he might say, or he might instruct her to tuck her hem into her belt, then continue her journey with her plump bottom still on show.

Just then a familiar voice called out her name. It was her Master's chauffeur, waiting beyond an archway, beside the limousine. Clacking and tripping on her high heels, she ran towards him.

Soon, they were gliding out into the countryside towards the residence. She was still burning with shame from the way the chauffeur had looked at her, his eyes insulting when he had briefly raised her coat. She presumed he had been instructed to make a check.

The limousine was very comfortable; very sensual in its near silent, leather-clad luxury. Without being able to help it she began to squirm her bottom, remembering the shame of the chauffeur's dismissive glance. What would happen if I touched myself here? she wondered, her fingers itching. What would happen if I raised my coat, parted my bum cheeks and pressed my naked anus against the cool of the leather seat? She imagined being held down, here in the car, to have her quim whipped, while the chauffeur jabbed her rectum with his finger.

Before she realised it, she was massaging her throbbing clitoris. And as an orgasm came, she jerked and quietly whimpered, then saw the chauffeur's cool grey eyes in the rear view mirror.

The car stopped. They were off the road, in a lay-by,

by a copse of trees. 'Come along. Hurry,' said the chauffeur, dragging her roughly from the back seat by her arm.

He was a handsome man, but nothing like her Master. His body was massive, and his hands and face were coarse. When they reached a clearing, he made her bend and touch her toes. She quaked as he tipped her coat up over her back.

The exposure was exciting, she could feel her sexual juices well again. For a few moments, she heard the chauffeur moving about the clearing, then, without warning, he lashed her bottom with a thin green switch.

The pain was fierce. She screamed. He struck again, then followed on with half a dozen more sharp blows. Her buttocks seemed stitched across with living fire. At least a couple of strokes had caught her in her furrow.

She felt humiliated, yet exalted by her punishment. Brought low because it was a servant who had lashed her; raised up because her bottom was marked for her Master's pleasure. She moaned in her throat when she heard the chauffeur's zip. She almost fell when he crammed his penis inside her slot.

The chauffeur fucked her coldly, brutally, then shot his seed without allowing her to climax. Yet, strangely, this added to the thrill, the shame, the debasement. Her sex was tense when he withdrew and fastened his flies.

'You're a slut,' he hissed and walked off towards the car. 'Comb your hair. Wipe your face. You look a mess.'

When she resumed her seat in the limousine, she remembered her Master's order, one that she had forgotten earlier. Sitting down, she lifted her coat from beneath her burning haunches, and pressed her stripes against the cool, smooth leather of the seat. She groaned softly and felt once more the urge to touch herself, then looked up and saw the chauffeur's narrowed eyes. He was watching her in the rear view mirror again.

Her Master's residence was imposing. It stood, grey and dour, in solitude, a few miles outside the nearest town. On the front steps his housekeeper waited, a beautiful young woman in an elegant grey dress, whose dark eyes regarded the penitent accusingly.

'Your shoes are dirty, and your coat is wet,' the housekeeper observed. 'And you're late. The Master won't be pleased about that.'

When she was ushered into her Master's study, the penitent felt herself blush. He was speaking on the phone, and he didn't even look up. She was kept for a full fifteen minutes, standing, feeling useless, off-balance. Reduced to a mere object, an ornament to decorate the room, she felt her sex moisten anew with humiliation.

The snapping of the phone into its cradle made her flinch. 'Take off your coat, please,' said her Master, looking up at her for the first time since she had entered.

The intensity in his eyes made her feel faint. They were golden, glittering, very stern. He seemed unmoved when she shed her coat and stood half-naked. 'I should like you to walk around the room a little,' he instructed, picking up a pen from his desk and toying with it, turning it end over end between deft fingers.

The penitent did as she was told, acutely conscious of her naked bottom and her girlish shaven sex. The perilously high heels made her mince as she walked, and the flesh of her rounded buttocks jiggle. She knew full well that her fresh lash-marks would be visible.

'Why were you late?' enquired her Master as she passed before him for perhaps the dozenth time.

'I – I –' the penitent stammered. The words wouldn't form.

'Tell me,' her Master insisted, his low voice silky. 'I want details. I want to know everything.'

The penitent managed at last to speak. Slowly, haltingly, she described the whole sequence of events to him;

even her *amour* on the train, which had no bearing at all on her late arrival.

'Stand still now,' he said as she finished her description of how the chauffeur had used her in the clearing. 'Here.' He indicated a place beside his desk. 'Lean over, please, and lay your body across the desk.'

Once again, the penitent complied without demur, pressing herself across the cluttered surface of the desk and feeling documents and paper clips adhering to her belly. With no warning, and no gentleness, her Master began an exploration of her sex and her anal groove, prodding with his fingers and pulling her slippery labia.

'You're a wanton creature, aren't you?' he whispered, pushing a digit through the tight ring of her anus and then waggling it in the channel within. 'You're insatiable.' He found a tender spot inside her and she wailed piteously, churning her hips against the edge of the polished desk. 'You're lewd. Easy. Too quick to come to pleasure.' He seemed to lift her with his finger, making her rise on to her toes. 'You have no self-control. I'll have to punish you very thoroughly.'

Thus immolated, the penitent waited, expecting her sentence to be carried out almost immediately. But instead her Master pushed a button on his desk with his free hand, and in a few seconds the beautiful housekeeper appeared again.

'Prepare her,' he said to the newcomer. 'She needs bathing, then a tighter corset and a pair of clamps. The silver ones with the long, onyx weights.' He didn't remove his finger until the instructions were finished, and the penitent let a sob of shame escape her. Her knees were weak as she was escorted from the room.

The housekeeper took excellent care of her. Within the bounds, that was, of an obviously dark and devious nature. The penitent was stripped of her bustier, her shoes and her stockings then made to step naked into a hot and scented bath. As she began to wash herself, the housekeeper dashed her hands away and took up the sponge instead, charging it heavily with thick fragrant lather.

The bathing was scrupulous, and soon the housekeeper abandoned the sponge altogether and began to use her hands on the penitent. And her fingers. Every niche and fold was explored, every sensitive hidden treasure. The penitent found herself brought to orgasm again and again, despite her revulsion at the other woman's caresses. Each time she came to her peak, she tried not to cry out, but found herself unable to stop herself gasping. Each time, the housekeeper laughed, then upbraided her just as the Master had done, calling her loose, licentious and a whore.

When the bath was finally finished and her skin dry and polished, the penitent was faced with yet another restrictive garment. The basque-like corset that had been chosen for her was made of soft black leather and reinforced with a series of stiff bones. She felt embarrassed as it was slipped over her head and she realised it covered nothing but her midriff and upper belly. She felt the onset of panic as the housekeeper began to lace it up. Unrelentingly.

Tighter and ever tighter became the basque, constricting her waist and deforming her inner organs. The penitent felt her breathing become shallow, and the whole contents of her abdominal cavity pressed down to create stress in her vulva. She felt as if she might burst. She felt as if she could climax at any second. She sobbed bitterly when the housekeeper knelt down and sucked hungrily at her clitoris. Another orgasm was teased callously from her flesh.

While she stood, still shaking and wet from her pleasure, the housekeeper attached long black suspenders to the lower edge of the corset, and then slid sheer black stockings up the penitent's shapely legs. The last preparations were a pair of high shoes, and the silver and onyx clips, as specified.

The penitent cried again as her nipples were put in torment, the tips first squashed then weighted down by the heavy chunks of onyx.

When she was presented to her Master again, he smiled narrowly but otherwise barely looked at her. He instructed her to stand beside his desk as he worked. She was desperately aware of the way her breasts and belly bulged because of the constriction around her waist. Her bottom felt twice its normal size, and the remaining tenderness from her switching seemed to pulse.

She had been instructed to look straight ahead, and stare at nothing, but she could not resist studying her Master. He went about his work silently, in total absorption, reading documents and occasionally making notes. The penitent was bewitched by the way his elegant, thin-fingered hands held the silver pen. His grip was light, yet controlled, and the nib skimmed across the paper. She imagined his grip on a cane or whip would be the same.

For about an hour, her Master attended to his paperwork, and during that time the penitent's nerves were stretched and stretched. She realised she was just a thing to him, a living accessory, attractive flesh that he could dispose of as he so wished. The thought of being his, totally his, excited her. She became so agitated that she rubbed her legs together, in a vain attempt to stimulate her aching sex.

Just as she was beginning to feel a slight tremor of pleasure, her Master looked up from his papers. He said nothing, but his eyes were gently reproving. The penitent shuddered once, then fell still.

Maintaining his silence, her Master pushed his chair back and rose from his seat. Taking her by the arm, he led her to a *prie dieu*, the very one she had sold him, which stood in the corner of the room. By means of a series of cool, controlled gestures, he bade her lean over it and offer up to him her bare rump.

The penitent heard a drawer in the desk being opened, and then there was a long pause while, presumably, he selected an implement with which to punish her. After what felt like a minute, the drawer was quietly slid shut again.

'I'm going to beat you now,' he said quietly. 'I'm going to give you ten strokes with this riding crop, and I want you to remain silent throughout.' He lapsed into thoughtfulness for a moment, then continued, 'I shall be pleased with you if you can keep quiet. Very pleased. But if you cry out, I may have to send you home.'

The penitent feared dismissal far more than any punishment and, clenching every muscle in her body, she braced herself, prepared to bite her own lips rather than make the slightest sound.

The pain of the first blow was excruciating. Squeezing her fingers into fists, the penitent fought the wild urge to scream. For the next stripe, she clapped her hand across her mouth, churning her bottom in an attempt to dull the suffering, but at the third, she was forced to gasp out loud.

'Have a care,' murmured her Master, then he went on to apply the remaining strokes.

The penitent managed to stifle her groans, but when it was over, she was not sure how she had achieved this. Her bottom was pounding, glowing, pulsating, each mark of the crop a band of fire.

'Stand up,' ordered her Master quietly, then he waited while she staggered to her feet, her knees threatening to buckle at any second.

'Turn around. Kneel before me. Open your mouth.'

When she obeyed, swaying, he unfastened his trousers and pushed his penis between her lips, then thrust roughly until he ejaculated down her throat. The penitent swallowed every drop of his thick, salty fluid.

'And now, the final test,' he said as he covered himself again. Picking up the phone on his desk, he summoned the housekeeper and asked her to bring the penitent's trench coat.

'We're going for a drive,' he said, when the penitent had been dressed – like a child – by the housekeeper, her coat again merely belted loosely at her waist.

Before he put her into his car, he gagged her, slipping a black rubber sphere into her mouth and fastening it there with narrow straps behind her head.

'There, that'll make things easier for you,' he said obliquely, then helped her into the spacious back seat. Instead of sitting beside her, he took the chauffeur's usual place behind the wheel, then put the car into gear and set it rolling.

They drove for some time, her Master not speaking and she, because of the gag, unable to. The night was dark and windy, and the lashing of the trees on either side of the road reminded the penitent of the stormy drama of being whipped. Would she be beaten again tonight? she wondered, still feeling the stripes and soreness of her last one. She wriggled her bare bottom on the leather of the seat, making the heat from her previous punishment flare. She wanted desperately to reach beneath her coat and stroke her sex, but she sensed that, like his chauffeur before him, her Master would be watching her closely, his eyes scanning the rear view mirror from time to time.

Their destination proved to be a pretty wrought iron gazebo in the corner of a small municipal park. Her Master parked the car, and then led her through the park towards it, making her stumble on her precariously high heels. The ornate little shelter was covered in on three sides with window panels of multi-coloured stained glass, but the fourth was both open to the air and to passers-by. It being late, however, there was no one in the park.

'Remove your coat,' her Master instructed, taking the garment away as she shed it.

Half-naked and shivering, the penitent allowed herself to be bound up with yet more leather straps. Her ankles and her wrists were each fastened tightly together, then the latter were attached to a hook that had been screwed into the wall. The hook looked quite new to the penitent's fearful eyes, as if it were a recent addition to the gazebo's fittings, and was positioned so she was stretched and couldn't move. Wearing only her tight corset and her stockings, her breasts and bottom were vulnerable, and she whined behind her gag in panic and fright.

'I'm going to leave you now,' said her Master, 'but first there is one more final touch.' He placed a black velvet mask across her eyes.

As soon as she was in darkness, the penitent felt him touch her weeping sex. He caressed her swollen folds perfunctorily, then, without warning, thrust a finger into her vagina. When she squirmed, he smacked her defenceless bottom. One, two, three fierce spanks, then he was gone, his footsteps echoing crisply on the gravel.

The penitent had been frightened before, but now she was terrified. Helpless and terrified. She was blind, almost nude, and unprotected. Anyone could come into the park, and anyone could touch her. They could examine her, or play with her, or worse. She was so exposed and available that she felt her quim ooze and flutter, roused to readiness and to openness by her plight. She was anybody's now; her Master had abandoned her. He had made a gift of her to whoever wandered by.

Would someone come? she wondered, imagining strangers reaching for her, groping her, defiling her. What if some late-night walker were to see her vividly striped bottom and decide to add to it by beating it themselves? Her silky juices ran down her thighs at just the thought.

The penitent's night in the gazebo was long and

wearying, but she was too uncomfortable and too excited to even doze. In the early hours, she heard first footsteps, then heavy breathing, close by her. After a moment, as she stood there with her heart pounding, strong hands carefully explored her naked bottom, then dived in crudely between her legs to make her climax. Her unknown caresser spoke not a word throughout this process, but his cologne was distinctive and familiar. Was it her Master who had sent the chauffeur to touch her and degrade her, or had the servant simply come of his own volition?

When morning finally arrived, her Master returned to her again, then gently unlocked her fetters and removed her slippery gag. Sweeping her coat around her body, he led her back to the limousine, and when they were settled, he began kissing her with tenderness and affection. The chauffeur kept his cool eyes on the road.

'See, my dearest,' said her Master as he paused to show her his watch, and she saw that the time was eight o'clock. 'Your 24 hours as my slave are now over. You're free now. You no longer have to obey me.'

But what if I want to? thought the penitent as the kisses began anew, and she realised, to her astonishment, that she loved him utterly.

She had spent a day and a night in the thrall of his dominion, but what she wanted was to belong to him forever.

To be his for *all* her days and *all* her nights.

A Pretty Weird Bloke

'I'm a pretty weird bloke, you know, Maggie.'

I always remember the first time David said that to me. We were in the wine bar, just around the corner from work, and I had just gone completely crazy and asked him for a date.

I was like that in those days: all impetuosity and emancipation. I had fancied David Devillier from the very first moment I saw him, and from the moment after that I had wanted to go out with him. And more. Much more.

But it had been difficult to tell if he fancied me.

'Brilliant, Maggie!' he had said, when I had first taken my ideas for the in-house magazine to him.

'You're as beautiful as you are clever,' had been the significant step forward when we studied the mock-ups together.

'You're marvellous, Maggie! Worth your weight in gold. I could kiss you!' he had said, *and* done it, when together we had got the firm's highest commendation from head office. But even then he hadn't asked me for a date.

It wasn't that he didn't show signs of affection. Or at least a degree of regard. When we met in the canteen to discuss the project in our own time, he always made a point of fetching the coffees. And paying for them. Not to mention bringing me a biscuit without having to be asked. One day when I had a migraine, he took me home, tucked me up on my settee with a blanket and a glass of water, then went out again to the chemists for special tablets. He praised my work – without being afraid to criticise it, too – and even recommended me for a salary increase. And he always laughed at my pathetically corny jokes. But he never showed interest in me as a woman.

Except of course, for the little 'touches'.

I was all set to hit the roof the first time David put his hand on my bottom; but when I turned around, my lips parted ready to emit a stream of feminist vitriol, I saw such an expression on his face of both yearning and remorse that, quite ridiculously, I apologised myself instead. David's own soft apology came out at the same moment, and he snatched back his hand as if he had burnt it.

You might think that after that, he wouldn't have touched me again, but funnily enough it began to happen fairly often. And after the first shock, I began to find I liked it. That I was waiting for it. Wanting it. By the time we had worked together for a couple of pleasant months, I was almost offering him my rear end on a platter!

By then we had fallen into the habit of having a drink together in the wine bar, just in a 'friends' context, and I was used to being seen about with him. Which did a lot for my image, I can tell you. David was handsome, in a discreet and elegant way; with shiny brown hair, a firm mouth, and light brown eyes behind his sexy metal-framed glasses. He dressed well, but not flashily; he drove a powerful car; and his job was good, and likely to get much better. In fact he was well and truly a 'catch' – and it wasn't even as if he didn't like women. He had told me when we started working together that he was a widower, and that his marriage had been sublimely happy until his wife had died quite young. It was talk of this, and his frank admission that he had dated a few women since, that had spurred me to put myself forward as the next one.

'What do you mean by "weird"?' I asked him, mentally running through a list of possible kinks. If it was saucy undies, I would be happy to oblige. I would even wear leather or rubber if he wanted me to.

'Oh, just a little – er – particular in what it is about a woman that turns me on,' he murmured enigmatically, clearly without realising my curiosity was going crazy.

'Well, I'm pretty broad-minded. I – I'm prepared to try anything. Why don't we go out together and just see what happens?'

To my surprise, he smiled devastatingly and agreed.

The first few dates were great fun, but frustratingly chaste. We went for walks, to the pictures, and for casual meals in small restaurants; but nowhere near either his bedroom or mine. We kissed very passionately on the safe ground of my doorstep, and each time, I was left craving for much, much more. I would lie in bed a little while later, stroking my sex like a demented thing, and fantasising about David's mouth possessing mine, and the feel of his long, cool hands upon my bottom.

My bottom. That was the one area where my civilised gentleman took liberties. He never touched my breasts, and he didn't grope my pussy, but my buttocks he handled often and with enthusiasm. As we kissed long and hard, his bold tongue subduing mine, he would reach down and grip my bottom with his fingers. I would feel his hands flex and cup my cheeks, moulding them this way and that, then he would massage both lobes in slow, arousing circles.

His touch was strong, and yet loving, gentle yet erotic, and as the days passed, it grew bolder and ever bolder. He would turn my back towards the door, and if I was wearing a skirt, he would lift it and fondle me through my panties. The first time he did this, I nearly orgasmed from the shock of it, especially when he rubbed my anus with his finger.

Soon he was putting his hands inside my panties on every date, and then pulling them half-way down my thighs to caress me, baring my bottom to the chilly breezes and the night air.

And I was going out of my mind! The way David stroked me had me dripping and desiring him, and I longed desperately for his explorations to go further.

'Let's go inside,' I gasped, one night when the delicious torment was too much for me. My sex was aching and my whole being was one big hunger. We were standing in the corner of my porch, with my pants and leggings around my ankles, and David's body my only shield from rude exposure. I could feel an erection pressing hard against my belly.

'No!' he said, almost violently, his eyes bright and tortured in the darkness. 'Let me kiss you, please, just let me kiss you.'

'But you *have* been kissing me,' I protested, feeling my bruised mouth as the tender, living proof of it.

'No . . . Turn around and let me kiss you,' he whispered, his fingers gently manipulating as he spoke.

The penny dropped. At last. Hobbled by my clothing, I turned around awkwardly, putting all thought of being observed by neighbours from my mind.

With what might have been a gasp of relief or ecstasy, David fell to his knees behind me, and in an instant his lips were pressed against my buttocks.

'So beautiful . . . So beautiful . . .,' he murmured, in between fervent kisses that seemed to devour my chilly flesh. It seemed bizarre, but I pushed my rump towards him. The heat of his mouth seemed to pass right through me and turn my aching sex to molten lava. Without thinking I reached down to touch my clitoris.

When he had finished kissing me, he put my clothes to rights and then turned and walked away without a word. His expression of remorseful yearning had come back.

The next day, an extravagant bunch of red roses arrived, accompanied – surprisingly – by a letter.

'Dearest Maggie,' it said. 'You're a bright, intelligent, beautiful, funny girl and I think I love you. But I don't want to fuck you as a normal man would. I said I was weird, and you're right to think I'm a pervert – but what I want to do is adore your gorgeous bottom. I want to kiss it, like I did last night. I want to stroke it, examine it, explore it, take photographs of it even . . . But most of all, what I want – what I need to do, is beat it. I want to spank your glorious bottom until it's burning red and fiery. I want to smack it with my hand, lash it with a crop, thrash it long and hard with a slender rattan cane, until it's black and blue and you're weeping with the pain . . . And when that's done, I want to press myself against you.

'So you see, my darling wonderful Maggie, I'm more weird than you can possibly have imagined, and if you don't want anything more to do with me, I understand.'

There was only one thing I could do. I reached into the drawer, took out a sheet of paper and began to write.

The meal had been magnificent, the wine superb, and the hotel was worth every one of its four stars.

'I couldn't believe it when I got your letter,' said David as we ascended in the lift, raising my hand to kiss it, his brown eyes as radiant as distant suns. 'It just seemed impossible you'd understand.' Drawing me close, he reached down and clasped the object he so adored.

'I'm scared, though,' I said, as his fingers clutched and kneaded.

'Don't worry, I'll look after you,' he replied.

The room was beautiful, the bed antique with brass

rails and exquisite lace-trimmed linen in shades of soft ivory and pale gold. Soft lighting enhanced its romantic aura.

'You might want to use the bathroom first,' whispered David, pausing to kiss me again, his hands still roving. 'So you're as comfortable as you can be while I'm seeing to you.'

I didn't think I would be comfortable at all, given what he had in mind, but I was nervous and I did need to pee.

'Yes, thanks. Shall I undress?' I asked uncertainly.

'No, it's all right,' he replied, smiling, 'I'll take off whatever I need to when we start.'

What have I done? What have I agreed to? I thought as I dallied in the bathroom. Earlier on, when we had just arrived, I had seen a riding whip of some kind in David's case. He was going to beat me with it, mark my skin, really hurt me, and all because he found it sexually exciting.

But didn't I find it sexually exciting, too? I realised to my amazement that I did. My creamy satin panties were sopping when I pulled them down to use the toilet, and beneath my silk camisole, my nipples were like stones.

'Are you ready, darling?' asked David as I crept out of the bathroom, and he folded me in a quick reassuring hug. He had taken off his elegant Armani jacket, and rolled up the sleeves of his dazzling white shirt. He meant business, and I couldn't disappoint him.

I nodded, and he said, 'You're wonderful,' then led me to the bed.

His preparations for my beating were as thorough as anything we had ever worked on in the office. First, he had me lie down on my front on the bedspread and stretch out my hands above my head.

'I'm going to secure you now, sweetheart,' he said, running his fingers across my rump. 'I'm going to fasten your hands to the rail, so you won't struggle.'

I felt a moment of panic as my hands were bound. There was no turning back now, I was helpless, I was trussed. The woven cotton bands that fastened my wrists to the bedrail were soft and non-chafing but they were also quite thrillingly unyielding.

His next act was to slide up my silky skirt, and fold it out of the way – both at the front and at the back – which left my undies, and the bottom beneath them, in plain sight. I was wearing everything matching in figured cream satin, with lace-top stockings in a beige a few shades darker.

'You're so beautiful,' he said, running his hands across my bottom-cheeks, then sliding his fingers beneath the elastic of my pants. 'We'll slip these down to your knees, I think, but we'll leave your stockings on you . . .' he continued, almost reflectively, 'It wouldn't do for you to catch a chill, would it?'

I didn't answer, but the thought of a simple cold did not bother me in the slightest.

'Just a few final preparations,' he said, moving efficiently round the bed, his voice almost ringing with excitement.

Sliding up my camisole, he bared my breasts to the embroidered bedspread – because 'it would feel nicer for me' – then lifted my hips and placed a cushion in beneath them. It was a rather firm little cushion, and he positioned it very carefully; so my pubis was pressed – with perfect accuracy – hard against it.

After that, he showed me the whip.

It was long and straight and rather beautiful in its own way, with a tag at one end and silver handle at the other. The whole of the shank was finely bound in black leather and its slender girth made me quiver at the possibility of being cut.

'Don't worry,' said David, reading my mind, 'you'll hurt, believe me, but you won't be truly damaged in the slightest. This whip is too old a friend to let us down.'

For a moment, I wanted to ask him if he had used the same whip on his wife when she was alive; but then it dawned on me that he must have. For them to have been so happy, she must have shared his special preference.

'Now, two last little preparations,' said David, laying the whip aside. 'I'm going to gag you – and then I'm going to stroke your clitoris.'

The first was achieved before my brain registered what the second one was. Another band of soft towelling was placed around my face and between my teeth, then fastened snugly in a knot behind my head. I could not cry out, but in a moment or two I longed to.

Considering that he had never touched me down there, or even shown a sign of wanting to, David's fingers on my pussy were very skilful. For what seemed like a lifetime, he delicately slicked my clitoris, using the juices from my overflowing channel; but as I began to writhe and almost climax, he drew back.

'Not just yet, my darling, not just yet,' he whispered in my ear, then straightened up and reached out to take the whip.

The pain, after the pleasure, was extraordinary; like a bolt of lightning cracking down across my buttocks. Without the gag, I would most certainly have howled loud enough to bring the hotel's security guard charging in on us, but as it was, I immediately began to cry. Every nerve along the impact line was shrieking and complaining, and in my frenzy I ground my pelvis against the cushion.

Another stroke fell then, like a shaft of horrific fire, and I waved my legs around to try and fight its heat. As I bucked my hips and wriggled, my panties went tight between my knees, and I felt embarrassed by their intimate constriction.

'That's it, my darling,' cooed David, from very close to me. 'Give in to it. Cry and struggle, but let it take you over.'

More blows fell, and made a pattern on my bottom, a blazing lattice that seemed carved upon my flesh. My buttocks were my world, and pain absorbed my mind completely. At least that was the way it felt to me at first.

I hadn't counted how many strokes of the whip David had given me – arithmetic was beyond my mental faculties at that moment – but after several, I experienced a strange phenomenon. I was in terrible distress, my bottom was swollen and pulsating, but between my legs I felt a new sensation simmer.

With the next blow, I squirmed almost languidly, surrendering to the agony while my clitoris kissed the cushion pressed against it. With the following blow, I had a different cause to sob.

'Oh, yes, my darling, yes!' cried David, throwing down the whip and climbing up beside me on the bed. 'I adore you. You're a goddess. You're perfect.' I heard the rasp of a zip, distinct and unmistakable, and simultaneously a supple hand was underneath me.

'I love you, Maggie,' he gasped, kissing my tear-streaked face as his finger wrought the purest of magic. 'I love you. I love you. I love you,' he groaned loudly as I climaxed, and through my pleasure I felt his penis seek my pain.

My last awareness was silken semen on my cheeks.

Since then, I've experienced a lot with my poor bottom.

We've tried everything David mentioned in his letter a dozen or more times over, and I've been to hell and back beneath his strong sure hand. I've been slippered and I've been hairbrushed; I've been slapped and whacked and cropped; and caned so hard once I couldn't sit in comfort for almost a week.

But with every awful pain there comes the sweetest rush of pleasure, and with every hour of torment, a night of soaring bliss.

I'm sitting on a cushion now as I write this. My bottom's throbbing like a tom-tom and beneath my robe it's crimson – but this evening I will be thrashed until I shout.

Do I like it like this? you might ask. Do I want these things to happen? I suppose I must do, but I really don't have much choice.

You see, my husband is *still* a weird bloke, and I love him to distraction.

Isn't it lucky that I'm pretty weird myself?

The Cure

Desperate situations require desperate measures, a friend had once said, and sitting in a bright, pleasant waiting room in an upmarket part of the City, Lainie Karelian *was* desperate.

Desperate about sex.

Why else would she have made an appointment at what was so cryptically called a 'fantasy therapy' clinic?

She felt so guilty sitting there in clothes Drago had bought her. Chic silks. Designer doodads. Guilty, even though a part of her said, 'Why?' She had come here for his benefit as much as her own.

It was the sneaking about that made it all feel so sleazy. Pretending to go shopping. Booking her appointment from a public comm-net booth. Using the last of her own money. All so he wouldn't know.

I bet *she* doesn't have this trouble, Lainie thought sourly, peering at the receptionist from under the brim of her hat. No, no love life problems there, obviously. The woman at the desk was serene and beautiful, a wide-eyed, fine-featured redhead with a pale but glowing complexion. Lainie had never seen such health, contentment, and general all-round unscrewed-upness. And no wonder, the lucky thing was pregnant; as big as a house and patently thriving on it!

Before she could stop herself, Lainie imagined the conception of that round, fertile bump. She saw the happy receptionist in bed with some tender, devoted male; their bodies locked in a close, murmuring love-fuck, his cock deep in her quim as he filled her and fulfilled her. Impregnated her.

It was a well known fact that pregnancy often increased the sex-drive, and Mother Superior over there was obviously one of the fortunate ones. She looked too pleased with herself to be otherwise.

Lainie pictured her as she would be now. Kneeling on all fours, heavy-bellied and graceful; her lover would be behind her, pushing in strongly but carefully from the rear. And as he fucked her, he would reach around and stroke her breasts. Touch the swell of his child. Slide lower to finger her clitoris. They would both be smiling and laughing and sobbing with pleasure. Orgasming together. Lainie felt like dying of jealousy.

Why the hell can't I have sexy ideas like this when I'm with Drago? she thought. If I could dream all this up when he was inside me, I wouldn't be such a wash-out. And he wouldn't give me those ominous, impatient looks of his.

'Tricksie? I'm ready for Miss Karelian now.' A woman's voice, disembodied but smooth and dark as chocolate, came floating out of the intercom. 'Would you ask her to come in, please?'

'Sure thing, boss!' the receptionist said cheerfully, and her soft smile made Lainie twice as envious. Even a close *working* relationship would be better than nothing. Especially if the doctor was as gorgeous as she sounded. Feeling nervous, Lainie leapt to her feet.

'Tricksie' couldn't get to her feet quite as quickly, and when the pregnant woman had levered herself up, she grinned and gave a rueful shrug.

'I'm getting too big for this lark now,' she observed as she led Lainie towards the consulting room, her tread surprisingly dainty for one presently so broad in the beam. 'In you go.' She opened the door and ushered

Lainie through. 'And don't be scared. She won't bite you unless you really want her to!'

Not quite sure what to make of that, Lainie nearly stumbled into the room, her pulse racing madly in spite of the receptionist's reassurances.

As she looked up, a slender white-clad woman was moving forward to greet her – and before she could stop herself, Lainie flinched and froze in her tracks.

After the voice, the face was a shock to say the least.

The fantasy therapist, dream doctor or whatever she called herself, was scarred. Appallingly so. A purple-red mark the size of a clenched fist nearly covered the right hand side of her face – from her mouth to her elegant browline.

God, what a shame! thought Lainie in the microseconds before the introductions began. If it wasn't for that thing she would be fabulous!

It was true. If you ignored her lurid stigma, the doctor was just as beautiful as her lovely receptionist, if not more so. Her bone structure was breathtaking, her skin like buttermilk, and her warm eyes and rosy lips were utterly sensual. And she had the most amazing hair. Swept off her face with two gold hairslides, it was a cascading fall of lush crimped waves that seemed to be several different colours at once. It was tabby, tortoiseshell, natural technicolour, and Lainie had never seen anything like it in her life. Even so, her eyes returned to the scar.

'It's okay, I'm used to people staring,' the flawed one said equably, her grin warm and winsome in spite of her lopsided face. 'Please, Lainie, sit down.' She indicated an upholstered chair, set to one side of her desk. 'I'm Isis, how can I help you?'

'I – I –'

Jesus, it was so difficult to talk about! Even with this weird but attractive woman who probably heard sob stories a dozen times a day.

'No need to rush,' Isis said gently, reaching out to pat Lainie's hand. 'It must be very personal or you wouldn't be here. Just take your time.'

In spite of her embarrassment, Lainie gleaned two facts from Isis' touch. One, that the woman had scarred hands as well as a scarred face; and two, that the touch of those fingers was mindbending. Bizarre as it seemed, it was a lover's hand Lainie felt against hers. She imagined Isis touching her in entirely different circumstances, in different places – and all of a sudden, she found she could talk.

'I'm frigid! I can't have an orgasm! And I think my boyfriend's getting tired of me!' she blurted out in the first cleansing rush. 'I left everything I ever had to be with him, everything I was, and if I lose him now I don't know what I'll do!' It sounded melodramatic but it was true. 'He's Jensen Drago, one of the richest, most handsome men in the City – and I can hardly bear him touching me any more! I don't know what to do! I'm desperate. I need something to make me respond to him in bed!'

She lost it in a flood of tears – and in an instant, felt Isis' arms close around her.

After several minutes of shaking and snuffling, Lainie wondered about pulling herself together. But as Isis had said, there was no rush – and those arms around her shoulders felt so warm. The temptation was to move in closer, snuggle up to those firm, rounded breasts, and find out whether there was lingerie beneath that starched white cotton, or just a bare and very delectably warm body.

'I'm sorry,' mumbled Lainie, blotting her face with the tissues Isis had produced out of nowhere. 'You must think I'm a complete idiot.'

'Not at all,' said Isis quietly, her silky voice very level and serious as she slid back into her chair, 'but I do think you should talk to Drago. Tell him how you're feeling. Let him help you.' She steepled her long, pink-scarred fingers. 'You could try partner counselling together. It'll take longer, of course, but I'll be honest with you . . . It'll be a hell of a lot cheaper than this.' She made a grand, sweeping gesture that encompassed whatever esoteric facilities lay beyond her airy consulting room.

'No! Please. . . I want to try it!'

Why so vehement, Karelian? thought Lainie, even as she spoke. What did she know about fantasy therapy anyway?

'Are you sure?' Isis said, her look saying she herself was not. 'I can certainly help you, Lainie, but I still think you should discuss it with Drago.'

'No! I want to do something now. As soon as possible.' Lainie felt panic rise, but not for the reason she had expected – the possibility of losing Drago.

If she left now, she might never see Isis again. Never see that strange, scarred face, be touched by those sensitive hands again, or smell that flowery perfume that was making her light-headed. Worse still, she would never feel that lithe, slender body against her again – or those heartbreaking, hard-nippled breasts.

'Please!' begged Lainie, more confused than ever. 'Let me start now . . . Oh, please!'

Isis was quietly amused. 'Don't you even want to know how fantasy therapy works?'

'Don't you just hypnotise me or something?' The hairs on the back of Lainie's neck reared up. Isis was smiling an almost devilish smile. Especially on her scarred side.

'Oh, it's a little bit more than that,' she murmured. 'You might change your mind.'

'No way! I won't change my mind! Whatever it is!'

'All right, then. If you're really set on it there's no point in waiting.' Rising in a swift, fluid motion, Isis led Lainie to the farther door, opposite to the one she had entered by.

As she followed her new mentor into the corridor beyond, Lainie still felt mixed up. She had come here seeking fantasy therapy to improve her sex life with Drago, but ever since she had walked into this peculiar facility, she had done nothing much else *but* fantasise. But none of it had been about him.

First it had been Tricksie, the earth mother receptionist, and a hypothetical vision of her child being conceived; and now it was an inner debate as to whether the slim figure walking swayingly in front of her was wearing knickers beneath her virgin white smock.

She's a woman, for Christ's sake! What does it matter what she wears? Lainie told herself. But even so, she could not stop looking. Scrutinising that neat, white-clad bottom and its lack of a visible line.

Isis showed her into a small but perfectly appointed bathroom. 'Are you sure you wouldn't like to talk about this first?'

'No, please . . . In for a penny, in for a pound as they used to say. Just tell me what to do and I'll do it.'

In spite of a stomach full of skydiving butterflies, Lainie felt more relaxed with Isis than she had in weeks. There was something so appealing about her, so downright seductive, that it was impossible not to feel at ease. More than at ease.

'All right then, Lainie,' the doctor said crisply, 'as the therapy involves your body as well as your mind, you need to make some preparations. What I'd like you to do now is take off all your clothes, empty your bladder, and bowels if you can, then join me in the treatment room, through there.' She pointed towards another of those mysterious, but promising doors. 'There's a robe in the closet you can slip on. Take all the time you need. I'll be waiting for you when you're ready.'

With that she disappeared, leaving Lainie open-mouthed in astonishment – and suddenly aroused.

This is a first, she thought as she obeyed Isis'

instructions. I can't work up a scrap of a turn-on for Drago, but when a woman I've known less than fifteen minutes tells me to strip off and do my business like a good little girl, I start feeling all hot and bothered!

'Come in!' Isis called out when Lainie tapped on the door a short while later.

Inside the treatment room everything was as pure and white and sparkling as Isis' pristine lab coat. It was quite small too, intimate and cosy, and at its centre was a couch, upholstered in white leather and looking not unlike a dentist's chair. To the side of this was a bank of computer gadgetry: digital readouts; keyboards; bundles of enigmatic wiring. Strings of figures were spooling across a monitor, and perched on a high stool in front of it, Isis was studying these closely, a tiny pair of wire-rimmed glasses balanced precariously on the end of her nose.

'Don't be scared,' she said kindly as she helped Lainie off with her robe and on to the couch.

Though the room was unnaturally warm, Lainie shivered. Whenever and wherever Isis touched her, she felt a delicious sparkly sensation, a kind of heady, erotic gooseflesh that had sadly long been absent in her between-the-sheets dealings with Drago.

'Relax, Lainie. Just relax.'

No problem, thought Lainie, closing her eyes and letting Isis adjust the head-rest beneath her. She was being coddled and cared for and she loved it. She felt fingers drift across her brow and smooth her hair, then glide over her face, her shoulders and her throat. With a desperation that shocked her, she willed them to go lower. To slide, explore, and linger. To hover lightly, circle and tantalise. To do all the small, sweet, loving things that Drago could no longer be bothered with.

The image of him spoiled things. Frowning, she opened her eyes.

Isis was frowning, too – a hair-raising sight with a

face like hers. 'You were getting loose then, Lainie. All nice and relaxed . . . What made you tense up again?'

'Nothing. I'm just nervous; wouldn't you be?'

'Yes, I think I probably would,' Isis replied, her impish smile returning. 'Now then, young lady, let me tell you how my gadget works while I prepare you.'

Lainie's uptightness promptly disappeared. It was the smile that did it – so weird but so wonderful – and the gentle, explaining voice. Between them they disolved all her tension.

'This treatment is a spin-off from an earlier project of mine . . . Perhaps you've heard of it?' For a moment there was something suspiciously like a leer in her voice. 'Pleasurezone Incorporated. It was, shall we say, a recreational service for people who wanted exotic sexuality but with no real-world risks . . .' She paused, and Lainie flinched as the doctor took hold of her foot. 'Don't worry,' Isis continued, her strong fingers kneading Lainie's instep and her toes, 'just a little reflexology, my sweet. Some clients find it relaxes them . . . Helps the process along.'

Relaxed just by Isis' voice, Lainie gave herself up to the gentle massage. She had never particularly liked Drago to touch her feet, but after only a few moments of Isis's manipulations, she began to experience a beneficial effect. She felt warmth, a curious mellowness, a lightness and a general sense of well-being. And something else too. Something far more easy to pinpoint; something oozy and slippy and tangible in the depths of her sex.

'Do you fantasise at all, Lainie?' enquired what was now the most beautiful voice in the world while its owner relinquished Lainie's foot. 'Do you think about sexy things while you're actually having sex?'

Lainie frowned again. Did she fantasise? No, not any more. Once she had indulged in all sorts of silly dreams while Drago was fucking her; most of them about white dresses and happily ever after. But nowadays she was always too tense, too scared he would see through her poor acting.

'No? Well, don't worry about it,' Isis murmured, 'because you will now. I'm going to turn your mind on for you, sweetheart. Make sexy dreams as natural as breathing. And when it's done, your body will switch on too; like an automatic loop. It'll be as easy as falling off a log.'

It sounded like wishful thinking, a fantasy in itself.

Suddenly Lainie believed it would be easy. Looking up into Isis' face, she felt a shooting flare of wonder, a surge of heat that hit every single part of her at once. And some parts harder than others.

The scar! Oh God, the scar! For some time, she had been trying to figure out what it reminded her of – without appearing to stare – but now, in this creamy dreamy state she was in, its nature was perfectly obvious.

Isis' scar was quim-shaped!

'Yes, I know,' the brain doctor said softly, as if Lainie's thoughts had flicked up on the screen with the other data. 'But it's *your* quim we're concerned with at the moment. And it's got to learn to do lovely things again for you.' She paused and laid her fingers delicately against Lainie's pubic hair; not stroking or probing, just ever so lightly touching. 'Do you ever masturbate, sweetheart?'

'No! Yes! Sometimes . . . But hardly anything happens. I don't seem to *want* to do it.' How depressing that sounded.

'You will in future.' Isis' elfish grin was as fierce in its own way as her scowl. And just as sexy.

Is that what a smiling quim looks like? Lainie wondered, studying the way the scar crinkled. Could a quim smile? More to the point, after all this, could her own quim smile?

'Now, Lainie, I want you to wriggle down on the couch until it fits the shape of your body. Can you do that?'

She nodded. By shuffling she found that the soft white leather moulded perfectly to her body shape; hugging her shoulders, back and bottom, its texture a caress against her skin. She had never felt so comfortable in her life.

'Okay with that?'

'Yes. Wonderful!' Lainie heard her own voice catch in a sob. It was true; she really was getting turned on! And barely anything had happened.

'What I'm going to do next is apply a series of sensor/transceivers to you. Minute conducting chips that pass messages to your mind and your body.'

Lainie felt a dab of something sticky applied to each of her temples, then a slight pressure and the feel of two small objects adhering to the gelid goo.

'These chips will transmit stimuli to certain areas of your forebrain. The jargonese is that they'll "alter your brain architecture", but in plain terms we're going to switch on your ability to fantasise. It might not happen all at once because responses are very individual. You'll probably only get vague images from this session. Pleasant drifting sensations . . . A general sexual glow. It might be useful if you thought about Drago and then you'll associate him with the dreams.'

Why? Lainie asked herself woozily. It was much nicer just to lie here, spaced-out, basking like a cat on a hearthrug. Thinking about Drago hurt; who needed it?

'Now we come to some other chips.' Isis paused portentously. 'The inducers. The ones that give pleasure and create the feedback between body and mind.'

Lainie knew what would happen now. Knew with those 'certain areas of the forebrain', perhaps, which part of her it was that was supposed to need curing.

She closed her eyes. Lying absolutely still, she felt as

if she were hovering on a white leather cloud. Waiting for an angel.

'Do you like having your breasts caressed?'

Oh, yes! Did she ever! Arching her back, she offered herself to Isis' gentle hands; to fingers that feathered and skated, their tapered tips circling her aureoles like moths, touching and tickling and pleasuring. It was a beautiful thing in itself, but even as her nipples tightened and stiffened, she knew it was just preparation. Opening her eyes, and looking down her body, she watched Isis dress each of her swollen teats with a small clinging cup made of some stretchy, nylon-like substance. From each of these trailed a fine red wire. Where the wires went, Lainie neither knew nor cared, it was the cups that were making her squirm.

'What now?' she croaked, as they tugged her and she imagined something even more daring.

'This,' said Isis, placing her hands on Lainie's hips and pressing her down firmly against the couch's hollowed surface. Her fingers were like brands on Lainie's skin, then like heaven as she ran a hand down the whole length of Lainie's right leg from the curve of her buttock to her ankle. 'The – the other sensors have to be fitted very precisely, Lainie . . . Would it bother you if I fastened you down?'

'Oh, no! Please . . . Do it!'

Now who had said that? Lainie wondered. Surely that sexy, throaty purr wasn't hers? That invitation to kinkiness and mischief?

Isis went about her task with frightening speed, fastening Lainie's ankles into softly-lined cuffs that held her long legs in position.

Being bound was amazing. She wriggled slightly, but the cuffs were deliciously unyielding.

'Bear down into the couch,' Isis instructed, her commanding voice only adding to the excitement.

Lainie obeyed, then squeaked in astonishment as

beneath the couch a mechanism whirred sub-audibly. With a well-oiled smoothness, the lower half of the couch began a slow divide into two, drawing her legs, her thighs and her sex wide open.

'Oooh,' she whimpered as the re-arrangement stopped. She was stretched now, her quim fully exposed, and the urge to close her legs again was unbearable. Seemingly unmoved, Isis started buckling up another stap, a broad white band that circled Lainie's pale belly and kept her bottom quite snug against the leather.

'Perfect.' Isis sounded pleased as she walked around to the head of the couch and looked down into Lainie's sweating face. 'Are you OK, my love? If you don't like it we can stop whenever you like.'

'No! I'm fine ... I feel fine,' murmured Lainie through lips that wanted nothing more than to rise up and kiss the mouth – and the scar – that hovered just inches above her.

'I'm going to touch you very intimately now, sweetheart. Are you ready?'

Always! All my life, thought Lainie wildly, feeling a surge of sweet adrenalin in her veins. Or was it something else? Something emotional, not biological. Whatever it was, she didn't care. It was heaven. It was bliss!

Drifting again, she heard a small snapping sound, then a second one, and when she looked up she saw Isis adjusting the fit of a pair of very fine white latex gloves.

Something went 'oof' in Lainie's chest and her vagina pulsed like a small, hungry mouth as she imagined the feel of those rubber gloves.

And then she was being touched. Very lightly. Between the legs. Isis' rubber-clad fingertips were as soft as mist against her labia – her wet, wet labia – and nothing short of divine on her tense, unsheathing clitoris.

'Oh baby,' the good doctor whispered, as much to

herself, it seemed, as to Lainie, 'I don't think you really need all this.' She nodded at her machine and its erotic peripherals, and her bright hair rippled like a curtain. 'You're so wet, my darling. So wet and ready . . .'

This last was so quietly said that Lainie wondered if she had dreamt it. That her imagination, loosened by Isis' calm and soothing presence, was already weaving its fantasies.

'Another sensor, Lainie.' She felt a push at the entrance of her vagina, rude but gentle, then her body gave gladly and let in an object that was firm and smooth and tubular. 'For Doctor G's little hot spot, sweetheart.'

Lainie moaned aloud, loving the stretch of the dildo inside her. It was silk-sleek and warm, and she could hardly tell where *she* ended and the probe began. There was an inanimate object inside her, a piece of plastic presumably, yet in that moment it meant more to her than any man who had ever breached the self-same portal.

'Just one more, love . . .'

What happened was what she had been wanting since her nipples had been tethered – and when Isis pressed the tiny stretchy cup over her clitoris, Lainie sighed in deepest of deep pleasure.

The little bud was so swollen and so sensitised, and the suction of the thing so luscious, that she climaxed immediately, one half of her wondering at the power of it, while the other just soared in its joy.

'Easy, Lainie. Hold still, my darling, let me get it on properly,' soothed Isis, her hands like starlight in the groove. Using all her physician's skill, she steadied the miniature sensor on Lainie's dancing clitoris. 'Oh, yes, young lady, I think this is going to be good for you . . . So very, very good.'

Going to be? thought Lainie blearily as soft fire washed through her loins and the dildo waggled lewdly in her channel. It *is* good, you crazy woman! Good? It's incredible. Beautiful. The best. What else do I need but this?

But as Isis positioned a plush-lined mask over her eyes, then kissed her cheek and murmured, 'Prepare to dream, my love,' Lainie knew it was only the beginning.

Nearly there! thought Lainie, grinning like a loon as the travelway sped her towards her goal. Jostled by other commuters, she clung on tight to the case that contained her belongings. The very few items she truly deemed as hers.

Yesterday, when she had left the treatment room, she had been walking on air. It had taken several hours, and Drago's return from his all-consuming business affairs, to remind her why she had even sought out Isis in the first place.

While they had prepared for bed, she had studied her partner's cold blond good looks more critically than she had in a long time; and suddenly found them annoying. Too perfect. Too flawless. Almost boring. And as usual, she had felt uninterested and sexless.

But as Drago had begun to caress her she had reached into her mind, as instructed, and nearly laughed out loud with elation. Images, feelings, and emotions had formed immediately. Her therapy dream all over again – complete with the same fantasy lover who had moved her and shaken her in ways that Drago had never done. Even at the height of her infatuation for him.

And as Drago the man toiled industriously in her quim, it was the dream lover who pleasured the greater Lainie. A formless thrust of golden sweetness passed clean through her skin and kissed her soul and her sex simultaneously.

In a weightless world of radiance, slim-tipped finger-tips slid slowly over her skin, blessing every pore they travelled over with a pleasure that was effortless and sublime. Lips kissed and licked and sucked her, tasting both sexual flesh and other, and making the whole surface of her body into one seamless erogenous zone. A sex, hot and engorged, smoothed its moist way across her trembling torso, its very passage the gentlest of sorceries. She felt a great white heat in her clitoris, an explosion that had nothing at all to do with Drago's mechanical shafting. The tiny organ became molten, mutable, burning; throbbing helplessly with a pleasure that was not of this world.

And as she orgasmed violently, she thrashed and screamed out a name – the name of her dreamlove, the owner of the fingers and the tongue. She hardly noticed that Drago was ejaculating.

'What got into you?' he enquired afterwards, half sarcastic, half suspicious, and Lainie felt suddenly liberated.

It was over. She was free.

And that was why she was here, walking into a place where something really *had* got into her.

Her cure.

And not just the healing of her sexuality, but of her boldness, her mettle, and her lust for life itself. Her ability to reach out, without fear, for what she truly wanted.

In the outer office, Isis herself was behind the reception desk and looking faintly hassled.

'Hello, Lainie,' she said, her strange, marked face showing surprise, perplexion, and something else Lainie couldn't quite fathom. 'I wasn't expecting you but I – I think I can fit you in. Things are a bit topsy-turvy today. Tricksie's resting. She's at home with her feet up and I'm trying to manage on my own.' She grinned wryly, 'And I don't seem to be doing very well . . . Please, come through.'

Lainie felt insanely excited as she sat down and dropped her case by the chair. Her heart was galloping, her pulse racing and lower down there were other parts preparing for action, too.

'What can I do for you, Lainie?' Isis seemed calm again now. 'Have you tried to fantasise yet?'

'Indeed I have,' Lainie answered, trying to keep her voice level and her roiling body still, 'but it didn't work out quite as you told me, Isis. It's all over between Drago and me. I've left him – and now I've nowhere to live, no money, and no job. And it's all your fault!'

For a moment that imperfectly perfect face looked devastated, and its owner on the point of tears. 'But you did so beautifully yesterday,' Isis said unhappily, her satin voice wavering. 'I just can't believe you couldn't fantasise.'

'Oh, I fantasised all right,' said Lainie, unable to contain her grin of triumph. And in the same instant she saw it reflected on Isis' peculiar physiognomy too; the good doctor was far too clever to be fooled for long.

'Oh, yes, Isis, I fantasised like a mad thing, and I came and came and came . . . But it was too good to waste on that self-centred bastard!' She paused, for effect, and let her gaze drift from the top of Isis' glossy head to the tips of her white-shod feet. 'So I've left him – and everything else, too. What're you going to do about it, doctor? It's your fault . . .'

'Well . . .' Isis paused, as if feigning deep thought, her off-centre smile making Lainie's loins quicken, then melt and run. 'I know of a place you could stay . . . And as for work, you can stand in for Tricksie for a while.'

'A temporary receptionist's job isn't quite what I had in mind,' Lainie said carefully, hoping against hope that Isis could read thoughts as accurately today as she had done yesterday.

'You're right of course, my sweet,' murmured Isis, her composure unassailable as she rose from behind her desk and moved forward. And as her slim fingers worked deftly on the buttons of her snow white smock,

Lainie's questions about her underwear were answered. 'You deserve far more than that.'

Isis was a vision before her, a therapy in herself with ivory skin, round, high-nippled breasts and a glorious tabby-coloured bush. Energised, Lainie set about dragging up her own tight skirt.

'Far more ...' Isis slid gracefully to her knees, and her fingers moved swiftly over Lainie's feverish skin: pulling off damp panties, drawing them down over stockinged legs, then flinging them away altogether.

'But tell me one thing, my angel,' Isis said archly as she leant into the open delta of Lainie's thighs and breathed delicately on to her pink and glistening quim. 'You're not having any problems responding now, are you? Admit it.'

Lainie did admit it.

First she nodded. Then she moaned. Then she screamed as her flesh turned to flame beneath Isis' flickering tongue.

Her dream lover's tongue. The very final element of the cure.

His Books, His Letters

'You have disappointed me,' her Mentor wrote. 'I gave into your care one of my most prized possessions, and what did you do? You treated it no more carefully than you would a cheap magazine or a sleazy tabloid newspaper. It was – is – an inestimable work, a volume of antiquity and value, and what did you do? You spattered it with droplets of coffee.'

It was tea, thought the Neophyte mournfully. Tea, Earl Grey, hot. But that wouldn't make things any better.

'I had hoped that when we met I could introduce you to certain delicate matters, and how they might be chronicled, in an atmosphere of peacefulness and harmony. But sadly, now, you leave me no option. I fear you must learn things the harder way, because to my sorrow, you have let me down quite badly.'

The Neophyte shuddered. She had wanted so much to win his approval. It was the reason for the books in the first place. Teach me! she had pleaded in her letters. Tell me what to read, so that I may better do what I do. I'm very ignorant but I do so long to learn.

And that was how it had begun.

In letters he had described, in the most exquisite and spine-tingling detail, the ways in which a person – that was, a submissive woman – might be punished. The classic rituals. The various traditional instruments. The portions of the body that were customarily beaten, whipped or spanked. Although attention was principally paid to the completely bared bottom, he told her almost casually, there were instances where a thigh or a hand might be smacked, as an aside or a penalty in themselves.

In the spirit of research the Neophyte had tried these pains for herself. And as the blows fell, usually delivered by a wooden or plastic ruler, she would wince with ecstatic excitement, and imagine her secret Mentor looming over her, his face – as yet still unknown to her – set in fine lines of elegant severity. She pictured him mature and knowing, his lips and his hands thin and firm.

Slowly his letters grew more intimate. 'When I bare your bottom,' he would write, 'you will experience a sense of overwhelming submission. You will want to cover yourself, hide your shame, yet you will bend your desires to mine. Your naked, trembling globes will be my property, my possession, and I alone will dispose of their condition.'

The Neophyte knew these were only words, the words she herself had begged of him, but in her mind there were often deeds, too.

With the letters, came books. Beautiful books, collector's editions lovingly preserved. Tooled leather covers, creamy, thick-papered pages, gilded edging and thin, silken strands of red ribbon to save a place where the contents were most choice.

The appearance of these books was sublime, and what was in them truly celestial. Descriptions of a hundred protracted corrections; cool, measured prose that stirred white heat in the Neophyte's poor loins. In his model writings, the Mentor often gave instructions that she should not indulge herself. But as they were simply examples – weren't they? – she had taken it upon herself to disobey him, then wallowed in a slough of deep remorse.

'Only after contrition may pleasure come,' he had written so tantalisingly. And the Neophyte had felt both wicked and fulfilled by disobeying.

Finally the day of their meeting had been set. Instructions given, many and detailed, and a map, too, supplied. With the letter outlining the when and the where and the what, yet another beautiful book had arrived. The most beautiful yet, its black, indented leather surface protected by a heavy amber-coloured jacket, and its pages, though old and thin, preserved in the most pristine of conditions.

The Neophyte cherished the book as if it were the Mentor himself, and yet even in her obsession she was unwise. Unable to part herself from its pain-filled pages, she had taken it to her bed, and read it whilst she had sipped her morning tea. And, of course, the inevitable calamity had occurred.

The splashes were few, but noticeable, and there was no way to defer their discovery. The Mentor had requested a swift return of this, his most rare and costly item.

The Neophyte had spent day after day of misery, expecting, and sure, almost, that in the next letter their meeting would be cancelled, or worse, he would banish her from his attentions forever.

But instead the appointment was to stand. She would still meet her destiny, it transpired, but now she feared it even more than ever, for it seemed that a veil had been lifted. Her literary delusions were crumbling.

'Come promptly and dressed in sober clothing. Your attire will be neat and discreet, and you will wear stockings, garters, and button-strapped shoes. Your underclothing must be white, and unadorned, except for petticoats, of which you may wear several, and all trimmed with a little cotton lace.'

The image of these clothes thrilled the Neophyte. Perhaps, if she followed his code of dress with precision, he would be pleased and forgive her for the book. Like a holy pilgrim she set off to do some shopping, for she had nothing quite so simple in her wardrobe.

When the day of the confrontation dawned, she donned her monochrome vestments as if each garment were made of cloth of gold. She was a handmaiden on a mission to serve her master, a sacrificial lamb about to yield its tender throat. Within the confines of her immaculate white panties, her woman's core burned and tormented her. She yearned for the Mentor, and this meeting, though she had never seen his face or heard his voice. His written words, in his letters and his prose, were sufficient to utterly command her; his clever, lucid sentences made her want to uncover herself completely, and offer him her bottom pale and naked. For his sake, she knew she could endure.

She imagined standing, but bent over, in the corner of his drawing room, her buttocks and haunches stretched and nude while he took tea – Earl Grey, perhaps? – with his friends and associates. She imagined a touch here, a pinch there, her nether parts assessed and handled before the most appropriate implements were chosen – with deep thoughtfulness – from a selection that the Mentor had waiting.

Part your legs, he would say. Show everything. And, embarrassed by her readiness, she would obey.

There were no cars outside the Mentor's house, so presumably no associates, but in answer to the Neophyte's knocking a young woman came to answer the door.

'Ah, you're here,' she said brightly, and ushered the Neophyte inside.

The Mentor's residence was old, with high ceilings, leaded windows and thick walls. Thick, thick walls that would absorb the very shrillest of sounds. Around her was all the beauty that the Neophyte had expected, but her nerves, and the presence of the strangely dressed young woman, made her less able than usual to take note of it.

Who is she? the Neophyte thought in alarm. A housekeeper? A lover? Another like me, here to learn at the great man's feet? Her companion seemed to know her way around all right, leading the Neophyte along a tall, gloomy hall with a polished parquet floor, then on, up a staircase, to a room at the far end of the landing.

But she can't be a lover dressed like that.

The young woman was tall and slender, and no doubt had long, lissom legs, but the Neophyte was unable to see them. Her escort wore a simple, almost spartan grey dress that reached all the way down to her ankles. Its collar was high, and its sleeves narrow and fitted, and with it she wore old-fashioned, buttoned boots. The severity of her garb did nothing to dull the young woman's beauty, and neither did the shortness of her hair – a cap of auburn that was dead straight and shiny. Her face was oval, almost nun-like and devoid of all paint, save a dab of crimson rouge upon her lips.

The Neophyte felt brash and overdressed beside this paragon of modesty, and she quailed when they reached a closed door.

'Don't be afraid,' said the young woman softly, reaching out to squeeze the Neophyte's sweating hand. 'He knows how to handle the nervous.'

The room beyond the door was a stronghold of learning, and clearly the haven of the Mentor. The Neophyte got the impression of row upon row of books, shelf after shelf of volumes, but she only had eyes for their owner – a slim, black-clad figure who stood motionless by the window, looking out.

'Ah, my dear, you've brought our new friend,' said the Mentor, turning on his booted heel, and facing in towards the room, the cropped one, and the Neophyte.

He was not at all what she had expected, although his brow was noble, and his eyes dark and piercingly sharp. The Neophyte could not have said precisely what she *had* been expecting, but even so his appearance took her breath.

'Yes, our most careless friend,' he went on mildly, although the attendant young woman had not answered.

'I –' began the Neophyte anxiously, then fell silent when the Mentor raised his hand.

'Oh, no, it's not your place to speak yet, I'm afraid. You're here to learn, to listen, and to reflect on a wealth of shortcomings . . . Not the least, your disrespect for my books.' Turning slightly, he nodded towards a beautiful highly-polished table, on whose top lay the open, tea-stained book.

'Such a shame, eh, Alice?' he murmured to his grimly-clad companion, although still she did not speak a word.

The Neophyte wondered if any woman was allowed to speak in his presence, or if it was only the ones who had wronged him who were charged to silence? The others could be just too awed for words. With an intellect like his that seemed likely.

'Perhaps we should begin?' he enquired pleasantly, striding forward into the centre of the room. The Neophyte almost gasped without thinking at his air of quiet force and the way the lamplight glittered threateningly on his spectacles. 'Alice, you may remain and assist me.'

The Neophyte felt the beginnings of real fear and embarrassment. Her letters from the Mentor were so personal, so intimate, and their contents were not a thing to share – no matter how much her own wayward writings might be peopled with legions of watchers.

'And what shall we call you?' he asked her, even though she was forbidden to answer. 'Pupil? Novice? Seeker after knowledge? You could be all these and more, given time . . .' He paused, seemed to debate. 'However, I think we'll use your own word. Will that suit you, my dear Neophyte?'

The Neophyte nodded, mortified that her pretentiousness should be revealed to Alice, and wondering if this, too, was a trait that ought to be discouraged. And – perhaps – chastised?

Oh, God! Oh, no! Oh, yes! Melting inside, the Neophyte saw a chasm yawn; not in front of her, as she had expected, but behind. It was a boundary. A borderline. An insubstantial Rubicon. One she had thought in her cleverness she could dance on, but which in reality she had foolishly long since crossed.

'Now you may speak,' said the Mentor softly, his voice closing a hidden gate behind her.

'Y – yes,' stuttered the Neophyte.

'Yes "what"?' prompted the Mentor, his eyes intent.

But what did he mean by 'what'? The Neophyte's heart pounded heavily, and she felt sweat bead in the small of her back. It was a trick question, clearly. Did he expect an honorific? An expansion of her answer? An apology? His cool face seemed to offer no clues.

'I don't know,' she continued, feeling helpless.

'Now that is strange,' the Mentor continued. 'You seem so full of opinions in your letters. So eloquent. Has your mastery of language escaped you? Is this another instance of your sad lack of care?'

She wanted to defy him. She needed to. But his aura seemed to reach out and take charge of her. She felt her brain turn to mush, and her knees suddenly weaken, and without thinking she fell down before him, kneeling on the rug with her head meekly bowed.

'Forgive me,' she begged. 'I'm so sorry about your book. I know I should have looked after it better . . .'

'Do you? Do you really know?' he questioned gently, his hand falling lightly on her head and ruffling the soft strands of her hair.

Shaking, her whole body quickened by one touch, the Neophyte felt off-balance and confused. Her Mentor wasn't really responding to what she had said, but to the things she had written, the things she had thought she had understood but clearly did not.

'Perhaps we can help you,' he went on as if she had somehow answered. 'Make you understand . . . Make you reverent towards that which must be honoured, and mark your duty in a way you'll be inclined to remember.'

Outside this room, the Neophyte would have laughed, and called the Mentor arrogant, perhaps even faintly ridiculous, but within it she now understood him. Perfectly. And understood – with fear – how the duty he spoke of would be marked.

'And shall I be your Mentor?' he questioned, lifting her face, looking down into her eyes, and using the word she had used only once in her letters, but constantly employed in her mind.

Half-dazzled, knowing she should look away, the Neophyte held his gaze and nodded.

'Very well, it begins,' he replied, turning her face away not cruelly but quite gently, although his voice was neutral and detached.

The Neophyte swayed, then slumped, her heart afeared, but her body singing with a deep, dark thrill. Every step of his booted feet, as he walked away briskly, seemed to vibrate through her moist, quaking sex.

It was Alice who helped the Neophyte to her feet, a sympathetic smile on her face. The pale, grey-clad young woman seemed to know just what to do, and turned the Neophyte to face her chastiser.

The Mentor was seated now, in a high-backed Victorian chair, with a thin yellow cane across his lap.

'No . . . Oh, no,' whispered the Neophyte, then felt Alice's shushing fingers at her lips.

'You may prepare her,' said the Mentor calmly, running his fingers along the gleaming, tapered rod.

'Lift your skirt,' whispered Alice, her lips close to the Neophyte's ear. 'Come on, hurry,' she urged when he hesitated, and folded her hand around his to guide her.

Although all this had happened time and time again

in the stories she had written, the Neophyte now blushed profoundly. Pulling clumsily at her skirt and her petticoats, she thought of her thighs, her stocking tops, and her panties, all on show before the Mentor's narrow gaze. As she struggled, the mass of fabric escaped her once, and fell down again, before finally she clutched it at her waist.

'Turn her,' the Mentor ordered quietly and the Neophyte felt Alice press lightly on her shoulder.

'Show her,' rang the command, when the Neophyte was turned towards the wall.

Eyes closed, and still clutching her skirts, she felt Alice move around to the side of her, then felt the woman's hands – both of them – take hold of the waistband of her panties. Slowly, almost ritualistically, Alice slid down the thin cotton garment, then let it rest at the Neophyte's quaking knees.

There was a silence. A long pause, pregnant with unvoiced meaning. For what seemed like hours, the Neophyte stood with her white bottom bare for the scrutiny of her Mentor, while somewhere in the room a clock ticked.

She could feel his eyes on her, his intense, dark gaze studying her soft, fleshy rounds and the shadowed furrow that nestled in between them. He was looking – staring – at the pursed and running place between her legs, rendered molten by her simply being before him. She felt shamed, out of control, quite ready yet *not* ready for his mercy. She would have given anything to touch her aching sex, but she knew that in this, as in everything, she must wait.

'Bring me wine, Alice, if you please?' the Mentor said suddenly, as the Neophyte stood still, with her body hot and dripping. She heard soft, even footsteps, the tinkle of glass, then the heavy creak of furniture or leather – the Mentor shifting position, crossing his legs comfortably in his handsome antique chair. As the time seemed to stretch unbearably, and her bared bottom to pulsate with desire, there came the slow, steady flick of turning pages. The Mentor had forgotten her, it seemed, and had settled down to do a little reading.

Did he drink one glass of wine, or two? How many chapters of his book did he read? Would she come soon, just from an agony of longing? It seemed to the Neophyte that she had been standing against the wall for a millenium, but at last she sensed the book being laid aside. She felt, rather than heard him retrieve his thin cane, then swish it slowly, in an arc, through the air.

'Now, Alice, if you would oblige us again?' he said, almost cheerfully, and once again, the Neophyte was handled. Guided by the silent Alice, she was led back towards the middle of the room, still clutching at her petticoats and skirt, then placed against the sturdy oaken table.

'Over here now, sweetheart. Let's have you ready,' murmured Alice, pushing steadily on the Neophyte's shoulders until she inclined herself face down across the oak.

The surface of the wood was coolly pleasant against the Neophyte's face, and smelt richly of lavender and beeswax. And as footsteps, the Mentor's slight but dominant tread, sounded deafeningly in the dense, ticking quiet, she felt her hands being gently clasped by Alice.

'This, my dear, is what we have read about and written of,' intoned the Mentor as his cane seemed to caress the Neophyte's bottom. She felt it rest there, light as thistledown, then almost float to and fro across her cheeks. 'The act of correction. The punishment for sins small, large, and imaginary. The retribution for all contrived wrongs . . .'

The cane lifted clear, and the Neophyte moaned softly and fearfully, sensing revelation but a heartbeat away.

'This, my dear Neophyte –' he purred, his voice

dangerous and seductive as the unseen implement rose, and Alice's hands tightened lovingly on the Neophyte's '– is the real thing, and nothing at all like my letters and my books!'

A line of fire seared the truth across her flesh.

Poses

She loved him, and she supposed she would do anything for him. As long as it was something she wanted.

'I'd like to bring some men home tonight, Mariette,' Jean-Paul had said. 'Friends of mine. I want to show you to them. Take a few photographs. You know the kind of thing. Then I'd like them to use you, while I watch. They'll be arriving some time around seven.'

In the afternoon, Jean-Paul went on a shopping spree, and returned with the clothes she was to wear for the session. Everything was very pretty, very feminine, and very expensive; and Mariette wondered about how they had been chosen. Had Jean-Paul sought the assistance of some accommodating vendeuse, perhaps? A middle-aged woman, hard-faced but chic, and worldly enough to understand the protocol of matters such as these.

'I'm sharing a woman with some acquaintances tonight, Madame,' he might say. 'She must look desirable, elegant, modest. She must be a gift for them. A sign of my respect for them. She must be the choicest, most feminine morsel they could possibly imagine.'

'Of course, Monsieur, I quite understand,' the vendeuse might say, 'Let me show you some suitable ensembles.'

Jean-Paul helped Mariette to get ready himself, no doubt concerned that she be faultlessly turned out for his friends. It was he who bathed her, running the sponge, charged with lather, across her body. He soaped her breasts, her sex, her bottom and her thighs, then took a straight-edged razor and removed her pubic hair. That he took pleasure in these intimate attentions was evident, although neither of them mentioned the large bulge in his trousers.

When her body was as exquisitely clean, and as immaculately hairless as it could be, he dried her off and anointed her with perfume, using a strong, flowery musk laced heavily with exotic Eastern spices. He might wish her to appear a lady for the delectation of his associates, but it was clear she had to smell like a whore. He applied the scent copiously across her breasts and on her thighs, massaging the fragrant oil into her skin with his fingertips.

Mariette was careful to hide her responses while he served her this way. Jean-Paul had recently read *L'Histoire d'O*, and very much fancied himself her master, but in truth he had never yet done anything with her, or to her that she did not like. To have him act as her maidservant both amused and excited her, and while he tended to her toilette she kept her legs closed as much she was able – feigning modesty – so he would not see the illicit sheen upon her quim.

Likewise, as he helped her into her clothing, her demeanour was both demure and embarrassed. She blushed prettily and looked downcast as he smoothed on her silk stockings, and shuddered as he fastened the tabs of her suspenders.

'There, I think you will please them,' he said proudly when the preparations were finished, and in silence, Mariette agreed. Her grey velvet suit was both shapely and feminine, its fitted jacket and narrow skirt defining her curves. To complete the impression of supremely elegant coquettishness, her heels were high and she wore a tiny hat and veil. Her slender hands were encased in grey kid gloves.

‘Yes! You are perfect,’ he exclaimed, adjusting the fit of a sleeve, then the line of her skirt. ‘Now you must wait here for us . . . We are to meet in the Cafe Trigonelle, and we may stay there for a few drinks. But you must stay still and silent until we arrive.’

Mariette remained silent – apart from a sigh or two – but she found it difficult to keep her body still. Every fibre of her being was on fire with anticipation, and between her legs her sex was a furnace, its heat stoked by a cavalcade of fantasies. She imagined herself exposed and demeaned in a score of different poses, her limbs arranged, and her clothing opened, to please the men. How soon would it dawn on them that such postures and contortions turned her on? That to be shamed and tormented was her pleasure? And just one of her many sexual whimsies.

Because it pleased her, Mariette sat on the black leather sofa, precisely as Jean-Paul had ordered her. The apartment was still and cool, a design poem in black and shades of beige, a perfect bland backdrop for the games that lay ahead. In her quietude, Mariette monitored her surroundings. She heard ice cracking in the insulated bucket; she smelt the distinctive tang of leather from the new upholstery beneath her bottom; she felt her lubrication trickle out into her panties.

Come *now*, Jean-Paul, she ordered in her mind, and from the lobby, she heard the sound of a clicking lock, an opening door. Footsteps followed, then murmuring, the tones masculine and full of bonhomie. Suppressing her smile, Mariette looked downwards, and studied the woven rug.

‘Ah, so this is the young woman in question,’ said the first voice, a light baritone, sounding confident.

‘Yes, this is she,’ said Jean-Paul a little eagerly. It was obvious he was anxious to please his friends.

‘A very fine specimen,’ commented a second unknown man, his tone rather cool and detached.

'Indeed,' added a third, who seemed to be in jolly high spirits. 'It's obvious she'll be marvellous to photograph. What do you think, Jimmy?'

There was no reply to this, although Mariette sensed a fourth stranger nodding.

'Stand up please, Mariette,' ordered Jean-Paul, whose voice was excited. 'Let the gentlemen see you properly . . . That's it. Stand straight. Arms at your sides.'

Mariette obeyed, very conscious of the rasp of her fine silk-mesh stockings as she shifted her thighs to adjust her position. She could feel her breasts rise and swell in the tight containment of her brassière, the nipples rude and pushing against the silk. She could hardly wait to remove her jacket and expose them.

'Is she obedient?' enquired the confident voice.

'Oh, very,' enthused Jean-Paul. 'She'll do anything I say . . . She's very pliant.'

'Oh good!' said the jolly one, and Mariette felt him step closer to inspect her.

'There are degrees of obedience,' the cooler voice observed, making her shudder with anticipation. It would be good to make this one's eyes open.

This one's blue eyes, she thought, when he grasped her chin, tilted up her face and made her look at him. 'She's proud, Jean-Paul,' he went on, his voice as refined as his perfectly groomed silver hair. 'I don't think you've yet schooled her sufficiently.'

With that, the silver-haired one lifted her veil and possessed her mouth roughly, pushing his tongue between her lips and stretching her jaw. Without thinking, Mariette fought back with her own tongue, swirling it around and flicking his with its tip.

'She's a slut, Jean-Paul,' he said coldly as they parted, shoving her away from him and making her sway on her high heels. 'She's far too full of herself.' He walked away and espying Jean-Paul's whisky, helped himself to a generously iced measure. As he turned away from the tray, his eyes met Mariette's and she looked down again, struggling hard not to smile.

'May we see her panties?' asked the very first man who had spoken, and Mariette heard him move across to mix a drink for himself, too, then quietly ask the others what they wanted.

'Certainly,' replied Jean-Paul, trying to sound expansive, but clearly a little rattled by his grey-haired friend's criticism. 'Is your camera ready, Jimmy?' he enquired of the as yet silent photographer.

'Yes, all set,' said a young voice, a very soft voice that Mariette found utterly delightful. A brief glance confirmed his face was just as sweet.

'Splendid. Raise your skirt then, my dear,' said the cheerful man, whose face was long and pale, Mariette saw, but whose brown eyes were extremely bright and merry. 'Let's see what you've got to offer.'

The grey velvet skirt was very tight, and Mariette had to wriggle to get it up over her hips.

'Oh, that's nice . . .,' said the man with the smooth, light voice. 'Very fine indeed. I do so love to see a young woman's knickers. Especially thin and silky ones like those.'

And I do so love to see handsome men like you, my friend, said Mariette silently, sneaking an admiring look at him through her long, mascaraed lashes. Of all Jean-Paul's friends this one was the best looking, a Middle Eastern type with black, curling hair and roguish eyes. His lips were very red, and slightly parted. And she could well imagine the sight he was panting over.

Jean-Paul had fitted out the flat with long mirrors, especially for occasions like these, but Mariette didn't need their assistance to see herself. She could plainly picture her slender figure, as she stood on the rug waiting, her torso half uncovered and half clothed. Her legs were long and slender in her smoke-coloured silk stockings, and where they ended, her naked thighs were pale and creamy, bisected by the narrowest of elastic suspenders. The panties she was wearing were pure white, as sheer as vapour, and full cut, up to the waist, with deep lace inserts. The fact that she was shaven was quite evident to all assembled.

'Not bad,' said the handsome Arab.

'Delicious,' said his good-humoured companion.

'Mmmm . . .' said the cool character assessingly, his blue eyes narrow.

The guests were all seated now; at their ease, in armchairs, each with a cool drink beside them. Jean-Paul was doing a little directionless fidgeting and the young photographer was making adjustments to his lens. Just watching him, Mariette felt hot and breathless. She imagined her own crotch as he would see it in his viewfinder, her pantied pubis at the centre, the focus sharp.

'May I try something?' the handsome Middle Eastern man said suddenly, getting up again, and walking towards her. 'These are very pretty, aren't they?' he said, touching the flat front panel of her panties, where it stretched tight over the equally flat plane of her belly. With one long dark fingertip he traced the division of her labia, then laughed softly into her face as she quivered and the visible damp patch at her crotch began to spread.

'She's very responsive,' he said to Jean-Paul, as he pressed a little harder, making her shaven lips part beneath the cloth. Mariette wanted to moan, she *needed* to moan, but she felt a greater need to retain her self-possession. She bit her painted lips, but she didn't make a sound.

The Arab, who really was quite beautiful up close, saw her efforts to contain herself and smiled.

'You'd like to come, my dear, wouldn't you?' he said, putting his face very close to hers. Mariette could smell the tang of whisky on his breath, as well as the spiciness of the ginger ale he'd taken with it. She wanted to kiss him, and make him touch her aching clitoris. But still she stayed silent and didn't move.

'Spread your legs a little wider,' he purred, his finger still poised over her sex. 'Tilt your hips . . . Push your cunt forward and give us all a better view.'

Mariette obeyed him, her breathing shallow, her heart drumming in her chest. The pose was lewd, almost ugly, but she felt enraptured; especially when her Arab nodded slightly towards the hovering photographer, who stepped forward, quickly adjusting his focal length.

'Begin,' said the Arab softly, and as he drew his hand away, Mariette heard the shutter start to click.

Making her mind a blank screen, she began to see what was being captured in the lens. Her thighs spread apart; her hips and pelvis canted at a provocative angle; her pudenda clearly visible through her panties. She could also see the evidence of her own juices, welling and flowing, making a dark, glistening stain on the gauzy silk. She could almost see the membranes pulse within.

'And now, a little variety,' announced the Arab, putting his long, dark finger into the picture. Letting it rest exactly where it had lingered before, pressing the sodden fabric into the divide of her love-lips.

Unable to prevent herself, Mariette made a high, faint, birdlike sound and felt her beleaguered sex gather itself and flutter. Little eddies of shamed reaction danced and rippled in her vulva, and her clitoris gave a single heavy throb. A hand gripped one buttock and squeezed it hard.

'Oh, please . . .,' she whimpered, feeling a maelstrom of conflicting emotions and sensations. She was coming, in a light and strangely inconsequential way, and both proud of it and angry that it had happened. She wanted to resist them, Jean-Paul and his friends, but at the same time she revelled in being wanton. She gloried in the fact that her flesh was weak and prone to pleasure; she exulted in the state of lost control. She pictured her love-juice running so copiously that it overflowed her panties and trickled in a rivulet down her thighs. She imagined urinating involuntarily, the golden stream gushing out of her, soaking her legs, her stockings and her shoes. Her clitoris leapt again at the dark, delicious fantasy – her humiliation preserved forever by the camera.

'What are you thinking of, my lovely?' whispered her tormentor, so quietly that the others couldn't here. His poised finger pressured her, making her orgasm fire and flare, while behind he besieged her anus through her panties.

'N – nothing!' she choked, her loins melting in his hands, while around them she heard faint murmurs of approval.

'I can't believe that,' he contested, still pushing, pushing, pushing, her thin silk knickers no barrier, no protection. As her hips waved, the infernal shutter went on clicking.

Then suddenly her gorgeous Arab was gone, and Mariette was left climaxing alone. On show, revealed and abandoned.

'Stop that! Immediately!' snapped the cold voice she recognised as belonging to the man with silver-grey hair. Opening her heavy eyes she saw him striding towards her. 'You're here for us, not yourself,' he said sternly, dashing away her hands, which had stolen to her crotch in the absence of the Arab's.

'You're a whore, aren't you?' he continued, grasping the waistband of her panties and pulling them down quickly and deftly to her knees. With no warning whatsoever, he thrust his hand into her vulva, fingers in a wedge, cruelly stretching the entrance of her channel. 'You're wet through down here.' Jerking upwards, he forced her up on to her toes. 'Swimming . . .' He flexed his fingers, moving them apart to stretch her more. Mariette moaned loudly, relishing the discomfort as she danced like a puppet, almost overbalancing, held up only by the one intruding hand. As he rocked her she grabbed his shoulder to keep from falling.

'You disgust me,' her torturer growled, but the tremor in his voice told her otherwise. His coolness was fast melting as he savoured her compliance, and when he kissed her again his tongue was wild and lustful. She had another orgasm, and he absorbed her shriek of ecstasy.

And still the camera clicked and wound, clicked and wound, clicked and wound; the pattern of sounds consistent as they used her. She seemed to see each tableau through the nervous eyes of Jimmy, and holding every pose, she committed them all to memory.

She saw her breasts exposed; her expensive jacket wrenched open, her brassière pulled down, her nipples pinched, then nipped tightly in silver screw-clamps.

She saw herself kneeling – naked but for her hat, her shoes, her stockings and her gloves – her mouth being ravished by the handsome, rampant Arab, while Jean-Paul held her head and kept her still.

She saw herself lying on the coffee table, her knees grasped by the silver-haired man, her bottom and haunches lifted, while his cheerful friend inserted a greased bottle-neck into her anus.

Mariette treasured all these poses, and conserved them in her memory, employing them later, when their guests had gone and Jean-Paul fucked her. As ever, on such nights, he was eager and pre-emptive – and completely uninspiring – but the shimmering slew of images made her come.

How fortunate I am, Mariette thought afterwards, tousling his hair fondly as he slept upon her breast. He was not very good in bed, and he never really had been, but he always kept her hunger amply served. His little 'session' had yielded satisfying fruit.

There had been four *cartes de visite* secreted amongst her abandoned clothing, the owner of each one no doubt pleased with his unique idea.

Mariette smiled. She had posed to please Jean-Paul, to give him pleasure and excitement; but in return, he had provided her with four new lovers.

Hugging her husband close, she wondered which to sample first.

Time is the Fire

A Thoughtful Interlude

Time is the fire in which we burn.

'Late again,' says Sebastian, his golden eyes mastering me as he fingers his precious antique fob-watch in a slow, somewhat menacing fashion. He always toys with the watch when he's planning something, so I have come to regard this apparently idle little mannerism with a rich blend of desire and shaking fear.

Time – as represented by that elegant, gilded chronometer – has become very important to us recently. I think of it as a steady ticking clock at the centre of our relationship; a beating heart that governs our life and gives it purpose.

Feeling foolhardy, I stare back at him in some small measure of defiance. I still have to do this, my wayward soul demands it.

Sebastian's answer is that piercing, almost metallic expression of his; the one that makes my poor heart leap and clamour.

'I'm sorry . . . I just got talking,' I mutter, throwing down my bag on Sebastian's leather sofa, and getting a raised eyebrow for slovenliness as well as my grossly late arrival. 'You know how it is.'

'No. Actually, I don't,' he replies airily, flicking open the beautifully engraved watch. He makes a big show of checking the time, then looking up again with that baleful facial cast.

Sebastian doesn't chatter. Sebastian doesn't even

make small talk all that often. And he certainly never wastes a scrap of time. Not a single second of his life goes by that is not utilised, and even in these few passing moments, during which he silently admonishes me, he finds a meaning and a source of sly delight. With his eyes squarely on me, unwavering and all-knowing, my body shudders and I feel my knees go weak. It's not hard to see the colour of his plans.

'Time is a very precious commodity, Miranda,' he says to me, quietly, his deep voice very solemn but still exciting. 'Some people say that it's the fire in which we burn. The predator that stalks us . . . The constant companion that accompanies us on our way.' Snapping the watch shut, he tucks it away in the pocket of his neatly buttoned waistcoat. 'And thanks to *you*, my dear, we two have lost an hour.'

I note he is wearing the black waistcoat today, the one with the elaborate, but understated embroidery that he often wears on occasions such as these. 'A cause for retribution, I would have thought, wouldn't you?' he continues, adopting an air of mock-reflection. 'A little punishment for the wasting of my life . . .'

It is on the tip of my tongue to point out that it's very likely I would have been punished anyway – but I keep my counsel, and intone a humble 'yes'.

'In that case, Miranda, you may go to the bedroom and make the customary preparations,' he continues, a tiny smile playing around his unusually pallid lips, 'And I will come to you in –' he slips out the watch again and studies it for another unnecessarily long period '– let's say fifteen minutes, shall we?'

I nod with a dour solemnity which matches his, then turn to leave the room. At the door, I get an overpowering urge to stop and drop a curtsey to him – his manner is so unrelentingly magisterial today – but as he might well interpret such an action as flippancy, or worse still disrespect, I decide to play it safe and just get out.

Fifteen minutes? It's not long in real terms, is it? But it's still plenty long enough to set my every nerve-end jangling and wind my spring as if I have become my loved one's watch.

The problem is my lurid imagination. Fifteen minutes can be an eternity when I am wondering what's in Sebastian's mind. What will happen when he comes after me *this* time?

On opening the bedroom door, the first thing I notice as I enter Sebastian's strange Victorianesque sanctum is the ticking of his mahogany long-case clock. Time again. The engraved brass dial and filigree hands read two-fifteen at the moment, and as it's taken me, perhaps, half a minute to reach the bedroom, I know that by two-thirty I'll be a quaking, quivering wreck. Well, inside, at least.

On the bed, Sebastian has laid out a nightgown for me to wear. It's white, voluminous, and virginal, with just some smocking and a little embroidery to lighten its plainness. Most of the men I've known in my life have wanted to get me into satin skimpies, frothy concoctions of spaghetti straps and lace that reveal far more of a woman's flesh than they conceal. But not my Sebastian. He likes to see me as some chaste and languishing heroine from a turn of the century melodrama; a beautiful, austerely-clothed penitent about to pay for some imagined domestic sin.

Stripping swiftly, I peel off my smart, tailored suit, my 'business' blouse, my undies and my stockings, then let the snowy gown slither down over my vulnerable body. The soft, slightly brushed cotton feels comforting against my skin, consoling. It fortifies my spirit and soothes my flutterings. I move even deeper into my lover's dreamscape, my heart now strong.

There are still some changes to be made, so looking quickly into the mirror, I use tissues to remove my make-up, rubbing away the subtle paint with trembling fingers. I dress well, and use cosmetics as a weapon these days, mainly because, you could say, I have bettered myself since I first met Sebastian. Drawing on his strength, I have succeeded at interviews I would formerly never have had the confidence to even attend. It's as if bending to *him* has given me the courage to conquer *my* world.

But it's time to lie down now, and abandon all thoughts of offices, jobs, and other forgettable, everyday trivia. I have no high status here in this room, no authority, no sovereignty; I'm simply Sebastian's, his willing vassal, and happy to be it.

The bed is inviting and very comfortable, with a pristine bedspread in nubbly white chenille. Settling carefully on to my front, I rest my cheek on one bent arm, then reach down behind me to adjust my billowing nightdress.

What must I look like now? I wonder when this task is done. I try to imagine the sight that would meet the casual intruder with a little time to spare.

Face down on the bed lies a moderately pretty red-haired girl in a white, antique nightgown. The visitor might be puzzled, though, at the paradox she presents. Her night attire is the very picture of modesty and innocence, yet she is wearing it in a most unexpected manner, drawn up at the back to expose her legs and buttocks. This visitor might be quite taken with the contrast between the cloudy white primness of her saintly cotton nightdress – and the shocking nudity of her bare, unguarded bottom. A bottom that is well-rounded and a little fleshy, and divided by a deep, rose-tinted groove. He might find that the thighs, too, are a handsome, tempting prospect – being also sturdy but still firm and rather shapely. If the visitor were Sebastian himself, he might ask, nay, command this young woman to open her plump thighs, so he could better see her awful, shameful eagerness and the lewd, unruly glistening of her sex.

Tick. Tick. Tick.

From where I lie I can easily see the clock. The yellow, afternoon sunlight slants conveniently across it, and shows ten minutes still remaining from fifteen.

Sebastian can achieve quite a lot in just ten minutes. It's an eye's blink in the grand and cosmic scheme of things, but during ten minutes with him I can pass from fear into certainty, and from untouched white into simmering pink, or red. As I have said, my love never wastes his time.

He might say something like, 'I'm going to cane you for ten minutes – and after that I'm going to play with you for five.'

I can almost feel the rod from just thinking about its hardness, almost taste its bite as it lands upon my flesh. Sebastian will never stop until those ten minutes are finished, no matter how much I carry on and struggle. And it's the same in the subsequent five. He will be equally, if not more resolute; he will persist, caressing me with great care and application, no matter how many times I come and come and come.

Tick. Tick. Tick.

Time. And Sebastian.

Sometimes he will order me to come to his house at a specific hour – as he did today – and thrash me once on arrival, and then again, every hour, as the clock chimes its steady, immutable passage. And on the half hour? Well, he will be as kind as he has hourly been cruel.

Another of his temporal tricks is to ring me at work, and instruct me to abandon whatever I'm doing and to go immediately to the cloakroom. Once there, I am obliged to stand in a cubicle for ten minutes, with my skirt pulled up to my waist and my panties around my ankles, and fantasise about some image pre-arranged. This might entail me imagining that I am being whipped with a riding crop whilst bound naked across a trestle. I might have to concentrate on an illusory scenario in which I have my thighs repeatedly smacked with a leather-soled slipper. My bare bottom walloped with a carpet beater. My buttocks held open and my groove lashed lightly with a ferule. Whatever it is, he makes it *really* happen – later.

Tick. Tick. Tick.

The tall clock shows that there are only five minutes to go now, but I can't help thinking about an event that occured precisely one month ago. Just remembering it makes my sex begin to moisten.

It could have been called a party, I suppose, but it was nothing like the tedious fancy dress frolic at which Sebastian and I originally met. This timely gathering comprised simply of Sebastian and several of his like-minded male friends – with me as their exclusive entertainment.

Marked out most punctiliously by Sebastian's golden watch, each man had sole use of me for a full thirty minutes, while the others sat round watching and sipping good wine.

The first guest, a sombre academic called Doctor Darius Brent, made me bend over, school-style, and clasp my ankles, while he raised my skirt and slip, then pinned them securely to my back. After that, he belaboured me rather stylishly with a tongue-shaped rubber 'slapper', and seared my buttocks through my tiny, lace-trimmed panties. His blows, though measured, made me sway and rock precariously, and my bottom seemed to swell with sizzling heat. I had a difficult time maintaining my uncomfortable pose throughout this exhibition, and when it was over he made me lower my sticky knickers. I cried freely as he slowly turned me round.

I was asked to retain my knickers for the next half hour, too, although around my knees instead of stretched across my bottom. The second disciplinarian was a young bearded man, unknown to me but strangely *símpatico*, whose dark eyes laughed while his mouth remained unyielding. In a universe where there had never been a Sebastian, I could have fancied him. As it was, I melted and obeyed him utterly.

This stern, hirsute maestro made me totter around the room with my pants half-mast and drooping, then drape my shaking body supine across his lap. His face and mouth were hidden while he repeatedly slapped my bottom cheeks, but I always imagine that he really *did* smile then.

I didn't smile. Not at all. I wasn't able to. Overlaying the fiery redness inflicted by the slapper, this superior spanking was an agonising trial to me. My new tormentor covered every square inch of me that had previously been walloped, and even seemed to find some untried areas. When his stint was finished, my plump buttocks were a sorry, pulsating mess. I remember looking towards Sebastian at the moment he released me – in a mute plea for mercy, I suppose – but all I received was his golden steadfast look.

Thinking of that look, I am forced – now – to wriggle, and then imagine the third and last of those 'half hours'. Chastiser number three had been a tall, silver-haired man with the coldest, bluest eyes I have ever seen. No one spoke his name but I sensed he was a VIP of some kind – a man whose identity was secret. In a voice that was glacial and weary, he ordered me to remove my clothing, then crouch on the table, bottom raised, completely nude. When I was in position, he thrashed my thighs with a long, thin switch.

'His Lordship', too, had been an artist with his implement. His cuts were lined up with an almost mechanical accuracy, and he returned frequently to the ones in tender places. I was whining loudly by the time he resumed his seat.

My darling himself used a ruler – his long-time favourite – but it felt like a horsewhip on a bottom so well prepared. He flicked my flaming buttocks with just the lightest, teasing strokelets, but each one became a swathe of crackling fire. I had to be held down by the bearded stranger and the Doctor – both while Sebastian beat me, and while he fucked me and I came.

Tick. Tick. Tick.

A glance at the clock reveals one minute still remaining.

The moment has come to compose myself, to stop all my squirming and my circling against the bedspread – and present my lover with a calm, quiescent bottom. Sebastian will be with me in less than sixty seconds now, his bright eyes glowing with that pure fanatic flame.

As I look towards the clock again, I see the delicate second hand sweep upward, then hear the creaking door and a soft, familiar tread. There's a click – the pocket watch being opened and consulted yet again – and with it, I hear a whispered, fervent, 'Yes'.

The time has come now, and he's about to make me burn.

The French Job

TEMPORARY POSITION. Wanted by French Businesswoman, Knightsbridge area, housemaid for light domestic duties. Must be amenable, discreet and very willing. Payment to be negotiated. Apply to Mme M-P Chaumier, Box 17.

Even the bedroom door gave her the shivers. Elizabeth stared at it for a full minute, wondering what lay behind its glossy, white-painted panels, what tasks and duties would be asked of her once she stepped into the room that lay beyond.

Remember, this is only a temporary position, she told herself, reaching out and knocking cautiously. For a limited period only. Whatever she asks, you can cope, can't you? Just remember it won't last for long.

'*Entrez!*' called out a clear, feminine voice, and with her heart bumping, Elizabeth put her hand on the door handle.

As she hesitated, eyes fixed firmly on her well-polished shoes, the white door swung open in front of her, and a tall, dark-haired women stood in the doorway, a narrow smile on her perfectly painted face.

'Come in! Come in! Do not dither out there on the landing.'

'I heard the bell, Madame,' said Elizabeth, her voice barely more than a squeak. 'But I – I wasn't sure if I should walk straight in.'

'When I ring I require you immediately, Elizabeth,' Mme Chaumier said gently. 'There is no need to wait outside. Now, let us see . . .' She moved off into the room, her kimono billowing around her, then forming to the sleek shape of her legs. 'I wonder if you would tidy up this room for me. I am afraid it has become a little disarrayed.'

'Of course, Madame.'

Elizabeth was new to this kind of work, but not alas, to untidiness. She set about her task as quietly as she could, intensely aware of Mme Chaumier's fragrant presence. The Frenchwoman was beautiful, her pale features finely-sculpted and impassive, but there was a sharp watchfulness in her wide-set grey eyes, an alertness that made Elizabeth shake and fumble.

'Elizabeth . . . That is such a formal name, *n'est-ce pas*?' said Madame casually, as Elizabeth picked a satin slip from where it lay discarded on the floor. 'So stiff, so strait-laced. I think I shall call you "Betty". Would you like that? I much prefer it.'

The words were soft, almost cajoling, but somehow Elizabeth sensed that no choice was being offered. She would be 'Betty' from now on, whether she liked it or not. 'Yes, of course, Madame,' she replied. 'Whatever you wish.' Bobbing a curtsey, and smiling tightly, she bent down to continue with her duties.

All was quiet in the room as she retrieved item after item of thin silk and sheer, expensive lace. Each soft garment had been worn recently; some seemed almost warm. The luxurious fabrics all smelt very strongly of Madame: her light talc; her floral perfume; the sharper, foxier tang that lay beneath them. As she gathered up her bundle, Elizabeth felt dizzy, imagining the body that had so recently worn these clothes.

What was Madame doing, she wondered, clutching a fragile pair of panties in her fingers, and feeling loath to consign them to the linen basket. Is she watching me?

Yes, I think she is – I'm sure she is. But why? I can't be as fascinating to her as she is to me?

Distracted by her musings, Elizabeth tugged at a stocking that was somehow tangled around a chair leg. It was as airy and delicate as a spider's web almost, pure silk, smoke grey, five denier, and she made a small sound of distress as it laddered.

'*Zut alors!* Betty, what have you done?' said Madame, her voice calm, as if she had been expecting such destruction. 'My beautiful stocking. You have ruined it . . . What a shame.'

'I'm so sorry, Madame,' murmured Elizabeth, holding out the ruined stocking like mist across her fingers. The desecration of something so lovely was horrifying. She felt the beginnings of tears and a lump in her throat. 'Oh, Madame, forgive me,' she begged.

Half hoping that her new Mistress would say that it didn't matter and that she had a hundred pairs of such stockings, Elizabeth began to twist the fine silk this way and that in an irrational manifestation of fear. A kind woman, a fair woman like Mme Chaumier would dismiss such a trifling mistake as this – wouldn't she? Surely a single stocking meant nothing to her?

'I would like to forgive you, Betty,' said Madame quietly, 'I would dearly love to . . . But I do not think that would do you very much good.' She smiled, her eyes bright with sympathy, with remorse. 'To overlook such an act would be to encourage further carelessness. Surely you see that?'

Oh, yes, how she saw it. How she saw what was coming next. Madame took the shredded stocking from her shock-numbed fingers, then surrounded Elizabeth's hand in both of hers.

'It is for the best, *chérie*,' she said, her red mouth a gentle, sympathetic shape. 'You will feel much better when we have dealt with this properly.'

I don't know! I don't know if I will! Elizabeth wanted

to protest, but she remained silent. Madame was already turning away from her, her eyes searching out what she required, what she needed for this 'dealing with'.

'*Ah oui, parfaitement,*' she said gaily, releasing Elizabeth. Moving lightly, almost floatingly across the room, she crossed to her crowded, cosmetic covered dressing table, and from the tumble of lipsticks, powder compacts, and multicoloured gilt-capped pencils, she produced a solid, serviceable hairbrush, looking surprised to have found such a plain thing hidden amongst the glitter.

'Come here, Betty,' she said, twirling the brush slowly in her long white fingers. 'I have found exactly what you need. Do not be afraid.'

Dreamily, her knees shaking, Elizabeth walked forward towards Madame. When she reached her, she froze before her, her fingers pleating nervously at a fold of her skirt, as cool sweat trickled down between her breasts. It was going to happen. Happen now, in this pretty over-decorated room, at the hand of this fey, dark Frenchwoman.

'Be brave, *ma petite*,' said Madame Chaumier, every line of her lovely body expressing compassion and tender concern. 'Think of how much easier it is to learn this way . . . How much better a maid you will be when we have finished.'

Elizabeth nodded, it was all she could do. She felt weak, powerless, like a doll without a will of her own.

'Lean forward, Betty,' urged Madame, clearing the top of her dressing table with a fine, confident sweep. 'Rest your arms on here and push out your bottom.'

Elizabeth did as she was told, conscious of the swish of her own skirts as she went over, and the way the blood rushed to her head in a blush. She was acutely embarrassed by her own vulnerability, and by the way, when she obeyed Madame, her backside was so raised and exposed. It wouldn't be long now. Any minute. She was afraid.

'Now now, this will not do. How can you feel anything through all this?' said Madame Chaumier, lifting the layers of Elizabeth's skirt and petticoats, as if it were not she herself who had stipulated a proper maid's uniform. 'Let us get rid of all these obstructions – so I can see you.'

If Elizabeth had been blushing a second ago, she was scarlet now, but fortunately her face was hidden against her arms. Madame Chaumier had exposed her ruthlessly from the waist downwards, lifting the skirt of her dress, and her frilly underskirt, so her knickers and her stockings were all on view. Elizabeth was mortifyingly conscious of how strange she must look in the long old-fashioned bloomer-like pants that Madame had insisted on, and of how loose and thin and silky they were. She moaned softly when a hand gently touched her.

'You have very firm flesh, *cherie*,' whispered Madame Chaumier, cupping the round of Elizabeth's left buttock and swirling it slowly with her palm. 'So resilient, so young and fresh . . . To chastise it will be *mon plaisir*.'

Elizabeth wriggled. The hand that held her was so warm, so seductive, she wished it would go lower, the fingertips pressing inwards to fondle her vulva. Suddenly she realised she was wet, very wet. Wetter, perhaps, than she had ever been – even though she was fearful and mortally embarrassed, and neither her sex nor her breasts had been touched.

She wanted. Desperately wanted. But what she yearned for she was not quite sure. Was it the punishment that she was so inevitably going to get? Or something more pleasurable? Or was it both?

'So naughty,' said Madame Chaumier, flexing her fingertips just as Elizabeth had prayed for and causing moisture to soak through the loose panties. 'I am afraid you are only making things worse for yourself, *chérie*. It is unseemly to be so eager – so lewd.'

The most subtle of pressures danced across Elizabeth's entrances, her labia, her clitoris. She pushed backwards, and the hand was removed.

'Enough!' said the Frenchwoman crisply. She sounded sure of her self. Indomitable. Imperious. Yet somewhere far back in the single sharp word was the very slightest ghost of a shake. Elizabeth felt the fingers that had explored her grasp the waistband of her knickers, hesitate, then pull it downwards across her buttocks and her thighs.

'*Un jolie petit cul*,' said Madame, her voice vibrant, almost trembling, 'Perfect for the brush. So white, with such soft and tender skin . . .'

Elizabeth felt a fine tremor pass across her naked buttocks. She had never been exposed this way in her life before. Never had her bottom uncovered for a woman. Only her husband had ever seen this sight before, and never in circumstances like these. She could hear Madame Chaumier breathing, quickly, almost gasping, as if she were balanced on the edge of excitement. She waited for another touch, a more intimate exploration, but the caress she now craved didn't come.

'*Très bien*. Let us commence,' said the Frenchwoman, her robe swishing as she stepped back, her tone brisk.

What will it be like? thought Elizabeth in the almost endless few seconds of waiting. She sensed Madame Chaumier fingering the brush, assessing its weight and hardness, and how much force she should wield. Be merciful! Elizabeth begged her silently. I'm new! I've never been punished! Be gentle or I'll embarrass us both.

The first stroke was appalling. Fiendish. 'Oh, no!' cried Elizabeth shrilly, one cheek of her bottom in flames. She wriggled, lost her position, aware of the grossness of her movements, yet helplessly surprised by the pain.

'*Ah oui*, Betty,' replied Madame Chaumier, sounding breathless. 'It does hurt, does it not? I am sure it hurts very much. But you must be a brave girl or you will never learn to be good.'

Again. A great clap of pain. But across the other cheek now. Elizabeth wanted to clasp herself, press her hands hard against her buttocks in a vain attempt to put out the fires. The palms of her hands were sweaty and hot, but against the heat in her buttocks, they would be glacial. Without thinking, she began to unfold herself up off the dressing table, then reach behind towards the two searing marks.

'Oh *chérie*, you must not do that,' chided Madame gently, abandoning the brush just long enough to grasp Elizabeth's arms. 'You must endure, Betty. Endure,' she said, re-positioning Elizabeth just as she had been before. 'If not for yourself, then do it for me . . .' Her soft lips brushed Elizabeth's cheek.

Elizabeth felt a wave of sweet weakness pass through her. Her bottom was throbbing, jumping, sizzling, and yet meekly she pushed it up higher.

'*Merveillieux* . . .' breathed Madame, stepping back again, and in an instant the pain bloomed once more.

The blows of the brush were solid, unyielding, meaty. Each one made Elizabeth cringe and yelp. Yet she no longer tried to resist them. She was hurting, burning, crying, and yet she courted each breathtaking stroke. Lured it. Sought it out. Lifted her bottom towards the impact of the brush even while it sped downwards towards her.

When it was over, she felt a huge sense of loss. After only seconds, she was missing the fierce bite of the wood against her bottom. Missing her own pathetic whimperings, and the kindly encouragements of her Mistress. The tears that streamed down her cheeks were not from the inferno in her buttocks, the crimson steaming radiance she knew must glow there, but from the aching knowledge that she couldn't have taken more. How could she be worthy of Madame now? Moving stiffly, she straightened from her pose against the dressing table, then pulled her knickers up across her punished rump.

'Shall I tidy up the rest of the clothes, Madame?' she asked, fighting the tremors in her voice and her body.

'Why, yes, of course,' replied Madame Chaumier, her eyes glittering. Her smooth pale cheeks were flushed with exertion, and her expression was distracted and a little wild.

'And will there be anything else, Madame?' Elizabeth said, very quietly, holding herself still, very still and expectant.

'Yes, *chérie*, just a small service,' murmured Madame, smiling. With a slight, graceful gesture she drew back her thin robe and uncovered the dusky triangle of her sex.

'So what happened next?' asked Geoff, his hand sliding possessively between her thighs.

'I tidied up the clothes,' replied Elizabeth, beginning to stir beneath her husband's loving touch.

'Liz! You know what I mean,' he persisted, one finger settling accurately where Elizabeth liked it best.

'I – I licked her,' Elizabeth stammered, her concentration wavering as the finger flicked and pressed. 'And she licked me . . . And that was it.'

'Wow . . .' Geoff nibbled her neck, and used more fingers now, but his attention was still as finely tuned to her words as her responses. 'And did you enjoy it then? All of it . . . Was it what you were expecting?'

'It – it was wonderful. I – Oh, yes, oh, God yes!' He had fingers inside her now, fingers moving, fingers pressing.

'Good . . . That's what I wanted to hear.'

As her body spasmed, Elizabeth's legs kicked and squirmed beneath the duvet, and sent a magazine sliding off the bed, its pages fluttering as it tumbled to the floor. She did not need to see it to know which section it had been open at, and which advert her husband had been reading.

TEMPORARY POSITION. Wanted by French Businesswoman, Knightsbridge area, housemaid for 'light domestic duties'. Must be amenable, discreet and very willing. Payment to be negotiated. Apply to Mme M-P Chaumier, Box 17.

'Five hundred pounds is a lot of money for one afternoon, love,' she whispered to Geoff when she was finally able to speak. 'Think of all the bills. All the things we need.'

'You're worth it, darling,' whispered Geoff as he levered his body over her, then glided into her on the wetness he had created. 'I'd pay ten times that if it'd get you what you want.'

Elizabeth swirled her hips, gripped him inside her, and suddenly it was Geoff's turn to gasp.

'And don't forget, love, we've always got the tape,' he panted, then kissed her neck as he began to thrust slowly.

Merveillieux, as Madame would say, thought Elizabeth, hugging her husband. '*Merci beaucoup, mon amour. Je t'aime.*'

Down at Heel

'Oh, God, Lewis!' cried Dora, her blue eyes flashing as she studied the Gold Card bill, 'This really is the final straw. I'm trying – so why can't you?' She flung down the incriminating document, reached angrily for her glass of wine, and downed the whole lot in one gulp.

As Lewis watched his wife top up her glass again, he wondered what she would say if he pointed out that it was she who insisted on good French vintages and not supermarket plonk. She who insisted on dressing like the wife of a plutocrat. Her chic little designer suits looked nothing special but cost him a fortune, and her shoes were always hand-made when something from Dolcis would have done the same job. Not that he didn't like her expensive shoes. Especially the black patent ones she was wearing now; the pair with the impossibly high heels, the sexily curved instep and the low, scalloped vamp. These particular shoes he considered well worth the money – because Dora had hinted that one night she might wear them while they fucked.

Dragging his mind away from that delicious possibility, he had to admit that, in the main, Dora was right. He spent far more than she did. Spent it. Mislaid it. Lost it. And worse, borrowed it. Borrowed it in ways he could never tell Dora about. He supposed he should really call it stealing; but his intention had always been, and still was, to pay the money back and get them back on their feet. But the sums of money he had clandestinely filtered from the company's bank account into his own had either been squandered, or invested incompetently and irretrievably lost.

Dora was suspicious already, he knew that, so how long would it be before Geraghty found out, too? And when that happened the sky would really fall in on them.

Charles Geraghty was Lewis's boss, the very man whose money had been purloined. And while he seemed benevolent – he was even letting them live in this flat, in his own house – Lewis sensed a very different agenda. Geraghty was like a sly reptile, basking on the rock of his own wealth and supposed generosity, but really waiting for the prime moment to strike and kill.

What was the bastard playing at? thought Lewis for what had to be the millionth time. The man had to realise that he and Dora were living far beyond their means, so why didn't he say something? They could have a quiet, man-to-man chat. Perhaps work out a strategy for recovery before things got too grotesquely out of hand.

But so far nothing had happened. Geraghty just sat back and watched them, clearly relishing the fact that Lewis was all too aware of the scrutiny. The man had the smooth, steely-eyed look of a Sixties secret agent, and though he was at least ten, or even twenty years older that they both were, Lewis knew that Dora fancied him like mad.

Why else would she be dressed like a siren when they were going upstairs for dinner tonight? She had slithered herself into a little black dress that Lewis had never seen before. It skimmed rather than grabbed at her elegant, voluptuous body, its sparse styling just an inch away from tarty. Lewis ground his teeth, knowing such simplicity was not cheap.

Still, as ever Dora looked well worth the exorbitant price she had probably paid. Her short blonde hair was gleaming, and fluffed into a new feathery, flirty style, and her lips were painted a succulent, livid red. All this for Geraghty, thought Lewis sourly, his temper growing.

'Are you going to drink all that?' he asked, watching Dora quaff down the second glass of wine. A second later, he regretted his sharp tone. Perhaps it would be a good thing if Dora got slightly tipsy. Alcohol had a tendency to make her amorous, and if things didn't go too badly upstairs, he might get the benefit of that good red vintage later. Conjugal relations had been somewhat thin on the ground lately, their libidos stifled by their growing lack of cash. The responsibility of debt often weighed down his erection.

Dora made some sarcastic comment he didn't quite catch, then abandoned her glass altogether. Flouncing from the room, she made it plain that she was eager to leave their ground floor battlefield, and get upstairs to the peace and refinement of Charles Geraghty's luxurious apartments. Lewis followed her, not wanting to look a fool by allowing his wife to arrive without him.

Dinner was both a gourmet delight and a stress-inducing nightmare. As usual. Lewis seethed as he ate his sole, and quaffed champagne. Geraghty had managed to out-fox him tonight in yet another different way. Their host was casually dressed in jeans, and a pure silk polo neck sweater, which made Lewis feel overdressed in his three piece suit and tie. Geraghty had the sort of effortless presence and style that Lewis knew he could never achieve himself, no matter how much he spent on tailoring and haircuts. His landlord's hair was sandy, slightly wavy – and if one was being critical, a bit overlong to be fashionable – but coupled with his strong yet languid body, it gave an impression of innate class, and inherited money. He made Lewis feel a clumsy, self-made ox.

'So, Lewis,' said Geraghty eventually, as he ran a finger around the rim of his brandy balloon. 'Don't you have something you want to tell me?'

They were sitting in Geraghty's comfortable and spacious lounge now; on chairs and a chesterfield in front of a real, open fire, even though it was spring, and the weather was soft and mild. Lewis, who had been perspiring steadily throughout the whole of the meal, felt sweat pop out anew in his armpits and his groin. Geraghty, of course, looked as cool and smooth as the syllabub they had eaten for dessert, but he had finally laid his cards on the table.

'Er – in what context?' said Lewis, stalling. There was no way he could wriggle out of this confrontation, and he knew he should be concentrating harder and more sharply than he ever had done in his life, but somehow, his eyes kept fixing on Dora. On the long, sleek expanse of her thighs, where her dress had ridden up. He kept imagining that stark division – between creamy skin beneath cobweb-fine nylon, and the dull, black gleam of silk jersey – moving upwards, ever upwards, until her stocking tops and then her panties came into view. She was sitting almost directly opposite Geraghty, and seemed to be lost in a reverie of her own devising. Her head was tipped back, and her eyes were closed, and Lewis was suddenly convinced that she was showing Geraghty her lace-clad vulva.

'In the context of debts, embezzlement, spending money that doesn't belong to you,' replied Geraghty mildly, swirling his brandy then taking a minute sip, 'Spending *my* money, Lewis, if we're being specific.' He paused, lifting the glass to the light as if some hidden truth might be evident in its amber contents. 'Not to mention the fact that I've yet to receive any rent from you for the flat.'

Lewis felt nauseated. He couldn't fool himself any more that there was a way out of this pit. His life was ruined; there was no help, no second chance. But he still couldn't stop staring towards Dora.

Her eyes were open now, but dreamy-looking, unfocused. She seemed oddly untroubled by their plight, and Lewis's sick feeling intensified. He didn't want to look at Geraghty, because he knew that the other man was staring at Dora, too. Covetously. Possessively. With a smug certitude, and lascivious anticipation.

Dora smiled as if tasting Lewis's horror. She was leaning back in her deep armchair, her arms along its arms, but suddenly she dropped a hand on to her thigh, and rubbed her fingers along the stuff of her dress, sliding it sensuously over the fine nylon of her stockings. Lewis heard the evocative rasp of friction, and to his revulsion, he felt his prick began to rise.

'Lewis?' prompted Geraghty softly.

'I – I don't know what to say,' Lewis said, his voice a hoarse whisper, his eyes still locked on Dora, and the slow but emphatic rise of her snug black dress. 'I – we're going through a bad patch. I've done some stupid things . . . But I'll pay you back. Pay the firm back. I just need a bit more time; a few months, that's all.'

'Time is money,' said Geraghty sagely, setting aside his brandy glass, and leaning forward in his chair. He wasn't hiding his interest in Dora now. He was staring directly at her crotch. From where Lewis sat, his wife's panties were still invisible, but it was obvious that Geraghty's view was of them was unimpaired.

I should hit him, thought Lewis, watching his landlord, his boss, his nemesis, smile lazily. He's seeing what only I should see. I'm her husband; she's my wife. I should smash his face in.

But he couldn't. He couldn't even move. And as Geraghty turned to him, something in the older man's eyes told Lewis what the price of that 'bit more time' was.

'Oh no,' he breathed, knowing even as the barely

formed words left his lips that his answer would inevitably be in the affirmative. It was either that, or bankruptcy. Prison. Total loss. And he would lose Dora anyway, if that happened. She hadn't done anything illegal. She was extravagant, but he hadn't told her the full story.

Geraghty did not speak, but a lift of his expressive eyebrows decreed his terms.

Lewis's queasiness intensified, but so – to his self-disgust – did his arousal. His penis throbbed heavily inside his silk boxer shorts. It was so hard and swollen that it seemed to be made of lead.

And although Lewis had not given the word, or the slightest sign of acquiescence, it seemed that Geraghty had received a message anyway. The older man lifted his hand and beckoned to Dora, who rose, like a sleepwalker, and walked towards him. Her high black heels made her sway a little, her lush hips wafting provocatively with each step that she took across the carpet.

Lewis felt as if his heart were about to leap from his chest, but when Dora reached Geraghty, and stood in front of him, it seemed time to at least try to minimise the agony that lay ahead.

'I'd better leave,' Lewis said, his voice coming out as a strangled squeak. He sprang to his feet and made as if to exit the room as fast as he could, given that his legs had almost lost their ability to support him.

'Oh, no, don't do that,' said Geraghty, not looking around from his intent perusal of Dora's lovely, nylon-sheathed thighs. 'I think you had better stay, Lewis, don't you? To monitor the transaction, so to speak,' he continued, slipping a hand behind each of Dora's knees, then letting his fingers trail up the backs of her legs. 'I'd like everything to be above board, for a change. Out in the open. So there's no dispute.'

'If you say so.' Lewis swallowed. His self-esteem seemed to be plummeting in an inverse proportion to the upward surge of his sexual excitement. He looked at Dora, his wife, and pictured her being serviced by their handsome, virile landlord. The image was vivid, electric, but there was no way it could be called a vision of lovemaking. What Lewis imagined was far too crude for that. He saw his Dora face down across Geraghty's leather-topped desk, which stood in the corner of the room. Her body was jerking as the older man thrust into her, taking her roughly, unfeelingly. In Lewis's mind, Dora was crying and protesting, but she was also writhing with blatant, sluttish pleasure, coming to orgasm as her body was invaded. And as her heels kicked and jerked, the slick black patent shoes flashed and flashed, again and again, like semaphore that mocked his very soul.

Wimp! You've lost her now, the glinting patent seemed to say to him. You've lost her for good. You'll never have her like this again. Not ever. Not ever. Not ever.

'Yes, I think it would be better,' said Geraghty, fracturing Lewis's dark dream with a reality that was just as bleak. The marauding hands were under Dora's dress now, hiking it up. Her lace stocking-tops and panties were on view. 'Come a little closer, Lewis,' he continued, 'I wouldn't want you to think I was taking liberties you were unaware of.'

I can't do this! I can't! thought Lewis, moving towards them nevertheless.

'You might see better from down there,' said Geraghty casually, removing a hand from Dora's thigh to point to a place on the carpet, just by her heel. The obvious inference was that Lewis should kneel down beside them, and watch whatever it was Geraghty had in mind from the closest of very close quarters.

Stumbling a little, Lewis slid to the floor, his suited knee just touching the narrow, shiny heel of Dora's shoe. He wanted to look away, but he could not. He felt hot and cold, his skin burning, yet clammy. Geraghty's hands were cupping Dora's bottom now, manipulating her rounded cheeks through the sheer barrier of her filmy panties, a wisp so frivolous it was as thin and light as smoke. Lewis could see, by the way his landlord's long, sensitive fingers were flexing, then relaxing, that he was caressing Dora right in the cleft of her rear, in the vulnerable division between her exquisite, fruity buttocks. He was stroking Dora's anus, stimulating her slowly and purposefully, and making her gasp and sigh and wriggle.

To Lewis's horror, his wife began to shimmy and thrust her hips, responding in a spontaneous, uninhibited way that she never did for him. He almost choked when she reached up and clasped her own breasts, mounding the resilient flesh in the same rhythm as Geraghty's probings. 'Oh, yes!' she cried, her fingers tensing, tensing.

Lewis didn't know what to do with his own hands. The urge to grasp his penis was like a silent order being shouted in his brain, but a lingering scrap of pride made him resist it. To show Geraghty, and his beautiful, treacherous Dora, that being humiliated turned him on would be the final nail of this crucifying punishment. Not that they couldn't deduce his feelings for themselves. If either of them had had sufficient time, and interest, to glance at his crotch, they would clearly have seen his huge erection.

'Oh, Charles!' groaned Dora, pumping her pelvis for the man who sat before her.

'Oh, Dora, my sweet Dora, what a choice little morsel you are,' countered Geraghty, still gripping her. His voice sounded proprietorial, patronising; it had a smug, sure ring to it that was lost on the half-enraptured Dora, but which made Lewis feel more sick, and hot, than ever.

'Now then, let's see what we've got, shall we?' said

their landlord suddenly, hooking his thumbs into the waistband of Dora's pretty panties. For a second, he glanced sideways and down, meeting Lewis's bulging eyes, then he returned his attention to the treasure he was unwrapping.

Geraghty drew Dora's knickers down slowly and carefully, easing them over the grippy lace tops of her hold-up stockings, then letting them settle, half-mast, around her knees. Dora's neatly trimmed blonde pussy was glistening and matted, already sticky with her juices, her excitement.

'Lovely. Lovely,' said Geraghty, his voice even and normal as if he were studying a new print for the wall of his sitting room, a piece of art for his extensive collection. 'But let's see a little more of it shall we?' Gripping Dora's thighs, he edged them apart, right to the limit her stretched panties would allow. She tottered for a moment, on her thin, spiked heels, but then grabbed Lewis's shoulder and leant on him for support. Her position now was an awkward splay-legged squat, her crotch thrust forward, her rounded bottom tucked right in.

Is this what I'm reduced to? thought Lewis, feeling the bite of her fingers through his jacket and shirt. I've given her a good life, much better than I can really afford, and I've always been faithful, and now all I am is a piece of furniture to lean on while another man has his way with her.

'Why not take your dress off, Dora?' suggested Geraghty, placing a hand confidently between her legs and beginning to masturbate her.

Dora nodded, tried to reply and ended up gasping. In an awkward, graceless, but obviously eager struggle, she managed to reach around and unzip herself, and drag the little black number off over her head – resting on Lewis from time to time to maintain her balance. Throughout the whole of this fumbling, jerky performance Geraghty continued to rub her oozing quim; Lewis could hear the evocative squelch of her juices.

Dora's bra was a match for her panties; a scrap of expensive trimming which cradled firm breasts that really needed no support. From his uncomfortable vantage point, Lewis could see that her nipples had stiffened considerably. They were like two small, ruby-coloured buttons trying to push their way through the sheer, silken lace, and looking at them – roused by Geraghty's presence and his clever fingers touching her – Lewis had a sudden horrid feeling that he might never be able to caress them ever again. Never put his mouth to each in turn; never lick and nibble them in the way he so liked to. She was Geraghty's creature now, his to manhandle, to explore, to kiss and suck.

Strangely, their landlord did not ask Dora to strip any further. He simply paused for a moment, surveyed the poem in cream and black that was her semi-clad body, then went back to work, with a vengeance, between her legs. His actions were direct, crude even; he thrust two fingers inside her, then methodically began to fuck her.

Dora, who had always complained at the slightest hint of clumsiness in Lewis's lovemaking, let out a long croon of delight and reacted with her gleaming, perfect body. Still clinging hard on to Lewis's shoulder, she swung her hips and thrust as hard as Geraghty was doing, pushing forward to get the best from each rude shove. Within moments, she was climaxing noisily, shouting and cursing with pleasure, while Lewis gritted his teeth in his silent, raging shame. Then, between his own legs, the final insult suddenly mocked him. His penis leapt, and disgorged his semen in his shorts.

'That was beautiful, Dora,' said Geraghty softly, 'Really beautiful.' She had slumped forward, panting, and her ravager had slid his arm around her back.

The gesture of caring was another knife slowly twisting in Lewis's gut. It was even worse somehow to see Geraghty being tender towards his wife, than it was to watch him ruthlessly molest her. And Dora seemed to appreciate the gentle gesture. She lifted her face, from where she had buried it in Geraghty's shoulder, then kissed the older man upon the mouth.

This kiss hurt Lewis the most of all. It was more intimate than the fondling and probing, a thing of the spirit as much as of the body, and a far greater, more conclusive betrayal. A duplicity that made his penis rise, renewed, in his boxer shorts. Stifling a groan of distress, he curled forward, as if hugging his own pain. Dora had collapsed against Geraghty, kissing him ravenously, and balancing precariously on his lap as his roving hands explored her near-nude body. Only her feet, in their beautiful but intimidating shoes, seemed to Lewis to remain his to worship. With a little sob he unfurled out of his huddle and pressed his lips against one spindly, glossy heel.

But as his mouth slid against the cool, flawless surface of the leather, and he heard Dora sighing with desire under the equally cool and flawless ministrations of Geraghty, Lewis became aware of a strange, uplifting notion.

This was it, he realised, his head filled with the lights of revelation. He was where he should be. This position of ignominy, crouched by the adorable, flailing feet of his soundly pleasured wife, was a greater high and a deeper thrill than fucking her had ever been.

Insanely, he felt at peace within his shame and humiliation. He could stay here forever, he realised – listening to Dora's uncouth grunting as Geraghty's hands reclaimed her. Even if he won the lottery, made a killing on the market, or found his fortune in some other way, he could not imagine ever wanting to change this fate.

He no longer bore the heavy encumbrance of

responsibility. Responsibility for navigating his way out of financial disaster; responsibility for keeping Dora in the manner to which she had become accustomed; responsibility – and an awesome one it was too – for providing her with orgasms in their bed. He had conceded all those burdens now to Geraghty.

Oh, yes, thought Lewis contentedly as he reached down to grip his penis. There were much worse lots in life than living down at heel.

Proud Helia

This is the 'Journal Intime' of Helia Christophides, begun, at the Woolstencraft Academy for Young Ladies on the 30th July 190–

I arrived today at this benighted hell hole, brought against my will by Mr Benjamin Reed, my guardian, God rot him!

I am nineteen, for pity's sake. Far too old to be mouldering in a dame school, even if it is so genteely called a 'select academy for special older girls' – which is a euphemism for disobedient, wayward hoydens! He, Mr Benjamin Reed, that is, says it is because I need a little polish before I can be introduced into society. He is probably right in that, but I know the real reason he has me incarcerated. It is because he lusts after me and my fortune, but wants me quiet and biddable so he can get his paws on both. He says that I am moody and wilful, but that it is quite understandable because I have lost my dear Mama and Papa. He says he cannot 'handle' me. Goodness me, I would never in a million years allow a pathetic excuse for a man like him to 'handle' me – neither metaphorically nor physically. I would rather die before be touched by his perspiring mitts!

Now if his hands were those of William, the boy who helps Mr Reed's gardener, things would be very different indeed. Now there's a pair of hands I do not mind at all. Oh, how I shall miss my William in this stupid, benighted place!

However, I digress. I must record my impressions of this place and its tiny band of 'inmates'.

Mrs Woolstencraft – our governess or whatever we are supposed to call her – came as quite a surprise to me. I was ushered into her sitting room, expecting a buxom, matronly figure with warts and a moustache, or some pinch-mouthed widow who probably froze her own husband to death and never let him into her drawers, except on his birthday, if he was lucky.

[As this journal is for my own eyes only, and to prevent me from going entirely dotty, I have resolved to be perfectly frank in the matter of my desires. Although if I were being frank, I would have mentioned the reasons why I particularly miss William. The little trysts we used to share in the potting shed. The way he would slip his wicked hand up my skirt and stroke my private parts until I had a crisis of pleasure – oh my!]

Another digression. How very ill disciplined of me. How silly!

Back to Mrs Woolstencraft. My new tutor, protector, wardress, call her what you will. As I said, she was, and is, a great shock to me. A far, far younger woman than I expected, she is one of the most handsome creatures I have ever set eyes on. Of refined and sober demeanour, as befits a teacher, she is slender, yet full-figured in all the right places.

It gave me quite a turn to realise how closely I was studying her body. I had never particularly noticed such things before. Things like the regal curve of her bosom beneath the midnight blue silk of her bodice; the way her hips flare out delightfully from her small, neat waist; her long legs, as I imagine them beneath the concealing weight of her skirts and her petticoats. She must be well-corseted, I am sure, no female form could be so harmonious without the assistance of good stays. And yet her movements are quick and light and seem unhindered. As she rose and moved about the room, first bringing the Academy ledger for Mr Reed to peruse, and then serving us tea, every action was graceful and flowing. As free as air; she floated like a wood nymph.

Why is it that I find her so enchanting?

As I said, she is handsome. She has pale skin, delicate, classical features, and eyes that are dark and very penetrating. Her hair is smooth, and just the same red-brown as a conker, and she wears it twisted elaborately at the nape of her neck. A neck, I might add, that is as long and swanlike as a ballerina's. A neck I found strangely alarming – because I felt a sudden peculiar desire to kiss it passionately, when she inclined forwards to point out something to Mr Reed.

Unfortunately, though, Mrs Woolstencraft does not seem to like me. Her expression is always watchful and cool. Assessing. Calculating. And yet, despite that, there is a kind of fire in her eyes when she looks in my direction. If I didn't know better I would say it was the glow of missionary zeal. Perhaps she wishes to 'convert' me in some way, but to what I simply cannot imagine.

'I hope you will be happy with us, Helia,' she said on greeting me. 'You will be given every opportunity to be happy – but whether you achieve that state is, of course, wholly in your own hands. The Woolstencraft Academy can only provide the environment . . .'

I did not know quite what to make of that, but the intent quality of her voice quite alarmed me. I felt excited in a sort of fluttery, helpless way that I would hesitate to reveal outside the confines of this journal. In fact, it is my intention never to show my feelings and weaknesses to others – be that Mrs Woolstencraft or any of her charges.

Charges? I have only met two of them so far. This is the holiday period, and it is only the most difficult cases – like me – who are in school when the 'good' girls are at home. Louise and Belinda, who I took high tea with, are probably in disgrace in some way too. They are certainly a rather rambunctious pair and they eyed me with an interest that seemed a little too familiar.

Louise is dark-haired, as I am, although her hair is not as smooth and straight as black silk, as mine is. Louise's mop is a mass of disorderly curls that seems in constant danger of escaping from her ribbons, but it does frame a very pretty face, with skin that is almost as fine and creamy as Mrs Woolstencraft's. A delicate pallor that I envy. I wish my own complexion could be as pale but, alas, my Aegean heritage dictates otherwise. I am a swarthy thing, my skin a burnished gold.

I am not so envious of Belinda, though. Her name means 'beautiful one', I believe, but her parents have played a spiteful joke on her. The poor thing has a handsome face but it is marred by a large birthmark, a prominent red splodge shaped vaguely like a flower. If it were not for this mark, Belinda would be exceptional, as her hair is thick and glossy, and her figure lithe and trim.

And she has a sense of humour, too. At least she makes her special friend Louise laugh. All through tea, as I carefully ignored them, the two girls kept whispering and giggling behind their hands. When not doing that they were exchanging warm, significant looks. As if they were lovers, not just a pair of girlish friends.

What peculiar notions I've begun to have! It must be this place. I had better go to sleep now before I dream up anything stranger.

31st July

A most extraordinary day! I do not know even how to begin to describe it. I will try though, while it is all still fresh in my mind, because if I don't it might seem later that I dreamt it!

The strangeness began before breakfast, with the

arrival of a servant to help me dress. Or at least that is why I *thought* she had come.

Yes indeed, Flossie Jenkins. A more insolent, uppity young baggage I could never have imagined, and it beggars belief that anyone in their right mind would employ her. And yet Madam Woo seems to look on her with favour.

['Madam Woo'. This, I discovered is the common nickname for our implacable custodian; one she is aware of, but doesn't discourage. I don't know why.]

Anyway, back to Flossie.

At six thirty, she roused me most rudely from my bed, looking a picture of liveliness despite the early hour. She is a redhead, freckled and jolly, and I could swear she does not bother to wear a corset. Her whole, lush body seemed to bounce and jiggle as she heaved the ewer of hot water on to the sideboard, and at every possible opportunity, she managed to press herself against me. Her limbs are sturdy and her breasts are soft yet firm.

'Come along, Miss Helia,' she said, when she had finished setting out my toilette. 'We've a little job to do before you get nice and clean.'

To my horror, she then proceeded to drag me along the full length of corridor and landing in just my nightgown, and to bundle me unceremoniously into the privy. 'Madam Woo hates girls with dirty habits,' she continued, closing the door behind us. 'That's why she likes me to check all the new young ladies . . . To make sure that they keep themselves clean. And that they're 'good' girls, if you know what I mean, Miss?'

I did know what she meant, and it took all my nerve to endure what happened next. Despite the fact that I informed Flossie that I was a grown woman, and quite capable of managing by myself, the wicked minx said that, no, she had her orders to 'supervise' me. Before I could protest, and so deftly I could not resist her, she whipped my nightdress over my head, then manhandled me until I was sitting naked on the lavatory.

Now, I am no squeamish, shrinking type by any stretch of the imagination, but I swear I blushed crimson as I sat there. Every bare inch of me. And Flossie would not let me up from the seat until I had done my business! In its wretched, embarrassing entirety! She stood smirking over me and watched the whole procedure.

How can I describe what I felt? The peculiar heat. The strange excitement. The sensation of an attractive young woman – and Flossie, for all her brass, is rather lovely with her ruddy, tumbling ringlets, her merry blue eyes and her buxom figure – seeing me naked was disturbing enough, but to have to perform the most demeaning of human acts under her surveillance? Even thinking about it has an alarming effect on me. The same effect that my sweet William used to induce in the shed, when he slid his clever, calloused hands beneath my skirts.

When it was over, I hung my head, and reached out blindly for my nightgown.

'Oh no, Miss, you don't need this,' said Flossie, holding on to it. 'You'll only have to take it off again to wash.' Before I could stop her, she had swung open the lavatory door, and bustled me out into the corridor. 'We're all girls here, Miss Helia. There's no need to make a fuss. It's just part of Madam's little game.'

Game, what game? I felt a weird little quiver in the cradle of my belly, and my bare feet seemed pinned to the parquet floor.

Flossie, however, was not to be gainsaid. It appeared she was intent on marching me through the corridors of the Academy without a single stitch of clothing on my body. Her fingers were hot on my bare back as she pushed me forward.

A game, is it? I thought. Well, I, too, can play games. I delight in them, and very rarely lose! Then and there, I decided I would show them that Helia Christophides is equal to anything the Woolstencraft Academy can throw at her. As Flossie shepherded me back to my bedroom, I went proudly and without demur: my shoulders straight, my head held high, my bosom flaunted. I was quite disappointed that the landing was deserted.

When we turned the corner, however, my boldness almost left me. Belinda and Louise were just emerging from one of the bedrooms, both modestly clothed in pretty blouses and long flowing skirts, with their hair already brushed and pinned up neatly.

'Good morning, Helia,' they chorused, the pair of them smirking and staring at my body. I felt a hot rush of scarlet across my chest and up my throat, but I stared back with all the sang-froid I could muster. I longed to cover myself with my arms and hands, but I stiffened my spine, squared my shoulders, and thrust out my breasts. I even shook my hair back, so it wouldn't mar the view.

'Good morning,' I said coolly, sweeping past them. As we reached the door to my room, I heard Flossie start to giggle.

'You'd better watch those two, Miss Helia,' she said, winking at me, and, to my astonishment reaching down to pinch my bottom. 'It looks as if they've a fancy to you!'

What on earth did she mean? I thought, rubbing the sore place her strong fingers had nipped. And why did I still feel that strange, exciting tingle down below?

After that, Flossie washed me as a nursemaid would bathe a child. I was not allowed to do anything myself, except raise my arms so she could sponge my armpits, and then stand with my foot raised, on a stool, so she perform the same service – at some length – between my thighs.

As she washed me there I started feeling rather giddy. Abandoning the cloth, she made lather with her fingers and rubbed it directly on to me. Four or five times, she soaped then wiped, soaped then wiped, soaped then wiped; exploring each fold and indentation of my flesh.

It took me just a moment to realise that she was touching me in just the same way that dear William had always touched me, in our stolen times together. After a few moments more, I cried out and fell against her, lost in the same delightful effect I had achieved with William.

'My, you're a quick one, Miss Helia,' Flossie said as she helped me to sit down. 'You'll do well here. Madam Woo likes a young lady with a bit of fire in her . . . She might say she likes her girls to be meek, and quiet and good, but mark my words, that's tommy rot! It's the frisky minxes who really get her going.'

Frisky minxes? And Madam Woo? What had such gloriously clandestine matters to do with her? Governesses were strict, and one of their prime functions was to ensure chastity and decorum in their charges. They were wont to do things like tying a girl's hands at night, to prevent self abuse. Or making her wear rigid garments so once again she could not reach down and caress herself. It seemed unthinkable that Madam Woo should *approve* of lust.

When I was clean, and my breathing and my heartbeat had settled as much as they could with an inquisitive young woman rubbing my naked body dry and examining every part of me, I stood waiting quietly for my clothing to be brought to me. It had become a matter of principle that I did not show my nerves.

'Right, we're going to see Madam now,' said Flossie cheerfully, her blues eyes as round as pennies and bright with mischief. She took me firmly by the arm and began to lead me.

'But surely I need some clothing? I cannot walk out of here naked again!' I protested, but to my inner horror, the cheeky trollop simply laughed.

'Oh no, no, no!' she said, pulling me forward, her sly strength defying my frantic struggles. 'It's another of Madam's little tests, Miss. Her special rituals. . . She likes all her girls to be brought to her in the buff on the first day. It cuts them down to size, she says. Some young ladies think they're better than the others, because they've got lots of pretty clothes and all. But with a bare arse, the whole lot of you are equal! Come on, Miss Helia, it doesn't do to make Madam cross so early on.'

So off we went again, with me stark naked, along the corridor. Happily, there wasn't far to go, and in a moment or two, we reached a forbidding black painted door, on which Flossie knocked quietly and respectfully. As we stood waiting, she gripped my bottom cheek and squeezed it. I was about to make some disdainful comment, and knock her hand away, when a voice from beyond the door called out for us to enter.

Madam Woo was seated on a beautiful chaise longue upholstered in wine-coloured velvet. She was studying some document or other, her fine eyes intent, her attention focused, but she glanced up at us as Flossie and I approached.

My governess looked even lovelier this morning than she had yesterday. She wore a prim white blouse with a tiny pie-crust frill at the neckline, a black brocade waistcoat and a long, and very full black skirt. Her hair was – as ever, it seemed – faultlessly coiled, her face was calm and saintly, and she wore a pair of tiny gold-wire framed spectacles, perched on the end of her small, straight nose.

'Helia! Good morning,' she said pleasantly, not rising from her seat, but holding her hands out towards me. With a push from Flossie, I moved a little nearer. 'Welcome to the Academy,' continued Madam, as if she had not greeted me yesterday at all. It occurred to me that the institution I had been admitted to yesterday, in the presence of Mr Reed, wasn't the same one I found myself in now. The Academy of Madam Woo had two entirely different faces, I realised:

one was a fine, upstanding, respectable school for young gentlewomen, and the other was a perverse and hidden enclave. And it was this second place whose rules embraced me now.

I was bare and unprotected in every way possible, while Madam Woo herself could not have been more clothed. Her high neckline, her beautifully draped skirt, and her long tight sleeves; all these seemed to protect and empower her. There was not an inch of her to be seen other than her hair, her face, and her white narrow-fingered hands, but of the two of us, she suddenly seemed the siren.

'Let me look at you . . .' She reached out to take my hand, and I suppressed a flinch. I must not show fear, I told myself, or any kind of weakening. I must make her believe that it did not trouble me to stand naked before her.

'You are a very beautiful girl, Helia,' she said, releasing my hand, then settling hers very lightly on my flank. The touch of her fingers was delicate and cool, yet something inside me seemed to burn. To burn for her. I could suddenly well imagine how it might be possible to put up with this, and even greater outrages, and still yearn for more in the pursuit of Madam's favour.

Her hand slid up over my body, cupping my breast for a second then releasing me. 'But you are proud, Helia, very proud. I can see that very clearly in you. In fact it seems the most important part of you . . .' She paused, adjusting her spectacles on the end of her nose, as if she needed to see me in even greater detail. 'Turn around!' she told me.

For a moment, I considered disobeying her. I wanted to rush from the room, to dress and pack my things and fly from this place as fast as was humanly possible. Then I caught the glint of her eyes, as they considered me from behind the miniature lenses. I saw the heat that I had seen before, and knew my pride had touched an added fire to it; so I turned, my head held high, my posture straight.

'Pride is no bad thing in certain circumstances,' murmured Madam, almost contemplatively as she laid her hands – *both* her hands – upon my bottom. 'And women have much to be proud of. They are man's superior in many ways . . . In almost every way, some would say . . .' Her fingertips palpated my flesh as if testing its firmness, its suitability for some as yet unknown purpose. 'But a woman must learn quietude and humility too . . .' Her thumb slid down the inner slope of one of my bottom cheeks, brushing the most delicate area, and making it difficult for me to keep my body still. 'Or at least a façade of humility . . . So that it may serve her to her advantage in certain situations.'

Dimly, I was aware that she was imparting to me a crucial verity, but her touch, on my naked flesh, confused my thoughts. It occurred to me, as she continued to assay the texture of my bottom, that the Academy might employ corporal punishment to keep its unruly students in line. As the spoilt scion of a loving family, I had never been physically chastised in my life, and the idea of being beaten was a shock to me. It both appalled me, and made me feel suddenly weak and very hot. A reaction that was so powerful I imagined Madam could feel it, too, transmitted through the tips of her fingers where they pressed against me, their touch both cool and fiery.

Bear up! Be strong! I told myself, trying to resist a peculiar growing languour. I straightened my back yet again, and as her thumb traversed my cleft, then slid down lower, dangerously close to my sex, I thrust out my rear to greet her hand.

'Oh, Helia,' said Madam, her voice soft, her thumb floating intimately against me. 'What a bold girl you are! I should chastise you for trying to entrap me . . .' Her face was so close to me, I could feel her warm breath on my naked bottom. 'But as it is your first day, I will excuse you.' With that she withdrew, denying my body her strange, tormenting presence. As she leant back against the chaise, with a tiny, breathy sigh, I became aware – to my chagrin – of my own overwhelming disappointment.

'That will be all, my dears,' she said, as if suddenly immune to my charms. I heard the rustle of paper again. She was reading. I was dismissed.

As Flossie helped me to dress – with all the usual decorum and properness I would expect from a well trained lady's maid – I felt confused. Had I been dreaming? Was I in the grip of some bizarre hallucination, brought on by lack of sleep and new surroundings? That could be an explanation for all the strange things that were happening to me, but if it were so, why did I feel so wakeful and so full of anticipation?

The rest of the day was really an anti-climax. Everything and everyone was ordinary. Meals, lessons, the behaviour of my fellow pupils, and Madam. I suppose I should have been grateful, but the wicked sprite inside me, the one that had quickened under Madam's delicate touch and Flossie's daring, probing fingers, seemed to prick me and demand some more excitement. Some test. Some lewd experiment. Alas, though, I was treated with only politeness and perfect solicitude. I only hope that tomorrow will different.

1st August

My prayers were answered! Although not immediately. I was even allowed to bathe myself today.

Breakfast was uneventful, although the kedgeree and kidneys were first class. The discourse around the table, between the four of us – Madam, the two other girls and I – covered only the weather, the curriculum and other trivialities. I alone seemed to be looking out for perilous undercurrents; the others ate, drank tea and talked as if everything at the Academy was normal.

The first part of the school day passed quietly too. We began with mathematics, a subject in which I am quite accomplished, followed by French, at which I also excel. Madam Woo is proving to be an able and cultured tutor; her scholarship extensive, but quite naturally conveyed. Even in the grip of other less explicable feelings, I can still respect her fine, sharp mind; but it made me shudder to see that white hand – the very one which had touched me so intimately – decline a French verb with such precision upon the blackboard.

It wasn't until the end of the lesson that the mood began to change.

I had been aware, all morning, that I was not the only one distracted from my studies. I was reading aloud from a primer, well aware that my voice was somewhat lacking in animation, when I also perceived an eddy of furtive whispering. And rustling. And sniggering. This went on a few moments, distracting me so much I mispronounced several words, and I felt anger began to seethe and make things worse. I finished the passage, red-faced and full of fury. I hated both Louise and Belinda for making a fool of me, and Madam for letting them. As I sat down, I closed my book with a ringing snap.

Madam gave me a long look, over the top of her tiny glasses. Her face was knowing, and faintly amused, and seemed to be promising me something which I could not quite make out. Then there was another giggle, and her expression turned to stone.

'Louise, would you care to share the joke with all of us,' said Madam, her voice a velvet threat. It made me tremble, and I wasn't even at fault.

'It wasn't anything, Madam, really,' claimed Louise Sutherland, rising to her feet and bumping clumsily against her desk.

'Belinda?' prompted Madam, still dour.

Belinda Gascoigne rose, too, with a little more

elegance than her friend, but still cowering. I had a strange premonition, a feeling of both dread and an almost sickening excitement in the pit of my stomach. I wanted to gloat, but I also wanted to do the most unexpected things, too. For a moment I wished myself alone . . . My belly seemed to clench.

'Well, it seems a shame to have to suffer the results of *nothing*,' said Madam Woo, with an odd but familiar edge in her voice. It was almost as if she felt the same as I did. 'But you must, nevertheless,' she added quietly.

Belinda and Louise looked at each other, their own expressions also peculiar. They, too, seemed full of apprehension, yet also thrilled. The spell that gripped the room seemed all-pervading. Louise nodded and then stepped forward.

'It was my fault, Madam. I'm responsible,' she said, sounding almost as if she was going to faint.

'You were both at fault,' said Madam, smiling thinly and reaching up to remove her spectacles. Folding them with a click, she then placed them on the desk. 'And you will both reap the consequences of your impolite behaviour. It will serve as a sovereign example of our code here at the Academy.' She turned to me. 'One that I hope that Helia will bear in mind when she next shows her temper.' She glanced significantly at the book I had closed so noisily.

There was a long moment of silence. I saw Louise clench her hands into fists.

'Well then, Louise, since you are so keen, why not step forward?' Turning to her desk, Madam moved a number of books and papers, clearing them to one end and leaving an unoccupied space at the other. With a gesture both imperious and graceful she pointed to the empty area, and Louise moved towards it, her steps suddenly reflecting some reluctance. Behind her own desk, Belinda drew a long, tense breath. I glanced towards her and saw that her eyes were fiery and yearning, their pupils huge black discs within the heat. It shocked me, as I could clearly recall seeing the self-same look in William's eyes, when I allowed him to put his hand inside my drawers.

When she reached the desk, Louise stood there uncertainly, her bosom heaving beneath her white blouse as if she had just sprinted a hundred yards. She was staring at her toes, able to look at neither Madam nor Belinda and myself.

'Louise, my dear, you know what to do, don't you?' prompted Madam, her expression and her voice steady although her eyes were flashing. 'We haven't got all day. Let's be having you. Chop! Chop!'

I had been expecting it, I realised, but I still felt a shock when Louise bent face down over the desk, her head cradled in the circle of her arms.

'Belinda! Prepare her,' Madam instructed, then turned to me. 'Helia, watch closely. And learn.'

With a speed and neatness that suggested this was a regular occurrence, Belinda moved forward to stand behind her friend, then lifted Louise's skirt and petticoats and folded them out of the way against the small of her back. Uncovered, the unfortunate girl's drawers gleamed snow white, becoming the very focus of all the free light in the room.

'As we're providing an example here, I think you may also lower her knickers, Belinda,' went on our governess, as if it were the most commonplace thing in the world to expose a young lady's bottom in the middle of the classroom.

The young lady in question made a small sound of protest, to which Madam replied with a very stern, 'Louise!'

Employing the same neatness she had exhibited with Louise's other clothing, Belinda unbuttoned her friend's drawers and pulled them swiftly down, arranging the pretty linen in a white frame around Louise's sudden, indecent nakedness.

Louise Sutherland is a slender girl, but her firm little derrière is quite curvaceous. And as I observed it for the first time – the twin lobes opulent within their frothy, lace and ribbon-trimmed boundary – I saw that she was shaking like a wild aspen in the wind.

More alarming even than the sight of her bare bottom, though, was the gleam of delicate moisture on her privates. The soft purse of her womanhood appeared darkened and swollen, and it shone like a rosy jewel between her thighs. Does my own look the same when I caress myself, I wonder? I know that stickiness is a symptom of excitement. I remember how wet my darling William used to make me.

But why, if that was the case, was Louise stimulated at this particular juncture? She was going to be punished, not pleasured. It did not seem to make a jot of sense.

Staring at the glinting groove between Louise's shapely legs, I experienced a sudden urge to look up, and when I did so, I met Madam's watching eyes. They were bright as stars – alive with passion in her calm, unflustered face. A message seemed to pass between us, a sense of recognition, I fancied. An acknowledgement that she and I had much in common, and that we were of quite different stuff to these charming but far lesser ones around us.

A second later, I believed myself to be imagining things again. Madam Woo had turned away with a look of scorn.

'I wonder if you would fetch me the tapette, Belinda,' she enquired, fixing Belinda Gascoigne with the same oblique expression.

A tapette? What can that be? I thought, as Belinda sped away to the cupboard in the corner of the room and returned with what looked like a battledore. It was the kind of bat used for playing 'Fives' or 'Ping-pong', only more extended and oval in shape. Madam Woo took this strange object in her hand, and hefted it experimentally, as if assessing its weight.

As I watched the movement of this ominous black leather blade, I felt a fluttering and pressure in my belly that was familiar, yet completely inappropriate. I was as stirred as Louise was by this situation, I realised. I felt a rush of dampness between my legs, a sudden sense of swelling that was both uncomfortable and delicious. I longed to press my fingers to the hidden place that irked me. I let my hand drop surreptitiously to my lap.

Though Madam was intent on Louise now, tapping the faux battledore against her hand and scrutinising her milky-skinned 'target' and the soft, gleaming folds of flesh that nestled beneath it, I got a strong impression that she was studying me, too. That she was monitoring my reactions to the lewd sight before me, and aware of my maverick emotions. This punishment was not just a test for Louise.

'I am going to give you a dozen strokes now, Louise Sutherland,' intoned Madam, her voice grave yet musical, as if she too was suppressing great excitement. 'Perhaps two dozen ... Or even three, depending on how you bear up and how you behave yourself.' She ran one long finger along the leading edge of the tapette, and then, to my astonished, almost horrified fascination, she let the same finger slide contemplatively down the deep crease between Louise's chubby buttocks. The girl mewled, and Madam's beautiful mouth thinned. I imagined she was more or less certain to get three dozen now.

'I will not expect you to make any sound during this procedure, Louise,' continued Madam, pressing her finger – with what could only be construed as pure devilment – against the forbidden orifice between the trembling girl's bottom cheeks. My heart raced furiously, on Louise's behalf, as our governess pushed harder and the clenched aperture suddenly yielded. 'And I will require you to keep perfectly still at all times ...' She twisted the finger, swivelled it slowly, and Louise's stockinged legs jerked and kicked wildly. 'Perfectly still, Louise,' she repeated, 'or it will be four dozen . . . And two hours in the garden on display. Do you understand me?'

The finger moved again, swirling, then gently pumping. Louise made an uncouth gurgling sound and waggled her hips as if trying to shake out Madam's digit. Beneath my desk, my own fingers rocked and pressed.

'Louise!'

'Y – yes, Mrs Woolstencraft,' wavered Louise, her voice high and full of tears. Before even one stroke of the tapette had fallen.

With merciless despatch, the finger was withdrawn, leaving the tiny hole gaping. I saw it pulse, like a little mouth, as if it missed its recent intruder, then my attention was drawn back to Madam. She had taken a step back, and raised her arm, then, with a speed that defied the eye, she brought down the feared tapette upon Louise.

Two things happened. One, there was a noise like a thunderclap, a mighty 'whack!' of quite unexpected volume; and two, after a full second, Louise caterwauled just as loudly.

So much for her not making a sound.

'Louise . . . Really,' intoned Madam Woo, her voice delicately pained as she hesitated a moment, then dashed away Louise's hands where the pathetic creature had clasped them to her bottom. 'You set a poor example for Helia.' She snapped the fingers of her free hand, and Belinda stepped forward, and – apparently without need of instruction – held down her friend's hands against the desk.

The tapette whacked down again. And again. And again. Each stroke impacted with a terrifying loudness, but a part of me began to wonder whether Madam had chosen the implement for exactly this reason. Some instinct told me that the bark of the tapette might be just a little bit more severe than its bite; and that to inflict real, dire pain, another device would most probably have been chosen. This noisy beating was a show put on for me.

And neither had Louise taken the slightest notice of Madam Woo's admonishments. She couldn't protect her own bottom now, with her hands held, but she continued to yowl loudly and struggle. Her legs scissored lewdly as she endured the tapetting, and it almost appeared as if she were deliberately trying to expose her sex to us. And to show us how much her pain aroused her. There was now a high sheen on her woman's parts.

And not only on hers, I could swear. The redder Louise's bottom cheeks became, the more distressed I became between my thighs. I was pressing myself hard now, through my skirt, my petticoats, and my drawers; rocking my fingers against my tiny, tender bud. The feeling of exquisite tension was greater, even, than anything I had ever experienced with William, and I began to panic, knowing what it was I was now compelled to do. By no means could I bear not to reach a crisis.

The schoolroom seemed to close in on me. Louise was making an awful commotion, and the tapette itself was noisy, but if I cried out, as I longed to do – as I needed to do – the others would most definitely hear me. Madam seemed to be engrossed in her task, as was Belinda, but the same sixth sense that had told me why the tapette had been selected also informed me that I was just as much the observed one as Louise. There was expectation all around me; a seething, a gloating. They were all just waiting for me to reveal my vice.

Yet still I rubbed and rubbed, and rubbed and rubbed. And when Madam laid down her tapette, and began to slide her narrow fingertips caressingly over the whole of Louise's be-crimsoned posterior, the sublime explosiveness beneath my hand became too much.

I bit my lip to contain my gasping cry, but as the waves of pleasure wracked my loins, I lost my fight. My heartfelt 'Oh!' caused a pair of heads to turn. A trio, even. Despite the fact that Madam's fingers were sliding, from behind, into her womanhood, the squirming Louise craned her neck so she could see me.

Madam spoke not a word, but her flint-dark eyes said everything, their stern look adding more delight to my transports. She was touching Louise, yet making promises to me. Issuing challenges. While my flesh still fluttered, I felt suddenly as if I were looking into a mirror, seeing myself in Madam Woo's handsome face. As my spasms began to fade, she turned away.

From a great and confused distance, I observed what happened next.

Belinda retained her hold on her friend's hands, because Louise was struggling once more. But for a different reason now. She was half climbing over the desk, but only so she could open her legs wider. Her bottom was scarlet, and so were her sexual parts. Madam Woo's fingers were alabaster against fire. She was tracing the gleaming shape of the swollen, pulsing folds, teasing Louise in a way that I could well imagine was both intolerable and divine. The unfortunate – or perhaps fortunate? – girl was stretched very wide now, and both orifices were visible. And twitching. Opening and closing like tiny dumb mouths begging for mercy. Beseeching their tormentor to fill them with the grace of her presence. Knowing that her tapered fingers would deliver and fulfil with all the efficiency and lack of remorse that they had employed to punish.

Still holding my own groin, I watched Louise buck and struggle like a filly, trying to entice Madam Woo to bring her off. She thrust her haunches backwards, as if to effect the impaling herself, but clever Madam kept her touch as light as air. I saw silvery fluid begin to trickle down Louise's thighs, and she moaned like a beast beneath the brand.

'Please,' the anguished girl begged. Would I have done the same in her place, I wondered. Or would I have held fast to my pride and remained silent? For a little while, at least.

Madam leant close to Louise, and whispered something in her ear. Louise's expression, as she listened, was complex; half-relieved, half-conveying a greater fear than before. I began to suspect that what she craved might demand an even higher price than she had already paid. Madam whispered again and her charge shuddered and closed her eyes. After a second Louise nodded her head, submissively, then lifted her bottom and haunches to facilitate Madam's access to her privates.

With no further delay, and almost brutally, our governess inserted a finger into the tender maw that craved it. Louise cried out softly, her whole body stiffening, her pleasure quite evidently delivered. As she quivered and crooned, I seemed to feel her sensations in my own body. I longed for penetration, recalling the feeling of William's work-hardened finger inside me. My own channel began to ripple and pulsate.

'You are dismissed, Helia,' said Madam without turning, still manipulating the moaning Louise. 'Tell Flossie to provide you with your lunch. There will be no further lessons today.'

And so I was banished from this darkly charmed circle. I felt bereft, angry, excited, cast down. My look of fury would surely have demanded retribution, but Madam had no time for me now. Louise, and later Belinda, were the twin foci of her suppressed desire, the familiar instruments on which to play her symphonies of pain and pleasure. I hated her, but longed to have her near me.

For the rest of the day, I brooded. Neither Madam nor Belinda and Louise appeared again after I had left them in the schoolroom, and I had only the smirking presence of Flossie to keep me company. Her knowing smile made me want to shout and break things.

The entire house was silent and brooding. Or almost silent. In the afternoon, not long before tea, I was taking a constitutional in the garden when I could have sworn I heard a shrill, keening sound emanating from an open window of the first floor of the house. It was a female voice, of course, but expressing some emotion or condition that was hard to decipher. Was it pain? Was someone being beaten again? The cry was agonised, yet I heard no smacks or slaps to accompany it. The only other explanation was that it was pleasure that was being inflicted, but pleasure of a degree so intense and extenuated that the manner of it defied my wildest imaginings. The poor moaning wretch was being stimulated in a way that rendered her as frenzied and agonised as a tapetting would have done. It was the sound of a woman gone beyond self control.

The most curious thing of all, though, was that this passionate wailing had a most distinctive timbre. It was not a girlish outcry, but had a sweet depth of tone that I could only ascribe to Madam.

As I write this now, something occurs to me which I should have considered before.

Does Mr Reed know what is happening here? Or does he believe the Academy to be a proper school? I suspect the former; and that he intends me to be thoroughly corrupted and prepared for his pleasures. I can just see his smiling, sweating face as he observes a young woman – me! – being thrashed and humbled. I imagine his pudgy fingers reaching out to touch my exposed privates, soiling me with his repulsive caress. I imagine worse things, too. Him unbuttoning his trousers. His organ jutting like a nasty red thumb; not a bit like my William's long sweet wand.

Oh no, no, no! It will never happen. I will do anything rather than fall back into his clutches. Madam Woo may whip me black and blue for the rest of my days if it means I do not have to surrender to Mr Reed!

2nd August

How to begin? There is so much to tell. And some of it almost too embarrassing to set down. Let me set the tone by saying that I am forced to lie on my stomach to write this account.

Louise was allowed to stay in bed late this morning. Because she was 'fatigued', Flossie told me, winking broadly. Belinda was in evidence however, though her manner was distinctly dreamy and rather distant. There was a slight but constant smile upon her face, an expression so intriguing that one almost forgot her birthmark.

Madam Woo was cool; her feathers, as ever, unruffled.

After breakfast, the first class of the day was drawing, and as the morning was fine and brilliant we were ushered out into the garden.

I don't know what got into me, but I couldn't concentrate on the subject Madam had assembled for us to portray – an arrangement of apples and oranges in a delicate Wedgewood bowl, which was set on a wrought iron garden table. It isn't that I cannot draw – quite the reverse, I have a special talent for it – but the inert and blameless fruits were so uninteresting. My mind was a miasma of darker, more fleshly images. I saw Louise, yesterday, across Madam's desk, her bottom bare, her female parts engorged and juicy. I saw William, as I remembered him from our last escapade in the tool shed; standing before me and smiling, his breeches open and his member rising proudly from his linen. I also saw Madam Woo in a picture that was both forbidden and irresistible; she was lying on a day bed, her skirts around her waist, being caressed between her legs by sly Belinda.

'Helia Christophides, that is not the subject I set you to draw,' said a soft voice behind me, and my face flamed as I focused on the paper. What I had drawn was what my mind's eye had envisioned. Pocket sketches of familiar figures drowned in lust!

There was a gasp, as Belinda leant across and studied my offerings, then Madam spoke to her, far more sternly than she had done to me.

'Attend to your own efforts, Belinda Gascoigne. Those look like marrows to me, not apples. Start again!'

Madam lifted the sheet of paper that was inscribed with half a dozen of my salacious interpretations. She looked very beautiful this morning in a pristine white blouse, with full leg of mutton sleeves and a high prim collar fastened with a dainty jet brooch in the shape of an elaborate curlicued seal. Her lovely skin was as pale, almost, as the fine stuff of her blouse, yet as she perused my meticulous, but incautious doodlings, a delicate haze of colour blushed her cheeks. She seemed, in a way that subversively delighted me, unable to lay down the sketches, and the longer she looked at them, the pinker her cheeks became. Her expression – of studied equanimity – did not alter, however, and the only other sign that I had discomfited her was the whiteness of her knuckles where she grasped the sheet of paper.

'You have a rare talent, Helia,' she said at length, finally setting down my work on the table, 'but you are disobedient. Wilful. And quite, quite disgusting. I asked you to draw the apples, and you have drawn –' the minutest pause – 'you have drawn something else entirely.'

Unable to face her, I scrutinised the inoffensive apples. Then felt the light touch of her hand upon my shoulder.

'You do realise, Helia,' she said, bending close and filling my head with her lily of the valley perfume, 'that this transgression cannot go unmarked?'

So this was it. I stiffened beneath her touch, recalling the grovelling and recalcitrance of Louise. Madam would punish me now, I was certain of that, but I would not make the poor showing that my fellow pupil had. I would not bawl and struggle and resist like a weak-natured baby; I would suffer proudly. I would neither move, nor yield, nor let one sound of pain escape my lips.

'Stand up, please, Helia,' she continued, giving my shoulder a brief, but strangely intimate squeeze, then reaching out to ring the little hand bell that would summon Flossie to the garden.

This made my heart hammer madly. It had been demeaning enough to have the servant girl watch me in the privy, but that she should see me punished too? That was too much.

'Mrs Woolstencraft, please –' I began, but was cut off. Madam spun me round, holding my arms, and looked into my face, her own as pure and hard as an avenging angel's.

'You will not speak, Helia. It is not your place to.' She squeezed with her thumbs and fingers, moved closer. I could smell the cool delicious mintiness of her breath. 'You will be quiet and suffer the consequences of your actions.'

She released me then, but I stayed where I was, frozen. I felt as if I were suffocating. My whole body seemed to swell with the strangest of sensations. My skin was sensitised, aware of every inch of my underwear against it; my bosom seemed to strain inside my corset. My bottom tingled as if it had been lashed already, and between my thighs the betraying fluid welled.

Oh, no! Not that! Not with Flossie here, too! My knees went weak, but I summoned every last ounce of my grit to keep them braced, as my mind presented the image, and the sensation, of the laughing maid pressing her fingers to my wetness.

'Floss, will you be so kind as to run and fetch the schoolroom cane for me? Miss Helia is in need of its attentions,' said Madam, after Flossie had appeared, run across the grass and bobbed her usual insolent half-curtsey.

I could not look at the girl. I knew she would be smirking. But when I glanced across at Belinda, instead, my scarred companion was staring, too, her drawing forgotten, a look of hunger on her face.

I was not the only one to notice this. 'Belinda, I am warning you,' said Madam silkily. 'Continue with your drawing or it will be two bottoms I have to see to, not just one.'

To 'see to'. What an odd expression. I was beginning to feel stranger and stranger. Quite detached and fatalistic. Perhaps I could survive this way? Use this almost serene state of mind to buffer me – no matter how painful and humiliating things became?

It did not take Flossie long to fetch the implement and, with a little show of pomp, she handed it to her mistress. Madam rolled it slowly and meaningfully between her fingers.

'Flossie, will you prepare Miss Helia for her caning now,' she said, her tone as light and normal as if she were asking for tea to be served. 'As it is a warm day –' she shielded her eyes and squinted towards the sunny sky '– I think it would be appropriate to remove some of her clothing.' She turned away, and began a series of practice swishes. 'Leave her chemise, her stockings and her boots, I think, but remove everything else.' She spun around, and fixed the maid with an intent but controlled expression. 'Do you have your pins with you, Floss? And the ribbons?'

I began to feel a little faint, a little sick. I was to be undressed again. Here. Outside. I looked around nervously. The garden wall was tall, but the house next door was much taller. What if someone were to spy on us? They would see me, in just my chemise, my bottom bare.

And furthermore, what dark functions could there be for pins and ribbons?

As Flossie closed on me, reaching for the buttons of my blouse, I resisted, knocking away her strangely delicate hands. She advanced again. I retreated a step or two, my own hands raised, like a pugilist's, to protect me.

'Now, Miss Helia, be a good girl,' she said, side-stepping as if she really feared I would cuff her. 'Don't be tiresome.'

Suddenly, I saw red. 'Tiresome! How dare you! How dare you speak to me like that!' I glared at her, my fingers curving into fists.

Before I was really aware of what was happening, a blur of black and white and tawny – skirt, blouse, hair – was upon me, and I felt a blunted streak of pain across my buttocks.

'And how dare you speak to Flossie like that!' said Madam evenly, yet with ice, as it dawned on me that she had struck me with the cane. Even through my good wool skirt, my drawers and petticoats, it had hurt like fire.

I wanted to fight, to strike out myself and resist her, but despite all that I remained still. There was a quality in Madam's steely, flashing eyes that subdued me. She held me pinned just by looking at me, the cane a potent symbol in her hands. And though I still fought inside, I let Flossie undress me.

With speed and efficiency, my clothing came off and was flung across my chair. Blouse, belt, skirt, petticoats, corset, drawers; I was divested of everything but my chemise, my stockings and garters, and my footwear. And even though I was allowed those, I felt more exposed than I had done yesterday, when Flossie had marched me naked along the corridor to see Madam.

All eyes were now upon me, even Belinda's. She was peeking up slyly from beneath her thick, silky eyelashes.

Flossie had finished her task for the time being, but under the guise of adjusting a fold of my chemise, she pressed her fingers into the groove of my bottom, then caressed one cheek, just where the cane had already impacted. That made me gasp, and Madam's eyes narrow.

'Come along,' she said, striding across the garden, skirts swishing, cane in hand. 'There's no time to waste . . . This has gone on long enough. It's time our young friend Helia was acquainted with our weeping willow.' Flossie pinched my bottom cheek to propel me along behind her.

What a fool I must have looked! Stumbling through the grass, in just my buttoned boots, my black stockings and my shift. And this last was such a thin, dainty confection, made from the finest Indian muslin and only reaching part way down my thighs in the new and daring fashion. I was well aware that any observer could see straight through it.

'Our weeping willow' is at the far end of the lawn, by the garden wall, a sturdy well grown example of its genus, with a garden name that is ironically and distressingly apt. As I trudged towards it, I saw to my dismay that a large staple had been driven into the living trunk, at a significant distance from the ground, and that there were two more, at its base, some feet apart. One did not need to be a scholar to deduce their purpose.

I balked again, but only for a second. I would show them what I was made of, I decided anew. I would do everything; I would take everything; not once would I exhibit fear or distress. They could tie me to their willow, but proud Helia would not weep.

From the capacious pockets of her apron, Flossie produced a length of black petersham ribbon and, looking her right in the eye, I sullenly held out my arms. Smiling, but with some admiration, I believe, she bound my wrists together and led me to the tree. Then, standing on tiptoe, she fed the strong, stiffened ribbon through the staple and secured me to the trunk with my arms above my head. With more ribbon, she fastened my booted ankles to the staples at the base of the tree, which left me stretched and helpless against the hard surface of the trunk, my limbs and body in the shape of an inverted 'Y'.

Quelling my fear, I studied the mottled surface of the bark, and listened to the tiny, normal sounds of a summer garden: an insect buzzing nearby, an unknown bird singing almost ecstatically in the higher branches of the very tree I was restrained against; the muted rustling of a breeze in the overgrown grass behind the tree. I heard a carriage bowling along the road, some distance away from us and, closer, I heard the low sussuration of a conspiratorial whisper. It was Madam issuing further instructions to Flossie, followed by a giggle from the maid, followed by a sharp but indecipherable word of reproof.

And then I was being handled again – in ways that it took me all my time not to protest. Reaching around from behind me, Flossie unfastened the buttons of my chemise and drew it open, pinning back the fine cloth so my breasts were naked against the tree. Similarly, she whisked up the garment's hem, too, and fastened that in a haphazard roll around my waist. I could feel a ridge in the willow's bark pressing against the little bulge of my pubis and, above my gartered stockings, my bottom and thighs were wafted by the same little breeze that played and danced amongst the grass.

I felt very peculiar in that shameful position, but not quite in the way I might have expected. Once again, my wayward mind presented images.

In the first, a line of people were queuing up to kneel down and kiss my bare bottom. They were all there: Madam, Flossie, Louise and Belinda, even Mr Reed and my dear mischievous William. As each pair of lips touched my rear, I felt the moisture of their open mouths upon my skin. I felt fingers prize apart my cheeks so that even more licentious kisses could be offered. I felt tongue after tongue probe my tiny nether portal.

And as I was kissed – in this dream – I was also touched. Whilst my bottom was licked and played with, other worshippers were fondling my breasts and my private female parts. I was squeezed and rubbed, pinched and palpated; I was driven to distraction by exquisite stimulation.

'Try and keep still, Helia,' said Madam Woo, her soft voice breaking into my raging fantasy. I realised to my horror that, far from remaining detached and unmoved by what was happening to me, I was making of myself a vulgar spectacle. Without really being aware of what I was doing, I had been massaging my body lewdly on the tree, rubbing my nipples and my naked loins against its surface. Full of shame, I became as still as if it were I, and not the tree-trunk, that was made of wood.

I heard footsteps, and the rustle of petticoats, and then I smelt Madam's light, floral perfume. She was close to me, next to me, just touching me; the cloth of her skirt brushed against my naked bottom. I sensed a small movement, then felt something cool, narrow and hard laid between my buttocks. It was the cane. She was just holding it there, resting in the groove, its lacquered surface delicately tickling my anal closure.

'I expect great things of you, Helia,' she murmured, her breath warm against the portal of my ear. She moved the cane, sliding it against the tiny pulsing rosebud in a way that made me want to squirm, to gasp and moan, to cry out loudly for I knew not what. My belly surging, my heart racing, I did none of these.

'Great things,' she repeated, her lips almost touching my face. 'You are the best, proud Helia. You are the finest . . . You are myself, as I was in the beginning.'

Her scent was making me dizzy, and despite my vows and my spirit, I jerked my bottom so it would rub against the cane. I would have something from this! Something that I wanted. I would have a little pleasure before I had to take the pain.

'Hush,' whispered Madam again, her hand on my thigh. 'Do not try to run before you can walk. There will be plenty of time for other things later.'

With that, she spun away from me, and I felt a sudden pang of unhappiness that had nothing to do with my coming caning. I wanted the perfume, the touch, the voice. I wanted Madam Woo, I realised, I wanted her to love me, but to love me on *my* terms.

'Will you cry out?' she asked, her voice level and businesslike now; no longer an intimate, breathy whisper. 'Because if you think you are likely to, we must fasten something across your mouth to prevent it. It would not do to attract undue attention.'

No! I would not! I would not!

'You may answer me, Helia,' said Madam, not hearing my passionate inner cry.

'No, Mrs Woolstencraft, I won't make a sound.'

'Are you sure? This is quite a test for a beginner . . .'

'I'll do my best,' I conceded. I had never experienced so much as a slap on the legs as a child; the kiss of the cane was beyond my imagining.

'Very well,' replied Madam, almost gaily. I heard a hissing swish, and clenched every muscle, but she was only testing the heft of her implement. 'Flossie can fetch something suitable, if you do begin to shout. But it will only be six cuts. Any more would be unwise on a first occasion . . .'

There was a long silence then. The birdsong, the sough of the breeze, the distant road noises; everything, even time itself, seemed suspended in readiness. Then, just when I felt the temptation to turn around and see if Madam had changed her mind and left me alone in the garden, there was a strange, high whistling sound, followed by a sharp snap like the report of a toy pistol.

I waited, for what seemed like a full second, but was probably only an instant, thinking, it's all right! It's all right! It's nothing! I can bear it! Then a line of pure, almost unimaginably intense sensation seemed to explode across my buttocks and in my brain.

Thinking back now, as I lie here on my face feeling the effects of that stroke and its five burning sisters, I find it impossible to adequately describe the impact of that slim length of rattan against my bottom. 'Pain' is not a sufficient expression of the feeling, either in severity, or in quality. It is more than a physical phenomenon, and infinitely more than a punishment. It is a circumstance derived from another world.

Suffice it to say that I *did* cry out. At that very first stroke. Despite all my avowals of iron will, my claims that I would truly be the best, I howled like a baby. Flossie was despatched to bring a large clean handkerchief from the house, and this was carefully refolded, then fastened around my face, between my teeth, to stop my cries. All the while I was waiting for this to be fetched, I sobbed and sobbed, tears streaming down my cheeks as my bottom throbbed and burnt. Just one stroke and I had been robbed of all my pride.

The remaining five strokes were both easier and more difficult to bear. Easier, because I was relieved of the embarrassment of screaming; harder, because each successive impact seemed to exacerbate the ones that had gone before. When it was over it took me some moments to discern the fact. My flesh was still reverberating, still rent by flame; my mind was still aloft in a high and shining place.

But as I sank to earth, I was in for some shocks. My downfall was wrought in more than pain. I thought of how I had writhed and struggled, flinging my body everywhere my bonds would allow it. I imagined what I must have looked like, crushing my sparsely clad torso against the tree, humping it as a cur mounts a bitch.

And Belinda had seen all this. My exhibition. My striped buttocks churning. My parted thighs pumping. My wet, and parted thighs.

Dear heaven, the ignominy of it. In extremis, I had lost the mastery of my bladder. I had wet myself, and now my inner thighs were gleaming and my stockings sodden. The smell of my own water was an accusation, a measure of how my mighty pride had fallen.

Yet for all this, it was not any of these things that galled me the most as I hung there, against that tree. Not the ravaged state of my bottom cheeks, not my childish accident; not my vulgar, exposed state. No, what troubled me was the torment between my legs. I bit down on the handkerchief, glad beyond reason that it was there to prevent me begging someone, anyone, any damnable person on the face of the earth, to slip their fingers between my thighs and rub my sex.

Madam was still close by. How sublime, I thought as my loins quivered, how wonderful it would be if she used the same strong hand that had wielded the cane to deliver me into my pleasure.

But I had not done well. I had not excelled – or been the best, I was sure of that. And I would not ask for a prize I had not earned.

When Flossie removed the handkerchief, I pursed my dry lips in stubborn silence.

'Nothing to say, Helia?' said Madam, her voice quiet, yet arch.

Was she asking me to ask? Was she asking me to grovel, to plead for forgiveness for the heinous sin of wetting myself? Of not being the paragon she had expected? Perhaps she was, but I would not give even her the satisfaction of breaking me. I kept my lips firmly pressed together, even when she ran a finger along one of my weals and turned it to a streak of pounding fire. I leapt like an eel, but I did not emit a sound.

'As you wish,' she said crisply, then bending closer, she whispered, 'my darling . . .' and touched her finger to my anus.

The tiny contact stirred me unbearably, and I tossed my head – but still I did not utter a single word.

Then Madam was gone, and I heard the sound of drawing materials being gathered, the purposeful swish of skirts, and Belinda being admonished to 'Hurry up!'

They were leaving me! *She* was leaving me. Leaving me in pain, in bondage, my legs wet and my body aroused. It was insupportable, and I opened my mouth to protest, then clamped it shut again.

I would not break. I would not give in. I would not yield.

But just as I thought I was to be abandoned altogether, there came, from Madam, a single order.

She said, 'Flossie, attend to her!' then she was gone, in a last swift flurry of skirts, inside the house and beyond my ken entirely.

I felt bereft, and for a moment, almost oblivious to my pain. It was submerged inside a greater feeling. The yearning, no matter how perverse it seemed, to be with Madam. In any way. At least when she was beating me, I was the centre of her attention. But now I was no longer interesting, and she had the vivacious and strangely attractive Belinda to entertain her.

'Don't cry, miss,' said Flossie, whom I had altogether forgotten in my dolorous crush on Madam.

The maid was close now, as close as her mistress had been, and observing the tears I had not realised I was shedding. My embarrassment, my degradation was now complete.

And yet as I blinked away the salty teardrops, then felt Flossie gently blot them up with the mangled handkerchief, there was a degree of comfort to be derived from the maid's pretty presence.

'There, there ...' she whispered, her body so close now that I had flinch from the brush of her starched skirt against my bottom. 'I know it hurts ... I really do ...' She slid a deft hand between me and the tree, and slowly rubbed my chafed and tender nipples. 'How do you think I feel?' She was using her thumb to strum one teat, and somehow, and most cleverly, managing to caress the other with the inside of her wrist. 'All these beautiful young ladies to see to ... Ladies of quality, from fine families.' I turned my head away, to hide both the effect she was having on me, and my frown of growing puzzlement. 'She hardly ever has time for me some days. I have to be really bad to get her attention. To show her how much I need her. How I need a firm hand just as much as you young ladies do.'

It dawned on me. Flossie was as much besotted with Madam Woo as I suddenly was. She craved exactly the same kind of personal treatment – punishment – that I had just received. She saw it as a gift, a benison, a treasured pleasure. Just as I did myself, in some dark inexplicable way. My buttocks had been hurt, and were still hurting, more severely than I had believed possible; yet the sensation was also a thrill to me. It was an exultation, inflicted by a goddess. A woman I adored, for a reason I could not fathom; a woman I desired, in a manner that defied all logic.

And this good-natured minx of a maid shared my passion.

As I continued to writhe, my arousal piqued by her tantalising touch, I felt a great sense of kinship with the sprightly, sensual Flossie. In the opinion of Madam's pampered and titled charges, my good Greek family would be considered little more than peasants, and of no more account than Flossie's working class relations. She and I were both underlings after a fashion, and I felt a wild, but intense urge to offer her the comfort she was attempting to offer me. At first I wasn't sure of what to do, but the answer wasn't difficult to work out. And short of transforming myself into Madam, I knew what it was that Flossie liked.

'Please touch me, Flossie,' I asked her, relaxing the iron-clad will I had hardened against her mistress. 'I – I feel so hot. So aroused. I can't help it. I think I'll lose my mind if you don't touch me between my legs.' I heard her breathing deepen and become ragged, and her fingers close roughly on my nipple. 'I need to come off, Flossie. My – my quim aches. I'm so wet . . .' I paused, considered my words, and my plans. 'You can do anything you like to me, Flossie. Whenever you want . . . If only you'll do this for me now.'

'Really, miss?' enquired Flossie, a shrewd edge coming into her voice. She was twisting my nipple now, making me wiggle in my bonds, and move my bottom about, even though it still stung and ached like the very devil.

'Yes! Anything!' I gasped, my state of desire more intense than ever. 'And I'll do anything for you, too. You can pretend I'm Madam Woo. Do the things you would like to do to her, but to me instead.'

'Right, Miss Helia, you're on!' said Flossie suddenly, giving my poor breast a last wicked tweak. 'I knew you were a sport, the first time I saw you.' Her hand slid downwards, past the pinned up bunch of my shift, and went straight to the core of my frustration. 'It's no trouble at all to bring you off, miss . . .' She attacked my swollen clitoris with all the gusto she had been using on my nipple. I moaned and my hips jerked. 'Just so long as I can handle your bottom as well.' Good as her word, she grasped my bottom cheek with her other hand and stirred its flaming weals so hard I had to bite my lip.

First in anguish, but after a second, in pleasure: rich, dark pleasure that bloomed as much in my well-thrashed rear as it did in the niche between my legs.

'Oh, my dear Flossie,' I moaned as my brand new friend delivered me.

She extracted her price, of course, later, when she had released me and taken me back to my room to be cleaned up; but to my sly delight it was a price I enjoyed paying.

And there was no loss of face in allowing Flossie to touch me, to pinch my weals, and even – dear God! – to lick me between my thighs, which was something that I had not even allowed William to do, even though he had pleaded that I let him.

Flossie and I are conspirators, now. Equals in adversity. She is going to come back later and give me something which will take my mind off my flaming bottom and help me sleep.

And somehow, I don't think it's going to be a cup of hot chocolate!

8th August

I write this in a state of high excitement. It is the first opportunity I have had to make an entry in this journal for a week, as the day after she caned me in the garden, Madam sprang something of a surprise on me.

'You're a very passionate girl, Helia,' she observed, as I stood before her, eyes lowered, every muscle and sinew tensed to keep myself from trembling with the very passion she spoke of, 'and passionate young women are wont to misdirect those strong and very particular emotions . . .' She reached out, lifted my chin with her cool fingers and made me look into her eyes, which were warm and laughing in her solemn, impassive face. 'So for your own good, I think we will have to restrain you at night. Just as a precaution . . .' Her lovely mouth twitched, and for an instant I thought her mask might crack, and she would genuinely snigger. But not so; her expression shuttered again and she went on, straight-faced. 'To prevent anything unseemly.' Lifting her glasses from her desk, she positioned them on the bridge of her nose, and looked down towards her papers. 'That will be all for now, Helia. You are dismissed. Return to your room. I will be with you shortly to administer your therapy.'

Cruel, icy bitch! I thought, storming from the room, not caring what penalty my haste might incur. The word 'therapy' had set me thinking too.

Whilst I waited – standing, then cautiously sitting, then pacing – I considered the ramifications of my recent brief interview.

I was to be bound up at night like a sinful little child, to prevent me, presumably, from playing with myself. What benefit to me this securing would be, I had no real idea. Touching myself, caressing my body to the inevitable and delightful conclusion, always relaxed me and ameliorated my temper. It made me sleep and wake refreshed and good-humoured.

No, my restraint was for Madam's well-being, not mine, that was for certain. She would have me bound and helpless, so my body was available for her to make free with.

But before that, I had to endure my 'therapy', and just thinking of that now evokes a shudder.

Like Louise before me, I was confined to my bedroom for the day, my morning clothes removed less than an hour after I had donned them, and replaced by a white flannel nightgown. The object of the exercise, Madam told me, when she had swept into my room like a dark, avenging angel, was to re-train me after my *faux pas* of yesterday.

At first I did not quite know what she was referring to. I had fallen from grace in quite a variety of ways. But an explanatory whisper from Flossie made me blench. Oh, no! How dreadful! How unthinkable!

Prefiguring my night-time disposition, she and Madam tied me to my bed, but securing me at my wrists and my ankles. After that came one or two refinements.

My upper torso, my arms and my shoulders were covered up cosily by the nightgown, a bedjacket and a shawl, and warm bedsocks were slipped over my feet. The area between, however, was left completely nude, with my striped bottom on splendid display, like a hunter's trophy!

To be left like this for hours on end would have been an ordeal in itself, but it seemed I was an exhibit for all and sundry. My contemplative solitude was to be broken by certain 'visits'.

But I am getting ahead of myself here.

Bound and confined in my room, my mind quickly focused on my predicament, and its paradoxical nature. I was wrapped up and cosseted in soft, warm clothes, on a comfortable bed, yet I was soon in an ever-growing torment. I had been made to drink several glasses of water before I was settled and made fast, and in no time at all, this liquid made its awful presence felt. A ball of lead seemed to settle in the cradle of my pelvis, a ball of lead that was ringed around with silvery spikes. I could find no adjustment to my position that would make this misery easier, and with every passing moment the weight and pressure grew and grew.

I began to sweat profusely, and the muscles in my thighs and belly twitched. I imagined the moment when I would finally be allowed to use the privy and between my parted legs my tender niche began to throb.

I had not expected this. Clenching every muscle to contain myself only made matters worse. My swelling, aching bladder pressed down on my seat of pleasure, and though I did not want it, I felt a rush of lust.

I tried to think of other things, to recite multiplication tables, remember stanzas of poetry, to name the countries of the world and all their capitals; but all in vain, there was no escape from my condition. From the need to pass water, and from the pulsing heat of my sex.

It seemed then that I started to hallucinate, imagining myself back in the lavatory, the other day, with Flossie. I dreamed of urinating freely, my golden trickle tinkling merrily against the porcelain, whilst Flossie, unabashed at getting her hand wet, gently played with my feminine centre whilst I peed.

I tried frantically to return to my maths and to my rhyming, but I could not seem to master my own mind.

Then, just as it seemed I was going to wet myself any second, the door opened and Madam swept into the room. She was followed by Flossie, whose face was alight with its perennial impish glee.

The tableau that ensued could only be described as a command performance.

'I expect you're feeling a little uncomfortable, my dear, aren't you?' enquired Madam Woo, sliding her hand between my belly and the rubberised sheet that had been spread out beneath me.

An understatement indeed, I thought, as much as I could think, biting my lips to keep inside my anguished shriek.

My sense of determination was probably my own worst enemy. I had swallowed down each of those glasses of water earlier, without a murmur, even though I had known what effect they would have upon me. I had suffered in stoic silence as my bladder had gradually distended, but now an even greater ordeal faced me.

I was to be tested. Probed and pressed. I felt Madam's fey, slender digits move slowly along the whole of my intimate groove, searching exhaustively for evidence of wetness . . .

Of which there was a great deal! But not yet of the character she was seeking. Or maybe it was? I was already *au fait* with Madam's special predilections. The way she relished the arousal of fellow females.

This rigorous test seemed to last for hours – even though in reality it probably took but a couple of minutes – the sensations hideous, yet jagged with an intensc, almost crucifying pleasure. Apparently satisfied as to the character of the fluid I was seeping, Madam's fingertips settled squarely on my clitoris, then began to manipulate it with great determination.

Jolts of feeling juddered through my loins and I pressed my face into the pillows to smother my cries. I lost the fight not to jiggle and jerk my hips, but biting the pillowcase, I emitted not one sound.

For several long moments, I saw stars behind my eyes as every muscle in my body twitched and clenched, but with shocking suddenness it seemed I was reprieved. Madam's tormenting fingers withdrew, and there was a flurry of whispered orders I could not hear clearly because my mind was thick and fogged.

Was it over? Was I to be released and allowed the privy?

No such luck.

A second later, I felt some oily, balm-like substance being applied to my bottom, right between the still smarting cheeks, and after another second my trial began again. Redoubled. Much, oh infinitely much worse than before. I chewed the disgustingly damp pillow so hard I swear I tore it, as a narrow well-greased digit pushed its way into my rectum, and at the same time my clitoris was found anew.

And as I suffered, I heard an angel's voice.

'That's it, my darling . . . What a good girl you are. You're learning . . .'

Or, 'Does it hurt, my sweet Helia? I'm sure it does . . . But it will help you to learn how to control yourself.

'Just think how useful a little training now will be to you. Imagine a glittering social gathering, people all around you. You're the centre of attention, and you have no chance to slip away. You will be able to smile, and laugh and dazzle, and no admiring gentleman will ever know about the delicious agony that lies within your drawers. He will be besotted by your beauty, enslaved by the lovely roses in your cheeks, and think that you are blushing because you like him . . .

'He'll never know your secret. How swollen you are . . . Your poor tender belly distended, pressing down, down, down . . . He will be quite bewitched by your poignant gasp as you sip your champagne.'

Looking back now, I know that this kind of talk is obscene and preposterous, like something out of a mad, laudanum-induced dream. Yet it did not seem so at the time. It was as if, within the walls of the Academy, all rules were changed, all standards of behaviour were warped and reconfigured. In our cloistered world there existed a different set of tyrannies.

But I digress again.

What Madam was doing to me was wicked. Wicked and unredeemably lewd. Yet I was conscious, even as the sparks of sensation stabbed my belly and my loins, that I was engaged, yet again, in a game with her. A rude, aberrant contest in which she leant over me, prodding her finger into my sore bottom, and touching my clitoris while I was bursting to go to the lavatory. And I, in my own wilful, provoking perversity, fought against her. Fought the pleasure. Fought the darkness in her eyes. The darkness of a sky on a night without a moon.

Ah, but it was a hard battle. My poor nerve-endings were totally confused. Overloaded with conflicting messages: messages of hurt, because my bladder was desperately swollen, and messages of exquisite sensuality, because that swollenness was jolting my clitoris from within. I didn't know whether to weep, or to scream and have an orgasm.

And Madam seemed to know – no! I *know* she knew exactly how I was feeling. She pulled away from me at the very second I was convinced I was going to deluge her. So cool, so apparently unperturbed, she kept me simmering away for what felt like hours and hours and hours, her clever hands walking a fine line of daring upon my body. Never too much, never too little; I came close to madness . . . And even when I was allowed to urinate – upon the chamber pot, like a little girl, and closely watched – the process was begun anew, without respite, and I was made to drink again. Glass upon glass of carefully chilled water, or steaming cupfuls of strong, stimulating tea.

As I lay in my near-delirium, I seemed to see Madam Woo even when she wasn't with me. Her face was my icon, both beautiful and sadistic.

But even while I worshipped I was plagued by other company. Soft of foot but giggling came Louise and Belinda.

They were guilefully evil.

'Not so proud now, eh, Miss Helia?' purred Louise, bending over me. The breath of her voice was warm and gentle against my ear, but at the small of my back, her little hand was hard and cruel. She pressed down energetically, forcing my belly against the mattress. 'We've all had this, you know,' she continued, rocking me and making me gasp and choke. 'She loves it! She really loves it! She'll be up in her room now, frigging herself senseless, imagining you bursting and trying not to piss the bed.'

The image was as taxing as the pressure. Madam on her bed, her dark gown around her waist, her long legs kicking, her hand a frenzied blur. Wanting to be there, I felt my own vulva pulse. Which was a bad thing as it pushed me closer to the edge.

'How does it feel, then?' murmured sly Belinda, coming to the other side of me and stroking my bare thigh. Her fingers traversed upwards, examining the oily residue that lingered between my bottom cheeks, then scratching a fingernail across my tender anus. 'I'll bet you're really swollen, aren't you?' she continued, toying with the tiny rear entrance that had already been violated by our governess. I buried my flaming face into the pillow and prayed for strength.

The fingers moved again then, and both girls began to assault me, tickling my sex and cruelly squeezing my Venus mount. The distress I felt was both terrible, and gloriously exciting, with each prod and probe I was convinced that I would leak. My clitoris bulged out between my swollen, silky love-lips, a perfect target for my pretty young tormentors.

Though it pains me to say it, I climaxed several times while they abused me. And very likely, I pissed a little, too. But not once did I plead with them to stop. It was a relief though, when the luncheon gong sounded and, laughing merrily, the two holy terrors fled.

That day, I can say without exaggeration, seemed to be the longest I had spent in all my life. And I admit that I was glad when it was over. Finally over in one last demeaning, but still voluptuous act; Madam releasing my pleasure whilst I was hovering over the potty. The urge to weep then – to howl, even – was almost irresistible, but I prevailed, enduring my spasms in a magnificent, tight-lipped silence.

And the days that followed have all had their own particular ordeals; I seem to be sinking deeper into a strange and alien landscape.

For one day, I became a little child again!

'You are so stubborn, Helia,' said Madam, her voice delicately pained when she visited me, very early, before breakfast. 'I swear I have never known a young woman more so . . . Not even the most juvenile of my charges, and that includes Louise, has ever behaved more like a mule. I think it's time to employ methods more appropriate to your nature. To the contrariness of a brattish little girl.'

And so, instead of one of my expensive gowns, or my embroidered silk blouses and well-made woollen skirts, I was put into the short, shapeless dress and cotton pinafore of a young schoolgirl. Which was bad enough itself, but really a ruse for a far greater humbling. One not unconnected with my interlude of being strapped to the bed.

I was denied my own underthings and dressed in those of an incontinent babe in arms. I admit that there was some pleasure in leaving off my constricting corset, but I soon forgot that in the shame of being taken back to swaddling.

I had to wear a napkin! A large square of towelling cloth, folded and pinned just as it had been when I was a tiny babe, and over this – presumably to hold in the moisture I was so grimly determined not to shed – a bizarre pair of oversized India rubber bloomers which rustled and squeaked with my every slightest movement. On top of these came a set of long knee-length cotton pantaloons, trimmed with lace, such as a child might also wear; but all the noise and commotion from beneath gave the game away.

'How pretty you look today, Helia,' said Belinda when reluctantly I revealed myself.

'Oh, yes,' chorused Louise. 'I love your dress and I really adore your hair.' In a final touch of ignominy, Madam had instructed that my long black hair be dressed in two childish bunches, complete with ribbons to match the trimming on my frock.

I have never felt such a fool, even when I was strapped to that tree in the garden, bare-bottomed and in just my flimsy shift!

But the childish clothing was just a part of Madam's agenda. When the others were dismissed for their morning break, I was detained. Not unkindly, of course; Madam Woo was too subtle to effect anything quite so obvious.

'How clever you are to have solved this problem, Helia,' she said, her eyes warm and merry for once as she leant over me, pointing to a solution I had expounded in my arithmetic book. 'It was quite complex. I didn't expect any of you to master it. Perhaps you could show me how you came to your conclusion?'

Witch! Perverse, exasperating witch! I thought as she drew a schoolroom chair up beside me and sat down. She placed her arm around my waist to keep me still.

It was the same game as yesterday, but played in a new arena; once again, I was being made to hold my water.

So be it, I resolved, realising in that instant that the awful pressure was starting to build. This dark and unspoken game was one of Madam's favourite deviations. I would indulge her, give her pleasure in it, satisfy her whims; but only because I, too, had become addicted to its charms.

I am becoming as warped as she is, I told myself, shuffling in my seat as I explained my elaborate theorem. And I like it! I flashed Madam a complicit sideways glance, and saw her rosy mouth twitch in a slight response. Beneath my girlish bunches my hidden ears began to blush.

At lunch, after almost waddling to the dining room, my private parts in ferment, it suddenly came to me that I, too, could change the game. I took a sip from my water glass, set it down upon the table, then fixed Madam with my keenest, steadiest smile. Her own features were alight with expectation; her lustrous eyes twin flames set in ivory. Holding her blazing glance, I relaxed my loins and finally released my gathered waters.

Oh, Madam, how divine that moment was! We were bound together by a secret chain of hidden feelings. As Belinda and Louise prattled on about some inconsequential nonsense, I throbbed with pleasure and drenched my napkin, and my lover blushed. Not the tomato stain of excited blood that rushed into my own face and throat, but the most delicate of misty pinks upon her cheekbones. She patted her lips with her serviette, in the slightest, most natural gesture, but I knew, even in my confusion, that she was masking a sigh. Her pale face was as calm as one of the carved, heroic goddesses that were still to be found in my Hellenic homeland, but her eyes held the polished, brilliant truth. Her delight in my clandestine wetting was as great as mine. We were soul sisters and she knew she had met her match.

When I could concentrate again, I felt smug. And hungry! I fell upon my lunch with gusto, enjoying the simple but well cooked food as if it were a succession of rarest gourmet delicacies. In a state of liberty I slaked my sudden thirst, with glass after glass of cool, pure water, and then brazenly wet myself again, whilst enjoying the delicious apple charlotte we were served for dessert. I held Madam's look again, and though she shook her head, she smiled.

The rest of the day was an idyll; there is no other word for it. In a fresh napkin, I was permitted to spend the afternoon in the garden with Madam, beneath the sunshade, reading a Gothic novel while she worked on prospecti and schedules for the new term that lay ahead. There was added and particular satisfaction in this, as Louise and Belinda were sequestered in the schoolroom, writing out the multiplication tables they had made a bit of a hash of earlier. A 'little girl' like me was not expected to study all day.

I did not manage to read very much of my book, entertaining though it was. My attention was mainly focused on Madam Woo.

She was the most perfect creature I had ever seen, I decided, and as delectable when she was tranquil as when she was stern. Her profile was as mysterious as that of a royal, exotic princess, and her little reading glasses added an extra glint of charm. I wanted to kiss the back of her neck as she inclined intently over her labours. One fine tendril of her burnished hair had escaped her chignon, and was coiling across her skin like a red-gold filament.

Flossie brought us home-made lemonade as the afternoon wore on, and – excited by my new found entertainment – I drank several large glasses. As the inevitable sensations began to build, I closed my eyes and painted strange pictures inside my mind.

Under delicious stress, I imagined Madam leaning gracefully over the dining table, her drawers lowered, and her linen held up, so I could kiss her glorious bottom. I imagined myself, strapped face upwards on my bed, wearing only my shift and my corset. I was helpless, my mouth filled with some scented item of Madam's lingeric, while she touched me, between my legs, for a long, long time. The last thing I pictured was *Madam* on the bed, the situations reversed.

At the moment when my dream-self crouched between Madam Woo's splayed thighs, tasting her salty pudenda and licking her clitoris, I blissfully released my inner burden, and soaked my napkin.

And imagined a soft, breathy voice saying, 'Well done, my dear . . .' Or did I imagine it?

The next day, when the vicar came to tea, was truly astonishing!

Now that I was a young lady again, we all dressed in our best afternoon gowns and took special care with our hair. I had a difficult time containing my smiles during Madam's long, prim lecture on the necessity for demure behaviour in the presence of a gentleman of the cloth. How could a woman so sensual portray a prude so very well? She was enjoying herself; there was no finer actress on the boards.

'You are all such good girls. Such sweet girls,' she said when we were gathered in the parlour for a last inspection. As we stood like three little maids in a row, she moved around us, her dark skirts swishing; sometimes stroking a cheek, or adjusting a curl, or rearranging a flounce. I could see, in spite of the shadowplay, that she was genuinely proud of us; even Belinda, with her vinous birthmark, was looking lovely.

'Even so, there is not one of you who doesn't have a tendency to be wilful,' went on Madam, her eyes assessing, her slender hands folded before her. 'I think, to be on the safe side, you should all wear a pacifier during the time the vicar is with us.'

Pacifier? What was a pacifier? I had not the vaguest notion what one of these could be, but just hearing the word gave me a strange, delightful twinge. Surely Madam didn't mean the device that was popped into a baby's mouth to occupy it and prevent it from crying? I had a sudden, silly vision of the three of us, Louise, Belinda and I, all sitting on the settee, sucking on infant's dummies. I had to giggle.

'You see what I mean?' said Madam, her eyes dancing. 'I can't have you tittering like hoydens while the Reverend Moulton is here. Pacifiers it is!' She rang the bell for Flossie, a small, but playful smile upon her lips.

When Flossie heard her mistress's request, she smirked, too, then went flying from the room, almost fizzing with glee. I looked towards my fellow pupils for some hint of a clue.

Belinda appeared dreamy, her eyes unfocused, her lips a little parted; Louise looked slightly sick but excited, and as Madam turned away, the slim dark girl pressed her hand to her groin.

It was some erotic thing then? Of course. Why did that not surprise me? The tingle in my loins, which had begun during Madam's homily, grew sharper and sharper.

Flossie returned with three curious looking black objects on a silver tray, as well as a small pot of what appeared to be ointment of some kind. These mystery items were made of India rubber but resembled nothing I had ever seen before. Their shape suggested a plug-like function; an irregular ovoid, a little tapered at the one end, and at the other narrowing to about an inch, before flaring out into a flanged circular base.

I could not imagine what Madam planned to do with them, then a second later, I knew the answer, absolutely and for certain, and my poor heart hammered.

Heavens! Oh dear Lord! How terrible! How delectable! I wriggled my hips in anticipation.

'Right! Let's get this over with quickly. Reverend Moulton will be here soon, and we don't want to keep him waiting,' said Madam briskly, reaching for the first pacifier. 'Louise. Over the arm of the chaise, if you please. Face down, skirts around your waist, bottom well up. Don't dawdle, my dear.'

'Please, Mrs Woolstencraft . . . It's all right. I'll be good,' pleaded the stricken girl.

'Louise!' our governess prompted mildly.

Louise took up her position and, without instruction, Flossie assisted her with her linen. In just a few seconds her trim white bottom was on show to us all.

'Now hold open your cheeks, my dear,' instructed Madam, drawing close to her, but not – I noted – obscuring either mine or Belinda's view of the proceedings. 'Flossie, please apply a little of the balm.'

Louise gave a little choked gasp, but obeyed, prising apart her buttocks to delicately reveal her nether closure. She started moaning as diligent Flossie applied the ointment.

'That's it, my dear,' murmured Madam gently, pressing the rounded end of the pacifier against Louise's well-buttered anus. 'You must relax now . . . Be quiet and good. Let it in.'

'Oh, no!' keened Louise as Madam persisted. She tossed her head, and I could see the toes of her boots digging and scraping at the carpet, but very gradually the little hole yielded and, almost with a 'pop', the black demon slid home into its niche.

The instant she was plugged, Louise began to make an uncouth gobbling sound and to waggle her pelvis furiously against the arm of the chaise. With a little 'tut' of resignation, Madam reached a slender hand beneath the belly of her charge, and almost immediately Louise wailed like a banshee and pumped her hips even harder.

It was obvious that Louise was well and truly pacified.

The procedure was the same for Belinda, although she only sighed, long and libidinously, as her entrance was breached.

And then, as the other two stood, ill at ease and slightly pink-faced, their long, full skirts beautifully smoothed to hide their secret, it was my turn to go face down, across the arm of the chaise, my rump in the air.

My nerves were already twittering. My two companions both had very pretty bottoms, and both wore the faint rosy glow of a recent chastisement. Had they each had a beating already today? I wondered. A private session, in their rooms, before we all assembled, appearing perfectly normal, to partake of our breakfast? The thought of that, and that those two beautiful, lightly punished bottoms were now stuffed and plugged by the infernal pacifiers, seemed to bring out the wanton in me. Dangerous though I knew it would be, I heartily longed for my own induction to this exotic form of calming.

'Now your turn, Helia,' said Madam, taking me by the arm and tipping me over the chaise. In a trice, my skirts were up and my drawers were down, and my derrière was uncovered to the world. There then seemed to be a long pause, a hiatus of quiet in which my pulse raced and pounded.

'Hold yourself open, my dear.' Madam's cool fingertips brushed across me, encouragingly. 'That's a good girl . . .'

More scrutiny. I felt all the eyes in the room on the rose of my anus.

'You're very tight, Helia,' Madam said, leaning over me, her perfume making me giddy, 'but even so, I think I'll try you with something a little bigger.' I shuddered as she sent Flossie from the room, then I allowed my stretched open bottom cheeks to close.

'Oh, no! Don't do that . . . Keep yourself open,' instructed Madam, touching the tiny orifice for a second and making me want to shout with hidden pleasure. I was almost fainting with the effort it took to cup a buttock in each hand.

After about a minute Flossie returned, and then she and Madam set about the task of greasing me. It seemed an inordinately thorough process, and was far more scrupulously performed on me than it had been with the other two. I gritted my teeth, and I dug in my toes, but I did not cry out.

Then it was time. Something that was enormous, and felt about the size of a cricket ball, was pressed firmly against the opening between my buttocks. I really did want to cry out then; to protest that it was far too big and would split me open, but I kept still and silent. Madam pushed the pacifier into me with a smooth relentless pressure and, after some moments, my anus finally yielded, and my protesting bottom was packed.

Oh horrible! Horrible! My innards roiled, and I felt a sudden, desperate need to rush to the privy. I jerked, began to panic, but then Madam laid a finger on the pacifier's outer flange and the dirty feelings steadied.

'There, isn't that better?' she whispered to me, rocking her fingertip a little and making tiny sensual frissons dance inside me. 'I always find that a well stuffed bottom makes me calmer and quieter. It focuses the attention, you'll see. Rids the mind of wayward thoughts and childish distractions.'

Poppycock! It didn't eradicate my wayward thoughts at all. It simply created new ones. I lay over the arm of the chaise, the soft velvet upholstery against my face, and tried to pretend that it was Madam there in my stead. I pictured the exquisite purity of her – her straight, commanding presence, her poised composure –

and knew that no pacifier, not even the hugest, could take her mind off sex.

I imagined her how she was dressed today, in the most severely cut, high necked navy blue silk dress – with just a piping of white lace at her wrists and throat – but with the outrageous licentiousness of a rubber-filled bottom underneath it. She would converse quietly, and move gracefully, but all the time she would be experiencing wave after wave of indecent pleasure from the bulbous bung inside her rectum. She might have an orgasm, yet show not a trace of it, save some colour in her cheeks.

'Get up now, my dear,' said Madam kindly, snapping me out of my reverie. 'I would like you girls to go down and make sure the parlour is tidy for our guest. I have just one little chore that I need attend to . . . I'll join you in five minutes.'

I struggled with my drawers and my petticoats, but my progress was slow and precarious. The slightest movement seemed to jostle the rubber intruder inside me, and that made me gasp and hold my breath. Judging by the rather ragged breathing of the other two, and the slow, very considered way they were moving, it was clear that they were experiencing the self-same problems. If it had not been such a perilous thing to do, I would have laughed out loud. What a trio! Three pretty bottoms all stuffed with wicked rubber! Three sedate young ladies descending the stairs, our knuckles white.

It was only a moment or two before the Reverend Mr Moulton arrived that Madam rejoined us. She appeared to be her usual immaculate, unruffled self but, uniquely attuned to everything about her, I immediately noticed a difference. Her dark eyes were sparkling like moonlight through raindrops, and across her cheekbones, in just the way I had fancied earlier, was a faint, but telling blush.

She was sharing our ordeal, I knew it! She, too, was stuffed, immolated, pacified; she, too, had a black and most thoughtfully shaped rubber plug inside her bottom. It was a hidden obscenity, an exquisitely luscious secret. I wondered idly if the others would guess it, too.

The tea party was both normal and surreal; an everyday occurrence, but with perversion beneath our skirts. The Reverend Moulton turned out to be younger than I had expected, and extremely attractive in a shy, quietly spoken fashion, and I kept imagining how he would react if he knew what we were hiding. He seemed a delightfully repressed young gentlemen. I imagined him fainting over the Lapsang Souchong and Madeira cake when we whipped up our petticoats to reveal our stoppered bottoms.

The more I thought about this, the more I wanted to wriggle about, or to throw up my skirts, reach into my drawers and play with my clitoris. What would the handsome Reverend think if he knew how much I wanted to play with Madam Woo's clitoris too? I imagined her bending over on the Turkey rug in front of him, while I held up her petticoats with one hand, and rotated the pacifier inside her with the other. I could almost hear her groaning, and see the silver stickiness that coated her lissom thighs.

'And are you enjoying yourself here at the Academy, Helia?' Mr Moulton enquired, his expression guileless. 'Mrs Woolstencraft is a most accomplished scholar, you know. You are extremely fortunate to be under her tutelage.'

'Why yes, thank you, Reverend Moulton,' I replied with a smile, then shifted ever so slightly in my seat to make the pacifier rock inside me. 'I love being at the Academy! If it were up to me I would stay here forever. I've learnt such a lot from Mrs Woolstencraft in only a few short days, but I know there is much much more to learn.' I pressed my thighs together discreetly, and felt a surge of wild feeling, 'And I'm really quite a glutton for – for wisdom.'

'Admirable! Admirable!' said the handsome young clergyman, a little bemused, I think, by my enthusiasm. And also – possibly – by the sudden attractive pinkness in my face.

I glanced across the table, and felt my pleasure quadrupled by Madam's slight smile. She may have nodded infinitesimally then, or perhaps not, but I knew my secret message was acknowledged. And even, dare I hope, answered?

Reaching for the teapot, to top up our guest, Madam Woo rocked ever so slightly in her seat, and for a moment then, she faltered. It was so brief a reaction that I swear no one else in the parlour noticed what was happening. But I did. I saw her thick, silky eyelashes sweep down, her mouth twitch in an instant of ecstasy, and I knew that she, too, was riding the dark intrusion of a pacifier; the violation of her supreme and beautiful bottom.

Listening with only half an ear to Mr Moulton's prattle about the benefits of education, and the simpering comments of Louise and Belinda – who were both obviously anointing their drawers over his pale and refined good looks – I longed to be able to approach my adorable Madam and investigate her secrets. I imagined the shock and desire that might appear in Mr Moulton's eyes if I were to ask my sweetheart to abandon her tea, and join me on the rug, where we might pleasure each other in a tangle of skirts and drawers, muslin and lace. What would it be like to lie top to tail with her, and feel her soft but muscular tongue licking my privates while she did me the same service down below? What would it be like to nibble the delicate morsel of her clitoris whilst playing with the black plug between her delectable fesses?

What would it be like to sup at the font of her soft,

swollen-wet femininity and bring her to a crisis she could not hide behind the mask of a genteel, unflappable hostess?

I wanted so much to touch and kiss Madam's privates that my fingers and my tongue began to ache. I had to put down my cup, my hands were shaking so much. My ears were filled with her illusory cries of rapture, so much so that I lost all sense of the conversation going on around me.

'And what is your favourite subject, Helia?' enquired Mr Moulton, and I realised to my horror that it was the second time he had posed the question.

I experienced a brief turmoil of discomposure, then, turning and staring directly into Madam's lambent eyes, I said, 'I do not believe I have a favourite, Mr Moulton. I relish all disciplines. Every task, every trial I am set is a challenge to me. And yet also a pleasure. The harder I am tested the more joy I find in it.' Then, in the guise of adjusting the folds of my skirt, I sat down hard on the damned black pacifier, and felt a great gust of sensation pass through me; a blend of release, of bravado and of triumph.

Of course, as a consequence of my resulting gasp and sway, I was deemed to have come over a little faint, and was escorted from the room by Flossie.

I was banished, but with Madam still in my heart.

She was there when Flossie removed the pacifier, and tickled the orifice it had sensitised until I was delivered yet again by her fingers.

She was there when Flossie got me ready for bed, then gave me a spanking – to warm my bottom and make it easier for me to sleep.

She was there in the night, when I managed to wriggle around, despite my bound hands, and work a thick fold of my nightdress between the lips of my sex.

She was there when I fell asleep, sticky and satisfied, and very proud of my own erotic cleverness.

But all that was yesterday, and last night, and now things have changed so much here that I hardly know where to begin.

'You are to see Madam privately this morning,' Flossie said when she first came into my bedroom. 'The others are banished to the schoolroom for the day, writing essays or something . . . So Madam can have you all to herself.'

This utterance made my heart trip and skitter, but I tried not to reveal my agitation to Flossie. I presented a cool, calm demeanour to my little friend, the servant, and even dashed away her hand when she tried to pleasure me. What I did allow was that she dressed me in my best black sateen skirt, with a French knot trim, and a particularly fine blouse of snowy cotton crepe, trimmed with pin tucks and inserts of lace embroidery. I wanted to look my best. There was a turning point ahead.

But even my best was rather plain beside Madam. When I entered her study I found her, as usual, in the most austere and ascetic of confections; a fine, shimmering dark grey dress that clung beautifully to her waist and to her bosom. At her throat was a little white jabot of frothy lace, and her narrow wrists sported the same pristine adornment. She wore no jewellery but her eyes shone like precious gems.

'Well then, my proud Helia,' she said, rising from behind her desk as I reached the centre of the room, 'what are we to do with you? It seems we are unable to humble you in any way, no matter what measures we employ.'

I said nothing in return, but stood straight-backed on the rug, with my hands clasped behind me, twisting my fingers to prevent myself from weakening. I met her fiery stare, but did not flinch or look away.

Standing before me, Madam sighed, which made her fine breasts rise and fall beneath her dress. 'So what are we to tell Mr Benjamin Reed?' she went on, still holding my gaze. 'He has paid us a great deal of money for our efforts to make you biddable. Shall we inform him the expense was all in vain?'

I compressed my lips at the sound of that hateful name, and I knew that Madam had taken note of my expression.

'Have you nothing to say, Helia?' persisted Madam when several moments went past in total silence.

'Nothing at all on the subject of Mr Reed, Madam,' I said boldly, inserting a note of dismissiveness into my voice, 'except to say that the expense is probably funded from the allowance he has been provided with to care for me . . . And that he most likely sees any such monies as a sound investment.'

'Why so, my dear?' Madam cocked her head to one side, with an elegant little twist.

'Because if I am "biddable" he will be able to coerce me into marriage, and then he will get his greedy paws on the inheritance I receive at 21.'

'Indeed?' Madam's sharp eyes narrowed. 'And what happens if you are unmarried at 21?'

'The fortune is mine to dispose of as I wish.'

Madam turned away from me then, her skirts swirling around her ankles like the sea about a rising Aphrodite.

'You said yesterday that you wished you could stay at the Academy forever,' she said, running one long finger along the edge of her desk, then picking up the school ruler that lay upon her blotter. 'Is that really the case . . . Or were you simply trying to bamboozle our poor, gullible Mr Moulton?'

'A little of both, Madam,' I said, wanting to surprise her. 'But mainly the former.'

Madam's soft, red lips quirked as if she were trying to suppress a smile. 'It may be possible . . .' She paused, weighing the ruler between her fingers. 'But I'm afraid that first, you must pass another test.'

Anything, I thought, bracing my spine and gazing at her proudly. Thrash me, Madam! Abuse me! Expose me! Demean me! There is nothing you can do that will make me love you less.

'I am happy to be tested,' I said quietly, feeling the familiar surge of heat between my legs. The wanton moisture of my lust was welling over.

Would I be stripped naked and thrashed with some fierce implement? Would I be made to exhibit my body in some embarrassing garb or posture? Would I have to wet myself? Allow myself to be fingered lewdly by my fellow pupils, Louise and Belinda? And by other pupils in the term that lay ahead? What would it be? What would happen? What test would my darling Madam set?

'If you fail, you cannot stay, Helia,' she warned, her bosom rising and falling beneath the fine fabric of her gown as if she were panting with anticipation just as I was.

'I understand,' I replied, feeling terror as an inkling of sudden insight dawned.

Could I do it? Did I even want to do it? Looking at Madam's slender waist, and the lush flare of her hips beneath her skirt, I began to smile.

In a wild, unwieldy gesture that was completely unlike her, Madam swept pamphlets, papers and various ephemera from the surface of her desk, clearing the area I now understood was necessary. Standing by the emptied space, her eyes full of drama, she half turned to me and held out the ruler – which I took.

'Well, then . . . Begin!' she cried, then with the fluid grace of a dancer she went over. Over her own desk. Her face down, resting on her folded arms; her bottom up, but still protected by her skirts.

The urges I felt then were most confusing. Astounding, even. For one second I wished I were a man. A young virile man like my William, with a fine member I could slide between Madam's thighs. I wanted her, I wanted to overpower her, but I realised there was only one sweet way.

'M – may I?' I stammered, moving forward.

'*You* do not have to ask,' she murmured, her voice taut, her face hidden from me.

Putting aside the ruler for a moment, I plucked at the hem of her dress and lifted it. Beneath, lay a delicious proliferation of luxurious petticoats that were of quite a different character to the severity of her gown, and under these were her embroidered and beribboned drawers.

I hesitated, in love with the divine curves of her bottom, even though they were hidden by the frivolously trimmed muslin. Her pose stretched the flimsy cloth tight against the shape of her, and between her thighs I could see a rapidly spreading dampness. Without thinking I pressed my hand into her crotch.

Madam gave a soft groan, and churned her buttocks to massage her privates against my trembling grip. It was just the sort of lewd, uncivilised response that in one of us, her charges, she would castigate, and the light of instinct told me the action was quite deliberate.

'Vulgar minx!' I retorted, giving her a rough squeeze, the withdrawing my caressing hand. 'As if it isn't bad enough that you have moistened your drawers, Mrs Woolstencraft . . . You compound the sin by drawing attention to it.' I touched her again, laying two fingers against her anus through the muslin. 'You do realise that I will now have to punish you, don't you?' I persisted, rubbing the thin cloth over the puckered bump beneath it.

Madam gasped, still moving her legs. Her self-discipline was no better than mine, it seemed.

'You are only making things worse for yourself, Mrs Woolstencraft,' I remonstrated quietly, remembering how Madam's low, precise tones were always more effective than strident shouting. I pushed a little harder against her nether opening, but this time she remained still, her muscles tense.

'Now then, let's get down to things, shall we?' I said, unhanding her. 'Will you reach behind yourself and pull down your drawers, please.'

With much rummaging, wriggling and tugging, Madam got her underwear down to her knees and revealed to me a bottom just as fabulous as I had dreamed of. Her skin was as snowy white as her linen, and as unblemished as a perfectly ripe peach. Her buttocks were a poem; trim, rounded lobes.

I picked up the ruler again, and fidgeted a little with it. How could I mar such a thing of beauty as the divine derrière of Madam Woo? What I wanted to do was fall down and worship it. To kiss it all over, and bury my face in its mysterious tawny groove. I wanted to bury my tongue between her cheeks, lick all her rude and private parts, and bring her to the pleasure she deserved, by my efforts.

But all that was not yet part of my final test.

Half remembering things that I had had done to me, and half following my suddenly powerful instincts, I drew the end of the ruler up and down her rear cleft a few times – testing her just as she was testing me. She tightened her arms around her face again, as I plagued her, obviously trying to hide the delight she was experiencing.

Then, at exactly the moment she began to weave her hips again, and pant with pleasure, I brought down the ruler across her bottom with abundant force. Madam grunted, whether in appreciation or discomfort I do not know, but I bade her, 'Be silent!'

To my surprise, and great joy, my task was easy. The sturdy schoolroom ruler seemed to fit in my hand as if made for it, and I relished the way it whisked and sang through the air, then impacted crisply with a satisfying 'slap!'. Within moments, Madam Woo's bottom was a mass of spreading, hot-looking magenta, and her private parts, nestling beneath it, were puffed and gleaming. When I lashed her squarely across her sex, she leapt and wailed, then bit her lip to reduce her cries to silence.

I laid the ruler on again, slightly harder.

Madam Woo jerked and squirmed, her whole body suffused with strain and effort, and within the circle of her arm, her face was taut.

This must be what she sees, I thought, striking at her engorged flesh again, then watching her tense white profile. The same grit, the same defiance; the same fight – on two fronts – against desire and pain. Madam Woo's eyes were closed, and her crimsoned buttocks were clenching and flexing. Her slender thighs, above her stockings, were juiced and glistening.

Incensed by the succulent beauty of her arousal, I thrashed her again and again with the ruler, my passion rising high in my savage, heaving breast. I know I was not hurting her nearly as much as she would have hurt me in the same circumstances, but in my own untutored way, I was determined to move her. Lay waste to her. Fill her with the fine, exquisite pain that created pleasure. When her cheeks were cherry-scarlet, and so hot looking I could almost imagine steam might rise from them, I flung aside the ruler and fell upon my darling's backside like a long-famished beast.

I pinched and squeezed and stroked her until she was throwing her slim hips from side to side on the desk and despite her efforts she could not restrain her sobs. Then, when she was moaning steadily, her hands clasped to her face to mask her tears, I thrust my hands between her legs and began to work her.

One I slid beneath her, burrowing through her linen, and then through her sodden feminine curls to touch her clitoris; and with the other, I possessed her backside and her dripping female entrance – my thumb in the former, and three stiff fingers, in a wedge, inside the latter.

'Have I passed my test?' I whispered into her ear, swirling my fingertip on her very most tender part. 'Am I good enough?' I asked, gripping her fore and aft with my other hand, gently massaging both her channels from within. 'Can I stay?' I begged, and kissed her shining hair.

With a great cry, Madam convulsed and took her pleasure, the supple membranes of her body rippling wildly. Her back heaved, her legs scissored, and her head shook as she rubbed her face against her arms.

She spoke no words, but I knew I had my answer.

There has been no school today at all – a fact which is not in the least surprising – although I myself have learnt some great and wondrous things.

How to endure the heavy burn of a hairbrush as it impacts against my upraised bottom. What the body of a naked woman feels like, when pressed breathlessly against my own, in the soft haven of a bed. How to give pleasure, with fingers and tongue, to my beloved Madam.

And so, it seems I am still stuck here in this hell hole. But it is a fate which I find thoroughly delightful. I still have much to master, and many difficult skills to acquire, but Madam Woo is a perfect font of knowledge.

The Academy is to expand, you see. In the coming weeks and months, many new pupils will arrive, some eager and some in dread of our rigorous prospectus.

The most exciting thing of all is that my dear Madam, accomplished and learned though she is, could never manage all these miscreants on her own.

There has to be someone else to wield the cane, the ruler and the paddle; someone else to insert the pacifiers, examine the virgin bottoms and the punished ones; someone else to supervise the regimens of submission.

And who better, might I ask, to perform these august duties, than one who has so recently been a recipient of their benefits? One who is still eager to study, by night

– by long, testing night – in the privacy of her cherished mentor's rooms?

So, here ends the irregular record of the haughty Helia – student, novice and general all round lascivious, defiant hoyden – and here begins a entirely brand new history.

The Daily Journal of Miss Helia Christophides, Senior Assistant Mistress at the Woolstencraft Academy for Young Ladies.

Life will not be easy here, that's a fact I know already. It might be harder to be a mistress than a pupil.

But my highest endeavour will be to make dear Madam proud!

NEW BOOKS

Coming up from Nexus and Black Lace

Nexus

Candida's Secret Mission by Virginia Lasalle
February 1997 Price £4.99 ISBN: 0 352 33141 0
Candie has a new job at a secret government establishment high in the Bavarian Alps. However, this is no ordinary employment; top-secret investigations are being conducted to measure female arousal and highly-sexed young women are needed to help research.

New Erotica 3 – Extracts from the Best of Nexus
February 1997 Price £4.99 ISBN: 0 352 33142 9
This is the third volume of extracts from the best-selling and most well-liked Nexus books of the past couple of years. The settings are as eclectic as the sexual peccadilloes of the characters. This anthology reflects the diversity of the Nexus imprint.

There are three Nexus titles published in March

Captives of Argan by Stephen Ferris
March 1997 Price £4.99 ISBN: 0 352 33145 3
When virgin Princess Nerina's kingdom is overrun by Prince Argan's invading forces, she is forced into a programme of corrective training and discipline. As she becomes addicted to these bizarre practices, however, she realises her hunger for Prince Argan, and vows to capture him by learning as much as she can about the art of arousal.

Susie in Servitude by Arabella Knight
March 1997 Price £4.99 ISBN: 0 352 33146 1
Susie has come to Madame Savage to learn about the fashion of restraint, but soon finds herself a keen student of madame's other services: discipline, correction, and the pleasures of spanking.

Eroticon 1
March 1997 Price £4.99 ISBN 0 352 31722 1
This unmissable collection of classic writings from forbidden texts features some of the finest erotic prose ever written. In its variety of people and practices, of settings and sexual behaviour, this exhilarating anthology provides the true connoisseur with the flavour of a dozen controversial works. Don't miss *Eroticon 2, 3* and *4*, also from Nexus.

BLACK
lace

The Master of Shilden by Lucinda Carrington
February 1997 Price £4.99 ISBN: 0 352 33140 2
When successful interior designer Elise St John is offered a commission at a remote castle, she isn't prepared for some of the more curious terms of her employment. She has been chosen to create rooms where guests will be able to realise their most erotic fantasies. She soon finds herself indulging in some fantasies of her own – which soon become reality.

Modern Love – a Black Lace Anthology
February 1997 Price £4.99 ISBN: 0 352 33158 5
Black Lace is the leading imprint of erotic fiction for women and the publishing sensation of the decade. This is the first anthology of the series with an exclusively contemporary theme. Seduction and mystery and darkly sensual behaviour are the key words to this unique collection of writings from the female perspective. Worlds of passion collide with unbridled erotic exploration and scintillating characters delight in the thrill of total surrender to pleasure and decadent indulgence.

Silken Chains by Jodi Nicol
March 1997 Price £4.99 ISBN: 0 352 33143 7
When sexually innocent Abbie flees from a dull marriage arranged by her guardian, she falls into the clutches of the attractive and wealthy Leon Villiers – the Master. Drawing on esoteric erotic practices, he introduces her to sensual pleasures far beyond her wildest dreams, but she is reluctant to submit completely to his will and, as her guardian's search for her continues, she knows that her liberty is in jeopardy.

The Hand of Amun by Juliet Hastings
March 1997 Price £4.99 ISBN: 0 352 33144 5
Naunakhte has been prepared from birth to enter a life of dark sensuality in service to the god Amun, performing rites which can only be described as indecent. When she is accused of sacrilege by a jealous rival, she is forced to flee, encountering Khonsu, a prince of the Egyptian underworld – and everything her body could desire. But fate draws her back to the temple, and she must choose between two lovers – one mortal and the other a god.

NEXUS BACKLIST

All books are priced £4.99 unless another price is given. If a date is supplied, the book in question will not be available until that month in 1996.

CONTEMPORARY EROTICA

THE ACADEMY	Arabella Knight	
BOUND TO OBEY	Amanada Ware	Feb
BOUND TO SERVE	Amanda Ware	Sep
CANDY IN CAPTIVITY	Arabella Knight	Jun
CHALICE OF DELIGHTS	Katrina Young	Mar
THE CHASTE LEGACY	Susanna Hughes	Aug
CHRISTINA WISHED	Gene Craven	Apr
CONDUCT UNBECOMING	Arabella Knight	
CONTOURS OF DARKNESS	Marco Vassi	
DARK DESIRES	Maria del Rey	May
DIFFERENT STROKES	Sarah Veitch	
THE DOMINO TATTOO	Cyrian Amberlake	
THE DOMINO ENIGMA	Cyrian Amberlake	
THE DOMINO QUEEN	Cyrian Amberlake	
ELIANE	Stephen Ferris	
EMMA'S SECRET WORLD	Hilary James	
EMMA ENSLAVED	Hilary James	
EMMA'S SECRET DIARIES	Hilary James	
EMMA'S SUBMISSION	Hilary James	Oct
FALLEN ANGELS	Kendal Grahame	
THE FANTASIES OF JOSEPHINE SCOTT	Josephine Scott	
THE FINISHING SCHOOL	Stephen Ferris	May
THE GENTLE DEGENERATES	Marco Vassi	
HEART OF DESIRE	Maria del Rey	